DRUID LORDS

INDIA DRUMMOND

Druid Lords

Second edition published in the United Kingdom 2013 by India Drummond

ISBN-13: 978-1492234609
ISBN-10: 1492234605

Author contact: http://www.indiadrummond.com/

Fae Name Pronunciation Guide

In order of appearance:

Oszlár: AHZ-laar
Yurnme: YURN-meh
Eilidh: AY-lee
Bran: BRAN
Griogair: Gree-GAIR
Tràth: TRATH
Konstanze: KAWN-stanz
Koen: Ko-uhn
Estobar: Ess-TOH-bar
Grenna: GREHNA
Vinye: VEN-yay
Dumvwere: dumv-WEHR
Flùranach: FLOO-ran-ak
Hon: HAWN
Leocort: LEE-oh-cort
Avin: AH-ven
Oron: oh-RON
Zdanye: ZDAH

CHAPTER 1

HUCK WEBSTER SAT BACK in the wooden chair and watched the other Amsterdam bar patrons with a smile. He enjoyed the occasional evening away from the Otherworld, being around humans from time to time. The other druids he worked with had lived in the Otherworld for six months before Huck came along. Even though he joined them willingly, certain he was ready to accept his new identity, the human realm continued to draw him back. Magic and wonders made up every part of his life in the Otherworld, but returning to the human realm grounded him.

Of the druids, only Huck had never touched the Source Stone. The ancient artefact had put the others through dramatic changes when they first encountered it. Munro was barely distinguishable from a faerie with his golden skin and pointed ears. The artefact's essence altered each of them enough that they were reluctant to approach its resting place in the Halls of Mist casually. Although enthralled with his developing magic, Huck didn't particularly want to have swirling eyes like the fae.

Huck had undergone some changes from his exposure to the Otherworld air. He became stronger, had more stamina. He had clear night vision, and the spark of his fire magic had come alive. With the sudden awakening of his druidic powers, the other druids hadn't needed to persuade him to leave behind his life working for a Texas oil company.

But even with the positive changes, Huck missed some things about human life. The others had changed so much that they didn't seem to appreciate human food or culture. Huck liked to sneak through the Otherworld gates to go to a movie or visit an art gallery or a park. He liked the way humanity buzzed. Faerie life moved at a snail's pace, and its political and social goings-on meant little to him.

After paying his bill, Huck left the bar and walked out into the spring drizzle. He had some time before he planned to meet the owner of a local coffee shop, so he took a meandering path.

He strolled through the narrow streets and peered into shop windows, listening to the sound of passing trams and the occasional trill of a bicycle bell. Amsterdam suited him for a lot of reasons. Most everyone spoke English, and he easily blended in as a tourist. He enjoyed the museums and galleries, which reminded him of the good things about humanity. Sure, faeries created some incredible things with their magic, but for him, that didn't compare to a work of art formed by nothing but bare hands and raw materials.

At the same time, Amsterdam showed him a seedier side of life: readily available drugs, drunken tourists, and in a certain part of town, women displayed in windows like merchandise. Without thinking, Huck found himself drifting towards the red-light district. The idea was civilised: make prostitution legal, and the women would be protected and the industry taxed. He liked the European attitudes, in general, but reality didn't quite live up to the ideal.

He walked by a set of fluorescent red windows, inhabited by young women standing and posing in sexy black underwear. What bothered him about the scene wasn't the women themselves, but the men standing around in the orange glow of the street lights. A small cluster of men in their twenties stumbled up, obviously drunk. Likely on a stag night, they jeered at the prostitutes and took a few photos. Before long, brothel security came out of the tall, narrow house and challenged the group. Huck shook his head and moved on before things got ugly.

He'd never paid for the company of one of the local working girls. Since moving away from the human realm, his attempts at relationships hadn't gone well. He'd met a wild girl with blue streaks in her hair in a Berlin night club and invited her back to his hotel room. Later, he found her rummaging through his wallet while he took a shower, and he kicked her out unceremoniously. She'd protested that she was merely looking for the room key because she wanted to dash out for some beer, but Huck didn't buy it. Another recent failure was with an American woman who worked as a translator in The Hague.

He'd quite liked her. *Erica*. But when he'd gone to visit her after their first encounter, she'd been incensed that he hadn't called for three weeks. She didn't believe him when he explained that where he lived, he couldn't get mobile telephone service.

Huck sighed as he thought about his situation. He missed sex. Not the act so much as being close to and touching another person. But trying to explain his lifestyle wasn't conducive to a relationship. After the second encounter, he'd never spoken to Erica again.

The drizzle turned to a bona fide rain, and Huck headed towards the coffee shop. Once inside, his senses were assaulted by the heavy smell of cannabis, and soon the expected headache started. The magical awakening the druids experienced when they came in contact with the faerie realm made them intolerant to certain foods, alcohol, and, he discovered recently, weed. Fortunately, he wouldn't have to stay at his meeting long.

The narrow building was deeper than it appeared from the outside. The shop nestled between a bookshop and a sculptor's studio, just down from a bakery. Because it was a couple of blocks away from the red-light district and out of the normal tourist loop, it boasted a healthy number of local customers. He also liked that the place wasn't as crowded as some similar establishments.

Huck realised he had no idea what day of the week it was. Faeries kept time by the number of nights to or from the solstice, or sometimes a particular festival or holiday. They tracked the time by the stars, and their stars looked nothing like the small, dim points of light over the human world.

He nodded to Maarten, who was showing a customer their house blend of marijuana called Golden Djinn. When he'd concluded his transaction, the tall blond man approached the door where Huck hovered. "What do you have for me today?" Maarten asked. "More than last time, I hope. I can't keep your hot-rocks on the shelf." He pointed to a table near the exit.

The dull ache in Huck's temples spread down to his jaw. He tried to blink the pain away, knowing he'd be fine as soon as he got some fresh air. Sliding his backpack off his shoulder as he sat, he pulled out a kidskin cloth. Unfolding it, he laid ten rocks on the table. "I added some runic art to these," he said. The runes were empty and meaningless, but the lack wouldn't mean anything to the customers, who seemed to like the designs. The rune that gave the stones their magical properties was invisible, even to his own eye. It disappeared into the heart of the talisman as he crafted the piece.

Maarten nodded. "Nice," he said. "My customers will like these. Can you bring more soon?"

Huck shrugged. "The process takes time." The truth was, the other druids didn't know about his little enterprise. He crafted the stones in secret, partly out of embarrassment for using empty runes for aesthetics. The problem wasn't so much that he worried they'd disapprove, although he figured they would, but more that he wanted some little corner of his life to be his alone.

"Same price?" Maarten took a piece of cigarette paper from his pocket and held it up to one of the runed rocks. Within moments, its edges blackened. Pulling the paper away before it ignited, he asked, "May I?"

Huck nodded. "Five euros more for each of the carved ones." It didn't take any more time to make them, but Maarten wouldn't baulk at the higher price. Hell, Huck could probably double his asking price and not worry the coffee shop owner.

Maarten picked up the rock. "I still don't understand why they don't burn my hands. Nice and warm though. I held back two for myself, and I keep them in my coat pockets. You're sure they're safe? Not radioactive or anything?"

With a chuckle, Huck shook his head. "They're safe. I have one other. Not sure if you'd be interested." He reached into his backpack a second time. "This one's just decorative." He pulled out a fist-sized piece of pink quartz he'd picked up from a shop that sold polished stones as healing crystals. He had managed to imbue a flame inside the heart of the rock.

Maarten took the rock and turned it, holding it up to the light. A flame flickered within, and the coffee shop owner whistled. "Beautiful," he said. "How much?"

"Fifty euros," Huck replied.

Maarten put the rock down. "A lot more than the others."

"Harder to make too. I broke four crystals trying to do that." He didn't mention the crystals only cost him a couple euros each.

"So what's your secret? Some trick of the light?"

With a small smile Huck said, "I can't give away my techniques. Then you wouldn't need me anymore." Maarten always asked, but every time, Huck gave a similar answer. Part of him worried that Maarten suspected the truth, but he shrugged off the niggling worry.

"Okay," Maarten said. "I'll get your money." His chair scraped against the wooden floor when he stood. He disappeared into the back room as a young woman walked into the shop. She smiled at the man who'd taken Maarten's place behind the counter. "Is Maarten in? I'm here about the job."

"He'll be right back," the man replied.

She nodded and turned as though she planned to take a seat at Huck's table, and she appeared startled when she realised the table was occupied. "Sorry," she muttered, stepping back, but she froze when she saw the stones on the table. "Where did you get these?" Her accent didn't quite sound Dutch, but then Huck was never very good at placing accents.

Huck looked the woman over. She was pretty, strikingly so. Her mid-toned skin and oval eyes made guessing her race impossible. Her delicate eyebrows arched over chocolate-brown eyes with flecks of gold, and she nibbled on her full lower lip as though unaware of the habit.

"I made them," he said.

She extended a finger and ran it over the runes on the sides of one of the carved stones. She yanked her hand back when she felt the warmth of the stone. After a beat, she reached out again, then ran her whole hand over the rock's surface. Still she frowned, as though frustrated by the runes. But that wasn't possible. Nobody without magical ability could read faerie runes because most of the meaning didn't come from the lines and shapes of the characters, but from the intent of the creator.

Her gaze remained fixed on the pink crystal. Huck was surprised she had touched it without asking, but he didn't try to stop her. She appeared entranced, and the longer she stared into the crystal, the more glazed her eyes became. "Fire-heart," she whispered.

Huck stopped cold. Those were the exact two runes he'd imbued into the crystal to give it that living spark of fire within. How could she have guessed? He rubbed his temple. Maybe his growing headache made him imagine what he'd heard.

Maarten returned as she picked the rock up. "Amazing artist, isn't he? A hundred euros for this one. It's one-of-a-kind."

She rushed to set it down as though the price shocked her. Maarten added, "Only fifty for the smaller ones." He handed Huck the agreed upon three-hundred euros cash for the entire lot.

She stared at Huck for a moment but flinched as she looked into his eyes.

Damn, Huck thought. Had she noticed the faint glow in his eyes in the dimly lit coffee shop? The gleam wasn't as pronounced as with some of the other druids, but he couldn't deny it was there. "I'll make you another," Huck said on impulse. "No charge."

Maarten threw up his hands in disgust. "You're killing me," he said. "She would have bought one."

The young woman dashed out the door. Huck grabbed his backpack and without a word to Maarten, he rushed to the shop's entrance, keeping his gaze locked on her short black hair bobbing through the crowd outside. He didn't know what possessed him, but he couldn't stop watching her. Was she a druid? An outcast faerie in disguise, hidden behind an astral illusion?

"When will you be back with more?" Maarten asked, but Huck didn't turn to answer. The girl had read his rune, and he had to find out who she was.

The nights in this part of Amsterdam were nearly as busy as the days, but with a different clientele. The bars and coffee shops throbbed with patrons, and further down the way, the red-light district and its sex shops and peep-shows would be doing brisk business. Huck wove amongst the foot-traffic and followed the young woman. She ducked through the crowds with purpose, and several times she doubled back and took an oddly circuitous route.

With the strength and speed and sharp night vision the Otherworld had given him, Huck didn't have any trouble keeping up. His head cleared as soon as he moved away from the cannabis smoke of the coffee shop, sharpening his senses even further. He kept to the shadows. Occasionally, she would stop and turn around. She shouldn't have been able to see him, but she tilted her head as though listening hard.

When she stopped, he did too, watching her closely. She looked terrified. Of what? Of him? The last thing he wanted was to scare her, but he needed to know how she recognised his runes.

Finally, she ducked into a small, narrow house, glancing over her shoulder after she put the key in the lock and turned it. Once she disappeared inside, Huck exhaled softly. Now what? He couldn't ring her bell at this hour of the night. He glanced at a street sign and made note of the address. He needed to think about this.

A pair of glowing eyes stared at Huck from an alleyway across the street. They blinked once, then reappeared. The sight startled him. Could it be one of the other druids? The fae almost never came into the human realm, and if they did, they avoided the cities. Plus, there weren't any Otherworld gates in Holland. He'd had to travel through Germany to get here. Huck moved forward, but the eyes shifted as though the figure turned. Although Huck never heard any movement, when he stepped towards the darkened alleyway, he found it deserted. Whoever had been watching had vanished. He cast his eyes upward, to the house the woman had entered. He didn't even know her name.

∞

"What do you think is happening?" Munro asked, meeting Keeper Oszlár's gaze. The druid scrubbed his hand through his golden hair, a very human habit he'd managed to keep, despite the other transformations he'd undergone in the past two years.

The ancient faerie frowned. "The gates are shifting."

Munro blinked. With everything he'd learned, from how to create objects of power to uncovering the true destiny of druids within fae society, there was still so much he didn't understand. For the fae, two years seemed like nothing. Their world was ancient compared to the human realm, and they lived much longer. Most faeries considered Munro's own fiancée, Queen Eilidh of Caledonia, almost too young for her station at only a hundred and twenty-seven. "The Otherworld gates? All of them? Shifting to where?"

Normally Oszlár was a patient teacher who found delight in Munro's discoveries and inquisitive nature. Today his tone was sharp and serious. "We must gather the queens at once." He raised his voice and shouted, "Yurnme!" Because of his advanced age, even by faerie standards, the name came out in a rasp.

"I'll get him," Munro said. Before Oszlár could protest the propriety of a druid lord running errands, Munro jumped to his feet. He trotted from the vast chamber below the library, up the winding staircase, and made his way to the keepers' study rooms. He found the sharp-faced Yurnme talking to a group of keepers. Bursting into the room at a jog, Munro said, "Oszlár needs you."

With a barely perceptible sigh, Yurnme stood. "Where can I find the head keeper?" he asked with just enough respect to save himself from chastisement.

"Below," Munro replied. The lower part of the library housed only one chamber, and that room held one object: the Source Stone, the most sacred and mystical object in the faerie realm. Munro had discovered a few months before that the artefact had been made by human druids, a revelation that changed the way faerie society regarded him and his brother druids.

Yurnme's lazy attitude annoyed him. At one time, Munro wouldn't have detected the subtle insult in the faerie's expression. Now Munro recognised the minute gestures, the flickers of emotion that had once eluded him. To snap the faerie into action, he added, "The gates are shifting."

Every faerie in the large sitting area gave him their full attention. Faces turned, and a cold silence fell over the already quiet room. Then, just as abruptly, the faeries leapt into motion, whirring as they moved with super-human speed. One approached him. "Will you be summoning Queen Eilidh yourself, my lord druid?"

"Yes," Munro replied. He hadn't considered doing so, but if something important was happening, she might want to hear the news from him.

"Then I suggest you make haste," the keeper said. "The queens must gather immediately."

Munro turned to go, urgency swirling around him. What did this mean? The Halls of Mist, which contained the Great Library, The Druid Hall, and halls for every one of the faerie kingdoms, connected to the kingdoms through a portal near the library entrance. The huge blue ball of light that allowed the kingdoms to connect in this strange, in-between place rested directly over the Source Stone. This, Munro had learned, was no coincidence.

When he arrived at the portal, two queens were already there. He didn't know either of them well, but then there were many faerie queens, all ruling independent nations, some small and some much larger. Eilidh's kingdom was, in comparison to most, quite small, at least as represented by its connection to the human realm. Faerie kingdoms were anchored in what he still thought of as the *real* world by a series of gates. The more gates a queen controlled, the more political sway she had.

He nodded to the two queens, and they inclined their heads, showing their respect. As he stepped into the dazzling blue light, he thought about how much things had changed. Not too long ago, faeries regarded humans with disgust, like some kind of talking animals. His discovery about the ancient artefact called the Killbourne Wall forced them all to reconsider those opinions, whether they wanted to or not. The runes on the wall told the faerie creation story and revealed that human druids were *draoidh*, sorcerers of ancient tales the fae revered above all others, even queens.

The draoidh once wielded almost unlimited power in the faerie realm, and Munro had discovered why. They were creators. Not only of runes and artefacts, but possibly of the entire fae race. The druids now living in the Halls of Mist had nowhere near the level of knowledge required to create sentient, living creatures. So much had been lost over the thousands of years since the original draoidh disappeared. But these modern druids did have remarkable abilities, and he had hope they would someday restore what had died out.

The moment Munro arrived on the other side of the portal, he felt a sense of belonging, of warmth and love. His bonded faerie, soon to be his wife, filled his mind. Something about the portal between Caledonia and the Halls of Mist dampened their connection, and her presence always relieved him.

The round portal shimmered on an immense circular platform, surrounded by Watchers. He saw one he knew. "Bran," he called and walked down the steps quickly.

"Yes, my lord druid," the Watcher said with a bow of his head.

"I need the queen to come at once," Munro said. "Can you send your fastest runner with a message?"

"If your need is official and urgent," the Watcher replied, "I will send a signal."

Munro hesitated a moment. "Do that," he said.

Bran nodded and turned to another. Raising his voice, he said, "The druid lord summons the queen." The somewhat younger Watcher's eyes went a bit wide.

Munro had only lived in the Otherworld for a couple of years, but he knew summoning a queen was a rare occurrence. He opened his mouth to explain, even though technically he didn't have to, when a familiar voice intruded into his thoughts. *How I love to sense your presence, Quinton. You seem disturbed. I hope you plan to stay in Caledonia for a while. I miss you.*

His inability to answer her frustrated him. He hoped she would receive whatever signal Bran sent and come quickly.

"If you'd step back, my lord druid. The beacon will become quite bright," Bran said. He lifted his right arm to the sky and whispered. All the Watchers in the circle did the same. From his fingertips came a blinding golden light. The beam shot into the air and joined with lights each of the other Watchers created.

Munro realised he didn't have cause to worry that she would miss the signal The higher it grew, the more the vast ball of light dwarfed the portal itself. Together the Watchers called, "Advance!" and the light flashed once, then zoomed away, leaving a glowing trail behind it.

"She'll come?" Munro asked Bran. He'd never seen them use anything like this before.

"Yes," Bran said. "Her majesty will most certainly come." He smiled. "That was exciting. We haven't sent a signal in a long time. I cannot help but express my curiosity," he added.

Munro didn't see any harm in telling the Watchers the news. Nobody had indicated he should keep the events to himself, and with the big ball of light flying towards the queen, his message wouldn't stay secret long. "The gates are shifting," Munro told him.

The faerie's eyes widened and swirled with a flash of magic. "Caledonia?" he asked.

"I don't know. The keepers are summoning all the queens."

"They always do," another faerie nearby said.

Munro didn't quite understand, but the Watchers were clearly worried about the implications of what he told them. "I'll send word as soon as I have some information."

Bran looked startled. "You are too kind, my lord druid."

With worry now weighing more heavily on him than before, Munro stepped through the portal and returned to the Halls of Mist.

CHAPTER 2

DEMI HARTMANN LOCKED THE DOOR behind her and pulled the bolt into place. The habitual action wouldn't stop *him*, locks never had, but the sound of the metal sliding into place comforted her anyway. Leaning against the door in the darkened entryway, she breathed for a moment. *Damn.* She'd needed that job. The savings she and her grandmother lived on wouldn't last forever.

Her grandmother called from the other side of the house, in German, of course, "Is that you?"

"Yes, Omi," Demi shouted. "It's starting to rain harder now." She unwound the long scarf from her neck and hung it on a hook near the door, then placed her jacket next to it. She shivered, but not from the cold. She didn't want to tell her grandmother she'd been followed home. She was tired of moving. When they left Berlin, they'd moved to southern Germany, then over into Austria. Then when *he* found them, they'd doubled-back to Zurich. The larger the city, the longer before he found her, but he always did. Omi had been the one to choose the Netherlands. Nearly three-quarters of the population spoke German, and even more English, which Demi had learned in school. Her grandmother's English was passable, but they hoped this time, they would have a while before he caught up with them. Part of her dared to hope he might not find her at all.

She tousled the damp out of her hair and made her way up the stairs to the main living room. By the time she arrived, she managed to paste a smile on her face. "Where's my little man?" she called through the doorway.

A small boy lay on the couch next to her grandmother, his head nestled on the older lady's bosom. He beamed through sleepy eyes. The bright smile melted her worries away. "Mama!"

"Come kiss me, Jago," Demi said with a tender smile. "Then it's off to bed. Omi shouldn't let you stay up so late."

Her grandmother stood when Jago toddled over to Demi. The boy planted a wet kiss on Demi's face and giggled.

"Maybe," Omi said, "Mama shouldn't have been out so late."

Demi picked Jago up. A healthy size at four years old, he was almost too big for her to carry up the stairs, but she loved to hold him. A flash of protective worry went through her, but she tried her best to push the feeling aside. She had close to two years before he would be old enough for school. "Mama had to go look for a job," Demi said in a playful voice to Jago, although she directed her words at her grandmother.

"I like it best when you stay with me, Mama," Jago said and yawned.

"Me too," she replied with a grin. "Come on. Bed time."

He laid his head on her shoulder with a contented sigh and fell asleep before they reached the upstairs bedroom he shared with his Omi. Demi kissed his forehead and tucked the blankets around him, then watched him sleep for a moment. Finally, she tore herself away to face her grandmother's predictable questioning.

When Demi went back to the living room, she found her grandmother peering into the street below. "Who is that man?" she asked.

Demi's heart filled with dread. She followed the older woman's gaze to a dark corner. The figure in the shadows barely moved. If she hadn't known he was there, she might have missed him altogether. "I met him at the coffee shop where I applied for the job. He must have followed me here."

"Is he—"

"No," Demi interrupted. "He's an artist."

"He may be working for Ulric."

Demi shuddered. She hated even the sound of that name. "He was selling his work to the owner. He wasn't there for me."

Her grandmother turned sharp eyes on Demi. "He's here for you now." Her tone held a warning. "You have to get rid of him."

"He'll go away on his own. He's only a man." Demi hoped she spoke the truth.

"Think of Jago," her grandmother insisted.

"I do," Demi said impatiently. "Every moment of every day." Tears stung her eyes, but she refused to let them fall. "He's only a man."

∞

Munro waited for the queens to gather, keeping back so as not to call too much attention to himself. That was not an easy task, because even after well over a year in the Otherworld, he and his druid comrades still caused a stir wherever they went. At least this time, the queens were too occupied with watching the blue portal to bother about him.

The queens arrived with their usual entourages, but quickly everyone except the queen herself and one or two others would make their way beyond the courtyard to their kingdom's Hall. Still, before long, the large courtyard felt crowded, and the keepers had not even surfaced from the chamber below. The queens didn't speak to one another, and most maintained an icy and calm appearance. Occasionally, Munro would catch one giving another a furtive glance. Clearly, something worried them.

After an hour, Munro wandered to the library entrance and took the downward spiralling stairs two at a time. Several keepers gathered in the back of the large entrance hall, and they glanced up when he entered. Their grim expressions, however, prevented him from approaching. He didn't see Oszlár, the head keeper with whom he worked the most. Of course, any of the keepers would have been happy to lend assistance to one of the druids. When it came to matters of important advice, however, they always referred him to Oszlár. Not wanting to talk to anyone else, Munro left.

Impatience bit at him. It might take several hours before all the queens arrived. Eilidh would likely have been at the castle at Canton Dreich. Even if she left immediately, the distance would require some time to cross. Faeries didn't use machinery or animals for transportation. Of course, they could run many times faster than a human. They also had more stamina and considered contraptions a human crutch, used to make up for the lesser race's lack of magical abilities.

Munro made his way through the crowd of waiting royals, wondering why they didn't wait in their Halls. Perhaps, he considered, they hoped one of the new arrivals would have more information. On a whim, Munro turned and walked over on the same bridges that led away from the courtyard and towards the grand Halls beyond. Beneath the thin bridges, thick fog roiled far below. The Source Stone emanated magic so strong, it created a mist that obscured the view of the gaping void under his feet.

He approached the open gates to the Druid Hall and looked up. He had a difficult time explaining to Eilidh why he wanted to live here instead of with her in Caledonia. He knew his choice disappointed her, but the decision felt right. Even with the discomfort of not having her near, he belonged here.

With help volunteered by many faeries from all over the kingdoms, they'd built their Hall in a surprisingly short time. The structure was more of a village than a single building, constructed to house hundreds. Cooks, gardeners, servants, and attendants all served the Druid Hall. Scholars lived in a special wing created for their use. When the druids would give them time, they'd question the humans, trying to scrutinise the unusual magic the men possessed, tracking its changes and development. This study included the bonding process druids could engage in with one faerie during their lifetime.

The architecture of the Druid Hall was an odd combination of fae design, modern influence, and ancient, moss-covered Scottish castles. Much of the place was still unfinished, and unlike the faeries, the druids did not have claim on any of the human realm, so this was their only domain. At least it was theirs. Except for the small amount they'd begun to grow in a small, rear garden, their food came from tributes from all the kingdoms, and the keepers had arranged for them to be supplied with anything they needed. The various kingdoms each tried to outdo the others with their generosity.

Although Eilidh had wanted the druids to stay within the influence of Caledonia, Munro was looking further to the future. As much as he wanted to give her anything she might desire, for the druids' sake, they should be affiliated with as many kingdoms as possible, to spread their web of influence as far as they could. They were building the foundation of a new society, one much bigger than him and Eilidh.

He worked his way through the gateway and beyond the wide, open garden at the front. He found Rory in the immense room they called their workshop. The ginger-haired druid sat at a rough-hewn table, bending over a carved wooden block and shaping it with his magical flows. He didn't notice Munro at first, but after a few moments, he came out of his trance.

A wide grin broke out across his face when he saw Munro. "Hey," he said. "How're things going at the library?"

Munro was glad Rory appeared so content and engrossed in his work. He'd been through quite a trauma not too long ago, one that left him wounded and angry for some time. As a result of his injuries, Rory would never be able to bond with another faerie. Munro didn't want to contemplate what that would be like. His bond with Eilidh shaped so much of what he had become. But Rory's bond had been stolen from him by a young faerie named Flùranach.

He had, in essence, become her slave, unable even to disagree with her, having to force himself to pretend to be happy, even about what had been done to him. Flùranach had been young, and she had been through a magical accident that left her unstable. Eventually, Munro had convinced her to release Rory, but not before the damage had been done.

Although Rory no longer suffered from the forced bond, the ordeal left deep scars. Flùranach had not been seen since. As far as everyone knew, she had fled to the human realm. Munro sometimes wondered where she'd gone. She'd once been like family to him. The idea of her, lost and alone on the streets of some human city, bothered him. Despite what she'd done, he hoped she was safe and well.

"What's up?" Rory asked.

Munro opened his mouth to answer when he heard Eilidh's voice behind him. "Quinton," she said, and Munro turned to her. "I received your call. I need to return to the courtyard to wait with the others. Will the druids be joining us?"

Munro turned to her. "What's going on? I know the gates are shifting, but what does that mean?"

Eilidh glanced over her shoulder, back towards the courtyard in the distance. "Our kingdoms do not intersect." Worry creased her brow, and her silver-green eyes swam with her concerns.

Munro frowned, puzzled. He knew each of the faerie kingdoms did not border each other, but only connected at the borderlands and here in the Halls of Mist. "I know that."

"Rarely, the gates shift from one queen's control to another. New kingdoms can be formed. Old kingdoms may die. Any of our kingdoms might be affected."

"What might cause such a thing?" Munro asked.

She shrugged, but her gesture did not disguise her anxiety. "Many things. Sometimes, but not always, the gates shift when a queen dies."

"You've had no word of a queen dying, have you?"

She shook her head. "No, but if this is the case, the event would be recent. This is one of the reasons we attend so eagerly. That and to determine if our own kingdom is at risk."

Rory interjected, "Wouldn't a dead queen's heir take the throne?"

Eilidh nodded. "Usually. Even when we deposed Cadhla, the gates accepted the will of the conclave and the Caledonian people and did not shift to another, but passed into my control. The artefact is a source of ancient magic none of us understands. In truth, I'm surprised the Stone accepted me." She set her mouth into a grim line. "It may even now reject me, if my kingdom has grown too weak to thrive."

"Are you saying the Source Stone chooses faerie queens?"

"Of course not," she said. "Griogair is waiting for me at the courtyard. By tradition, only the keepers and royal families are present when the Stone reveals its new pattern, but no one would deny your right to attend." Her voice had an almost imperceptible quaver. Through their bond, Munro sensed her nervousness.

Griogair was Eilidh's husband, and he had become Munro's friend. When she and Munro married in a month's time, she would be the only living faerie queen with two mates. The tradition of polyandry, he had learned, had once been common, but she would be the first in well over a millennia to resurrect the practice.

"Of course we'll come." Munro lifted an eyebrow in Rory's direction.

The other druid nodded in agreement. "Aaron is upstairs. Douglas is away with Tràth, as usual. Huck hasn't come back from his trip to Ashkyne yet. He may still be gone for a day or two. You know how he is."

Munro nodded. The new American druid hadn't settled in quite as easily as the others and often made trips through various kingdoms to visit the human realm. He always came back, though, and Munro believed he would eventually view the Otherworld as home. "Get Aaron?" he asked Rory. "I'll meet you there."

Turning to Eilidh, Munro asked, "Did Tràth come with you and Griogair?" The youngest druid, Douglas, had bonded with Griogair's son, Tràth, making them the only other bonded pair besides Munro and Eilidh.

"No," she said. "I haven't seen them for weeks."

Munro took Eilidh's hand. Her fingers trembled in his grasp. He kissed them lightly, happy he could make such simple gestures openly. They'd had to spend the first six months of his time in the Otherworld hiding their relationship. Now that the druids had status in the faerie realm, Munro was able to claim his place by Eilidh's side.

A rush of gratitude came through their bond and warmed Munro. Eilidh appeared strong and resolute, but inwardly, she quaked, terrified she would soon be deposed. Munro didn't pretend to understand. How could an artefact determine who was queen? Why would it turn against her, and what would happen if it did?

As though sensing his disquiet, she said, "The Stone has not awoken for many hundreds of years, since long before my birth. Usually, we are left to our own choices."

"What happened last time?"

She frowned, her silver eyes swirling with dismay. "An entire kingdom disappeared."

CHAPTER 3

HUCK NEEDED ADVICE. He couldn't stand outside this woman's house all night without risking the police being called. So, sometime before midnight, he headed towards the Ashkyne-controlled gates just over the German borders. Fortunately, his enhanced speed, strength, and endurance allowed him to make the seventy-five mile journey in a fraction of the time a normal human would need. Otherworld gates were always located in the countryside, far away from human habitation. He'd tried to map them out, but because he relied on the patience of the faerie queens who controlled them, finishing the project would require some time.

Unlike the familiar gates in Scotland, the ones in the Ashkynen borderlands were positioned farther apart, spanning several European countries. He'd travelled through one and ended up in Romania. This western German gate was as close as he'd dare go to Queen Vinye's territory, which included England, Wales, and part of Northern France and Belgium. Because of some conflict she had with

Queen Eilidh before he came to the Otherworld, Vinye was all but openly hostile to the druids.

As he raced through the countryside to the wooded copse where the Ashkyne gate stood, Huck's thoughts centred on the woman he had encountered. Considering every nuance of her appearance, her reactions, every flick of her eyes, his instincts told him she was different, special. She'd read his runes, without a doubt. Normally, he would have pursued the puzzle alone, but he had less experience and perhaps lesser talents than the other druids. Unlike them, he'd never touched the Source Stone. He hated to admit it, but he needed help.

As he drew near the gate, he became aware of the Ashkyne Watchers. Of course, they had observed his approach. No human could come near a faerie gate without the Watchers' consent. Only those with the blessings of the faerie queen would be permitted close enough to see the magnificent, glowing arches.

He passed through the gate, and once on the other side, he breathed deeply. The Otherworld air was thick with magic and had a loamy scent that felt fresh and clean to his lungs. With a sense of purpose, he turned north, running back to the glowing blue portal to the Halls of Mist. He moved quickly, but a part of him resisted leaving the human world behind. He sensed the loss every time and wondered if he would ever feel at home among the fae.

In another hour, he came to the portal. In addition to the usual Watcher contingent, faeries filled the area. The atmosphere hummed with anticipation. A group preparing to enter the portal drew his attention. Queen Konstanze met his gaze and stopped short. She glanced to the portal, as though eager to be on her way, but she seemed unwilling to turn her back on Huck. With a tilt of her head, she acknowledged him and waited.

Huck suppressed a sigh. The brown and gold of her swirling eyes reminded him of the woman he'd met in the Netherlands and the urgent business that pushed him forward. He didn't want to speak with the queen, but she had been gracious about allowing him free roam and had given generously to the Druid Hall, so he couldn't snub her. With a smile plastered on his face, he approached. "What a pleasant surprise, Your Majesty," he said. "What takes you to the Halls today?"

"Lord Druid Huck," she replied, with an odd emphasis on his name as though she found it somewhat distasteful. He wondered if perhaps his name meant something rude in the ancient fae tongue. "We received word the gates are shifting. How fortunate you will be there to witness the flow of power." Although he didn't know what these events might mean, he assumed from her slight smile she expected to benefit.

"Does this happen often?" he asked.

She blinked at him, as though just remembering he might be unfamiliar with fae history. "The last time was when the seven Reshkin gates came to be part of Ashkyne."

Huck nodded solemnly, even though he had no idea what would have caused one kingdom's gates to transfer to another. Some druids didn't mind exposing their ignorance, but Huck knew several queens didn't like showing deference to humans in the first place, much less humans who understood so little about their world. "Of course. Then, we should go at once," he said.

She tilted her head again, and he returned the gesture. Despite her cold manner, he liked Konstanze, or at least, he respected her. To save her the embarrassment of allowing him to go first as propriety would dictate, he indicated the portal. "The matter is urgent, Your Majesty, so I insist you go ahead. You were kind to stop to greet me, but I shouldn't keep you. Please."

"As you wish, my lord druid," she replied, turning to signal to her entourage. Without another word, the group stepped through the blue orb of light and vanished.

He waited for her entire group to disappear, and then waited a few moments to allow her time to move away on the other side. None of the faeries who stayed behind spoke to him, although he sensed their gaze on him as he stared into the blue light. One thing he did like about faeries—they were patient. As he stood in silence and stared, they appeared to think nothing of it.

With an intake of breath, he stepped through. The difference between the Halls of Mist and the faerie kingdoms was as large as the difference between the Otherworld and the human realm. Where the kingdoms were lush and forested, the Halls of Mist was constructed and artificial, made of smooth, too-perfect stone and bridges that arched a touch too high. Each of the kingdom Halls was large and imposing, floating away from the main courtyard, suspended over an impenetrable, lifelike fog below. Wisps of mist wended over the edges of the narrow paths like ghostly tendrils.

Every eye in the courtyard turned to him expectantly, but once the faeries recognised him, the crowd looked away as though disappointed. He'd never seen so many queens in one place. He glanced around, spotting the other druids standing together. Munro hovered beside Queen Eilidh of Caledonia, his fiancée. Rory and Aaron stood a little bit behind, with Prince Griogair and a few other faeries Huck didn't know well.

He made his way towards the familiar faces and greeted Munro with a whisper. "Konstanze told me the gates are shifting. What's that mean?"

Munro appeared even more serious than usual, and that was saying something. "From what I understand, the Stone dictates which queen controls which gates. At any time, the Stone can transfer one or more gates from one queen's control to another's, shifting the balance of power."

Eilidh stepped closer and nodded to Huck. "Hello, Huck," she said. Although none of the faerie queens typically showed much emotion, she looked markedly nervous.

Huck got along well with Eilidh. Of all the queens, she treated the druids like normal people, saying things such as, "Hello, Huck," instead of "Greetings, Lord Druid." The gesture was a small one, but it put him at ease. "Hi, Eilidh," he said with a smile. "So, what are we waiting for?" he asked.

"For the last two queens to arrive. Well, one really. Queen Grenna won't come, no matter what."

"No?" he asked. "Who is Grenna?"

"The queen of the sea fae. I've never met her. As far as I know, none of her people have visited the Halls of Mist in over two thousand years. Some believe they've died out, but if those rumours were true, the gates would have shifted to another queen's control."

"Who else isn't here?" Huck glanced around, but was too unfamiliar with the faces to be able to determine who was missing.

"Vinye of Andena," Eilidh said, her white eyebrows knitting together in a frown over her swirling silver-green eyes. "We thought you may have been her. On the other hand, she may be taking her time to show she isn't worried."

Huck could understand both the concern and the posturing. Losing one gate would mean losing access to part of the human realm. The fae visited altars in the human realm to ask for the Mother of the Earth's blessing of fertility. From what he'd gathered, they couldn't reproduce without going through that ritual. If a fae kingdom started losing the ability to reproduce, they would certainly die. "What if a kingdom loses all the gates?" he asked.

By the anguished expression that flashed over Eilidh's face, he knew she feared this scenario the most. "Throughout the Otherworld, faeries will now gather near the gates. When the gates shift, the kingdoms will be torn. If the queen loses one gate, she loses any territory close to that gate, and her citizens gathered around it will owe their loyalty to their new queen. The lands could be divided and shifted physically to be part of the new kingdom. If the entire kingdom passes to a new queen, the new lands will meld with hers, creating a new region in her kingdom. She will gain the property, possessions, and citizens of the former queen."

"Sounds terrifying," Huck muttered. He couldn't imagine the upheaval, both figurative and literal.

"The receiving queen will provide whatever her new citizens need to transition well, and all will welcome their new neighbours. It is a great honour to have the power of your kingdom strengthened, so residents of the receiving kingdom will be glad to aid those who add to their numbers."

The system sounded like it provided quite a few opportunities for disaster. Huck understood why Eilidh was so worried. "And what happens to the queen who has her gates removed from her control?"

"If she loses only a few gates, she will return, her kingdom diminished and some of her people gone." She paused, looking away. "If she loses them all, she loses her crown. What is a queen with no people and no kingdom?"

"But what about her?" Huck persisted.

Munro cast him a dark look. "We don't know what's going to happen. There's no need to dwell on the worst possible scenario," he said.

"It's all right," Eilidh said softly to Munro. "If my reign has come to an end, I can't stop the inevitable. This is magic as old as the fae themselves." She turned to Huck. "If the victorious queen will have me, I would become her subject. The queen of Reshkin lost her throne this way. She was mated to the receiving queen's youngest brother. The pairing allowed for a more graceful transition by providing the queen the protection of the other royal family. I would be fortunate to be offered such an arrangement, should I lose my throne."

"But you already have a mate, almost two," Huck said with a glance at Munro.

She nodded. "Of course the outcome depends on who takes my throne." Her gaze shifted to Konstanze. "Some queens are less accommodating than others. Griogair is a prince in his own right, cousin to Queen Zdanye of Tvorskane. He will always have options, no matter what." She hesitated before adding, "As a druid lord, Quinton is not dependant on me for shelter or status."

"If Caledonia's gates are lost, you can become a part of the Druid Hall," Munro said. He squeezed her hand, but Eilidh didn't seem buoyed by the offer.

"Eilidh," Huck began, "what makes you so sure your kingdom is the one at risk?"

She smiled, but there was no happiness in her expression. "My kingdom is the youngest and the least stable. I was a usurper to begin with, and my reign has been plagued with treachery, murder, and near chaos."

"If you're right, who would take your gates?" he asked.

Munro interrupted before she could answer. "She's not right. Nothing indicates the gates will shift away from Caledonia."

Eilidh ignored Munro's response. "Konstanze, most likely," she said. "She controls a huge swathe of the human realm, more than any other. Another contender might be Vinye, of course. We share control of a group of human islands. Our gates are near to one another's. But in truth, human geography matters less than a queen's influence. No one has more influence than Konstanze."

Huck located Queen Konstanze in the crowd, and he was surprised to find her watching the three of them closely. When their eyes met, she gave a slight smile. Huck didn't care who was queen of what place or who controlled which gates, but Munro had been the one to help him after his druidic powers were unlocked. If Konstanze gaining control of Scotland meant Eilidh and Munro wouldn't be able to get married and that Eilidh would lose everything, Huck didn't like the idea.

"Why is Vinye tarrying so long?" Eilidh muttered to herself. "If she isn't here when the portal closes, she cannot be eligible to take control of the new gates. No queen, no matter how haughty," she said with a glance towards Konstanze, "would miss the opportunity to add to her power."

"What if she's the one who is losing her gates?" Huck asked.

"Vinye?" Eilidh said, surprised. "Impossible. She's been on her throne for hundreds of years."

"But didn't you dole out some humiliation to her last year?"

Eilidh chuckled. "Politics is full of humiliations. No, if the Stone shifted every time one queen had a political triumph over another, our people would be dizzy from the perpetual upheaval."

Huck opened his mouth to ask another question but was silenced by a loud rumble.

"She's not here," Eilidh whispered. "The portal is closing." She sounded almost hopeful. Perhaps, Huck thought, this meant Eilidh wouldn't be losing out to Vinye, whom even he knew she hated.

The blue orb began to dim, but before it closed completely, two figures stepped through.

"Vinye," Eilidh said, but broke off when she realised the figures exiting the portal were male.

Huck recognised one of them immediately. He was Vinye's mate, an elder faerie with greying hair and cloudy blue eyes. Streaks of blood splattered his tunic.

A gasp went up in the crowd. "Vinye is dead," said the prince-consort.

"Who's the other one?" Huck whispered to Eilidh.

"Vinye's son and only living heir, Koen," she said, her attention riveted on the arriving pair.

Huck was surprised. Because none of the kingdoms were ruled by men, he hadn't realised men could be heirs. Surely this wasn't the reason the gates were shifting. Of course, on the other hand, the blood on their clothing indicated something more was amiss.

"What happened?" asked one of the queens, but her question was drowned out by the murmurs around her when the gate turned black and began to solidify. The blue light had vanished, and as the new arrivals moved away from the platform, the familiar glow was replaced by a solid, black granite disk.

The disk began to spin slowly clockwise. A series of runes appeared on its surface, each one glowing brightly. Then the disk stopped and one rune burned brightly, then disappeared.

"Vinye," Eilidh whispered. "That was her sigil." She closed her eyes and her lips moved as though she was again talking to herself.

"What happens now?" Huck asked softly.

"Now we see the rune of the queen whose kingdom will enfold Andena." The disk ground around and jerked from time to time. Eilidh watched closely as each rune approached the top of the disk.

At one point, the gathered queens gasped. Both Munro and Huck looked to Eilidh. She seemed puzzled. "It passed over Konstanze's mark."

A few minutes later, the hushed crowd began to shout with disbelief. "What?" Huck said over the uproar as he peered at the stone. "Whose sigil is it?"

Before Eilidh could answer, the crowd parted in front of her and the two princes made their way through. The elder, Vinye's mate, stood back while his son strode up to Eilidh. "Your Majesty," the younger man said, falling to his knees, looking pale and shaken. "I pledge fealty to Caledonia and beg your mercy on my house." He glanced up. "If you will not spare my life, at least spare my father, who shares no blood with my mother, who was your enemy."

Eilidh stood in silence, staring down at the young prince whose head was bowed low. She glanced around in disbelief, then glanced again at the stone portal. It quivered, as though ready to name another if she rejected the boy's loyalty.

"You and your family have nothing to fear from me if you had nothing to do with the murder of my people."

Huck awaited his answer as eagerly as everyone else in the crowd. Everyone present knew well that Vinye had plotted to destabilise Caledonia last year, and her plot included ordering mass murder, which she attempted to blame on Eilidh.

Prince Koen looked up, still kneeling, and met Eilidh's eyes. "I swear I had no part in that monstrous plot. It shames me to the core. I would give my life to undo the horror my mother visited upon our race."

"Then you will find shelter in Caledonia."

His father spoke up, his voice shaking slightly. "And what form will this shelter take? Will you offer my son to mate with a faerie of your own bloodline?"

Eilidh hesitated. "I have no sisters, nor female cousins. I am my mother's only daughter, as she was her mother's only daughter."

Much to Huck's surprise, Konstanze swept forward, her eyes gleaming. Eilidh's rune appearing on the disk must have been as much of a shock to her as to Eilidh. "I will give refuge to you, Prince Koen. And you will find shelter in my bloodline. You will become the mate of my sister's daughter."

As soon as the words were out of her mouth, the disk began to turn, and the glow behind Eilidh's rune dimmed. She watched the artefact in horror.

"No," she said. "Koen has pledged his loyalty to Caledonia, and I will offer the shelter of my bloodline." The runestone growled, and the light behind her sigil did not dim further. "I will take Koen as my mate, third to Prince Griogair and Druid Lord Quinton Munro."

Munro didn't speak, but his jaw flexed as he ground his teeth.

Prince Koen paused and licked his lips nervously. "Although we are most grateful to Queen Konstanze for her offer of haven in this difficult time, I humbly accept your offer, Queen Eilidh."

With a growling shift of the stone, Eilidh's rune once again shone at the top of the disk. The other symbols shifted, leaving no sign Vinye's sigil had ever existed. With a quiet whishing sound, the stone dissolved into darkness, which then burst into a glow. The blue portal retuned, blazing brighter than before.

The prince rose and stood aside, he and his father both keeping their heads bowed to Eilidh.

"Prince Estobar, how did Queen Vinye die?" Eilidh asked.

The dead queen's consort shifted uncomfortably. "The circumstances are unclear, Your Majesty, as her body was discovered only half a night ago. We believe the kingdom Watchers were acting at the direction of certain members of the Andenan conclave, but I have no proof of this."

Eilidh frowned, then nodded. She signalled to her entourage. The crowd parted, and with a glance towards Munro, she stepped towards the portal, crossing through first, followed by her mate Griogair. Last of all were the two Andenan princes, Koen and his father.

"What does this mean?" Huck asked Munro, who stayed rooted in his place.

"It means Eilidh is growing more powerful," he replied, his mouth set into a grim line.

"Will she really marry this guy?"

Munro looked at him. "Eilidh will do what she has to for her people, as she's always done." Without another word, he turned and broke through the murmuring crowd, many of whom appeared anxious to return to their own kingdoms. Munro headed towards the Druid Hall, and the other druids followed.

For the first time since he stepped through the portal, Huck remembered why he'd returned, and the mysterious woman he'd followed through the streets of Amsterdam.

CHAPTER 4

FLÙRANACH ADJUSTED THE HOOD covering her face and her distinctive, flowing red hair as the queens dispersed. Her gaze travelled to the furthest bridge over the mists, a bridge only recently created.

She didn't like the Halls of Mist, this strange, in-between land with no sun or moon, no connection to the human realm, no earth but that which was brought in from the faerie kingdoms.

Flùranach grew up in the human realm, born in exile when azuri talents were still punishable by death in any kingdom. She had planned to return there after she released Rory from his false bond, but she'd not been able to take the final step through the gate. Shame burned within her at the memory of what she'd done. She blinked to keep tears from flowing freely.

The crowd had vanished through the portals or to the Halls. Flùranach stood alone and unnoticed at the back of the courtyard, near the library entrance.

She stared towards the Druid Hall. Rory. Aaron. Douglas. Munro. Huck. She'd only met Huck once, on the day she found him and unlocked his druidic talents, but she observed him closely today. She felt his druid magic stirring, less developed than the others, but strong. In addition to the astral powers she was born with and the voice of time that stayed with her ever since her encounter with the void, she possessed an affinity for druids. She sensed their powers, even when they themselves did not recognise what they were. No other living faerie was known to possess her ability. Other faeries could only touch those with whom they would be a compatible match for bonding. If not for her, they never would have discovered Huck. Despite her achievements and talents, her crimes forced her to stay hidden.

Flùranach took a deep breath. She was about to turn towards the library entrance when a voice spoke to her from behind. "You shouldn't dwell on the druids," Oszlár said. "It's not time for you to approach them yet, child. Focus instead on your own development."

"Not dwell on them?" she repeated softly. "He is in my heart, day and night. I cannot forget. He looked good today. Healthy and strong. He is healing well."

Oszlár's voice became sterner. "The deepest wounds are not visible to the eye, child. Come inside. You took too great a risk venturing out today. I shall build a cell for you if you find you cannot control your impulses."

Flùranach shook her head and turned to the ancient keeper, the oldest fae alive and the wisest of them. "That will not be necessary, keeper."

He nodded without smiling. "I worry for you. Rory is healing, but are you?"

She wiped away a tear and turned to go down into the library complex. "I will heal when Rory forgives me," she said.

Before he let her go, Oszlár put a hand gently on her arm. "No, child. You will heal when you forgive yourself."

"Do you have time to read with me today? Or shall I ask Dumvwere?" She couldn't face the painful truths Oszlár so often wanted to talk about. Over the months she'd hidden among the keepers, she'd found it easy to change the subject. Oszlár was persistent, but not unkind.

"I must go to Caledonia to offer my assistance and counsel to Queen Eilidh. It is traditional, but I imagine her joint conclave will have her ears buzzing with advice for many weeks if not months to come." He paused. "Do you like reading with Dumvwere?"

A young scholar, Dumvwere was handsome and, unusually for a faerie, had a quirky sense of humour and laughed openly. No doubt Oszlár hoped Flùranach would find him attractive. The old faerie thought she obsessed over the druids, especially Rory. He didn't understand the magic compelling her to stay close to them or the deep connection she'd shared with Rory for a brief time. It didn't matter how the bond came about or that she'd severed the connection. Rory would forever be part of her.

"Yes," she said with a smile. "He's very patient. Good journey to you, keeper." She moved towards the long, spiral stair leading down to the library. This time, Oszlár did not try to stop her.

∞

Rory followed the others to the Druid Hall, but his thoughts stayed in the square. He'd felt Flùranach's presence, much like he might notice a familiar scent. That particular vibration in his soul wasn't the sort of thing he would forget or fail to recognise. What would she have been doing at the Halls of Mist? As he walked away, the notion faded. By the time they reached their Hall, he wondered if he'd imagined the sensation.

Flùranach is gone, he told himself. He wondered where she'd been, as he so often did. Was she still alive? As soon as he voiced the question, he dismissed it, certain he would be aware if she died. Now that some time had passed, he found himself more kindly disposed towards her. Six months ago, he swore he'd never forgive her for stealing his bond, marring him magically so he could never bond with another. She'd trapped him in the kind of slavery no man would like to contemplate. He hadn't even been able to disagree with her without horrific pain.

Once, he'd been so attracted to her, but then she'd betrayed his trust and everything changed. On the other hand...

"Rors?" Aaron said.

Rory looked up, startled to realise he'd stopped walking and just stood in the doorway, staring into space. "What? Oh, sorry." He shook his head as though trying to clear the cobwebs. This happened more often than he cared to admit. Yes, the deep anger had vanished and even the sadness and depression he'd experienced for a while after Flùranach left, but he wasn't the same. He felt distant from the others. No matter how they tried, they could never understand what he'd lost, especially Aaron and Huck, who'd never bonded.

"You okay?" Aaron was the one Rory had known the longest, the one who years before had introduced him to the faerie who unlocked his powers, and the one who tried the hardest to keep Rory from retreating into his own shell.

"Yeah, I'm fine. Just thinking about today." Not that he'd tell any of them he thought he'd sensed Flùranach. They'd get worried all over again, think he was going 'round the bend.

"Never saw that coming," Aaron said. "So Eilidh now controls all the gates from Scotland, Ireland, Wales, and England?"

Munro nodded. "Not just that. Iceland, the Faroe Islands, the Isle of Man, Guernsey, Jersey, and the northwest quadrant of France and most of

Belgium." He frowned, his dark mood creeping out from him like a black fog.

"As if she didn't have enough going on with the wedding coming up," Aaron said. "Now she's got a kingdom doubling in size, if not more, overnight."

"But this is a good thing, right?" Huck asked. He sat on the low, fae-made settee in the back of the room and kicked off his shoes. "It's a helluva lot better than if Vinye took over her kingdom, which is what Eilidh thought would happen."

They looked to Munro, but he stayed silent.

Aaron broke the awkward silence. "Eilidh always worries. You know her. She's a better queen than all the others put together, but she's insecure because she's so young. This will have to boost her confidence."

"Or scare the crap out of her," Rory said, leaning against the entry archway. "It sure would scare me. She had trouble believing she had a grip on things after the mess last year. Now she's got twice the responsibilities and a new fiancé she's never met before. That can't be easy." Munro twitched at the mention of Prince Koen. Rory was surprised he seemed so upset, considering he hadn't minded that Eilidh also married Griogair, but the three of them had a strange and complicated relationship.

"I've got to go," Munro said. "I'll be in Caledonia for a while."

"Wait," Huck said with a sudden note of urgency. "I need to talk to you before you leave. Can you spare a few minutes?"

Munro stopped and raised an eyebrow. Huck never asked for help. He was the independent type, so much so that the others never saw him half the time.

"I was just coming back from Amsterdam to talk to all of you. I know everything is a mess, but I think this is important."

"Sure," Munro said.

That was like him, Rory thought. He would always put his own stuff aside to help someone else, especially one of the other druids. Even though Aaron had been around the longest, over time, Munro had become the real leader. Even the queens sensed it because he was the one they deferred to the most, the one they looked to for decisions.

"I met this woman," Huck began, staring down at his hands.

Aaron broke into a smile. "Aw, our little Hucky has a girl."

"Not like that," Huck said quickly, then paused. "She's different...like *we're* different. She read one of my runes. I think she might be a druid."

Munro sat back down, his own problems immediately shifted to the side. "Tell me from the beginning." Rory joined them as well, careful not to fall out of the fae-made swing chair. He still hadn't gotten used to the bloody things.

Huck reluctantly came clean about selling his druidic talismans at a few out-of-the-way shops in Scotland, Switzerland, Ireland and the Netherlands. Munro frowned but didn't interrupt. Huck went on, describing how he'd met the woman, the way she read his rune and then ran when she realised he'd seen what she did.

"You're sure she wasn't fae?" Aaron asked. "There are probably quite a few exiles out there living in secret. Just because Caledonia doesn't execute azuri fae anymore doesn't mean all the kingdoms are on the same page or would welcome back those they'd kicked out."

Huck shook his head. "Round ears and normal eyes."

"But astral fae can cast illusions to change their appearance," Rory reminded him.

"I don't think so," Huck told him. "She didn't move like one of them or even like we could after we'd been to the Otherworld. She definitely didn't want to be followed. If she could have moved faster, she would have."

"All she said was 'fire heart'?" Munro asked, deep in thought.

"Yeah, but those were the exact two runes I put into the crystal. It wasn't a coincidence. She read my intent."

Rory understood why the American druid wanted so much to be believed. He was the newest, and in some ways, an outsider. The other druids had been born in Scotland. All but Munro were water druids, so they had something central in common. More importantly, they'd gone through so much together in the past couple of years. Huck was a lone wolf, but perhaps they hadn't worked hard enough to make a place for him.

"If she can read runes, her powers have already been awakened, which means she's encountered a faerie sometime in her past. Unlocking doesn't just happen," Rory said, wanting to show solidarity with Huck.

"I think someone else was watching her too," Huck said. "I thought I saw a figure in the alley near her house, but when I looked again, there was no one there." He shrugged. "For all I know, the whole thing was my imagination."

Rory felt another pang of compassion. Huck was making excuses and not trusting his instincts, the same way Rory did when he thought he detected Flùranach's presence at the square today.

"How can we be sure?" Aaron asked. "Maybe we should talk to her. We've discussed how we would approach another druid, but dropped the idea. Now that we can't find them…" He faltered, obviously not wanting to mention Flùranach and her talent for detecting druids. "I had put those plans out of my mind, to be honest."

"We can't be certain," Munro said. "Not unless her talents are already manifest and she can make talismans herself. If she's developed enough to be able to read runes, though, she surely knows what she is. The real question is, if she is a druid, where is the faerie who unlocked her? In my experience, the only ones who can uncover latent talents in humans are either a compatible faerie, or a faerie with the ability to detect a druid."

"Like Flùranach," Rory said absently. The others looked at him uncertainly. Why did they think he would fall apart at the mention of her name?

"Could she…" Aaron glanced at Rory before continuing. "Could she be in the Netherlands? Could she be the one who unlocked this woman's talent?"

"Possibly," Munro said. "On the other hand, this woman might have been unlocked by an exile we've never heard of. We shouldn't jump to conclusions."

"We need to get back on track looking for other druids," Rory said. He wasn't the same wreck he'd been before. He didn't like being treated like a fragile mess. Sure, he'd become a little distant, maybe, but he wanted to get on with life.

"How?" Aaron asked. "Without someone like Flùranach, we can't find them. We can't even prove this girl of Huck's is a druid without just walking up and asking her."

Huck chuckled. "I doubt she'd be open to that. I suppose we have no choice. If she is a druid, maybe we can help her."

Determination surged in Rory like he hadn't experienced in a long time. "I have an idea where Flùranach went."

Every eye turned to him, and the silence stretched for a few minutes before Munro asked quietly, "How?"

His sense of her in the courtyard had been fleeting. Nothing would make that story sound sane. "Just a hunch. I want to check it out."

"What about the girl in Amsterdam?" Huck asked.

"Give me a couple of days. It probably won't take that long. I think...I think Flùranach is closer than we suspected." Rory bore the weight of their expectant stares. No one wanted to question him about how or what he knew. "You know how she was before. She couldn't stay away even then. I don't think much has changed."

"You think she's here in the Halls of Mist? Which Hall?" Munro asked.

"I'm not sure, but I believe she was at the gathering today." He nodded in the general direction of the distant courtyard.

Aaron said, "We can't trust her. Even if she is close, we should take the news as a warning, not as the solution to our problems. Don't the rest of you remember what she did to Rory? How she viciously attacked him?"

A flush of shame reddened Rory's face, and he hated showing the weakness. "I think if I'm ready to at least talk to her, the rest of you should be willing. I knew six months ago we'd need her if we were going to increase our numbers, but I refused to forgive her when she asked. It's my fault she's gone. I had the power to stop her, but I let her go."

Aaron was still angry, but Rory understood why. The other druid was afraid. He didn't want to end up a magical cripple like Rory was. Flùranach had the power to maim any of the unbonded druids. "And you have forgiven her now?" Aaron asked.

Rory didn't have an answer for that. "I'm at least willing to find out if she'll work with us. I'm planning to find her and talk to her, no matter what we decide about the rest. I have to. For my own peace of mind. At least as a druid, all of the Halls will receive me. I think I'll know if she's near enough, even if they stonewall me."

"Okay," Munro said. "Do you want help? I'll come with you. Just say the word."

"No, but thanks for offering," Rory replied. "You should be with Eilidh. She'll need you right now. Huck can tag along to the Halls since he has more frequent contact with the queens than I do. Some of them may still be around after the shifting today. If we find Flùranach and can convince her to work with us, we'll take her to Amsterdam, assuming Konstanze will give us passage through the German portal."

Aaron glowered at them. "Fine," he said. "Find her if you must. I'll be the last person to say you shouldn't deal with your own issues, but keep her away from me. Far away."

Rory gave a nod of agreement. After all, what were the chances he'd actually sensed her presence? He might never find her. If he did, could he face her? Despite his brave talk, he felt vulnerable, confronted with the reality of encountering the woman who'd scarred him for life.

"All right," Munro said. "I'm off to Caledonia, and I'll talk to Douglas while I'm there, tell him what we're planning and find out when he's thinking of coming back." Douglas still spent most of his time in Caledonia with his bonded faerie, Prince Tràth. He was the only one of them who didn't make their permanent home at the Druid Hall. Munro gestured to Huck. "Can I have a word alone?"

Rory stood and made his way out, saying he wanted to grab a few things before they left and promising to be right back. Munro was going to chide Huck for selling those talismans, and he didn't want to make the ordeal worse for Huck by giving them an audience. Rory understood why Munro would be cautious. If the humans found out about the fae, who knew what might happen? Sure, faeries had magic, but they were far outnumbered. The entire race could be wiped out in a trice by guns and modern weapons. Although they had the option to retreat into the Otherworld, that would mean a much slower, but equally permanent, death of their race. Without access to the human realm, faeries couldn't offer the required sacrifice to the Mother of the Earth to ask for the blessing of fertility. By peddling his fire rocks, Huck put the secrecy of the entire fae race at risk.

CHAPTER 5

AFTER TALKING TO HUCK, Munro immediately headed through the portal to Caledonia. On the other side, he gave polite congratulations to Bran and the other Watchers, who greeted him as they celebrated the growth of the kingdom and the addition of new gates.

His mind was far away, though, with Eilidh and her promised *third* husband. As soon as Munro could make his getaway, he hurried on. Travelling to the castle at Canton Dreich, Munro thought about the time not so long ago that he was merely Eilidh's secret lover. Eilidh's first marriage had been a political one, and Griogair didn't want to come between Eilidh and Munro. The pair shared a deep, magical bond and were so much a part of each other, sometimes he couldn't tell if his moods were his own or a reflection of Eilidh's.

Over time, Eilidh had fallen in love with Griogair too. They hadn't expected the romance to blossom. Coming from a traditional Scottish background,

Munro never would have believed he would accept a three-way arrangement. In the end, he and Griogair had become like brothers, both loving and supporting Eilidh in a role that had already cost her so much. Munro and the prince worked things out, gave each other space, and understood the other always had Eilidh's best interests at heart.

This new guy, Prince Koen, threatened the delicate balance of their arrangement. He barely even looked old enough to shave, but likely he was over a hundred. Funny how Munro had come to believe a century was young, when he himself was only in his mid-thirties. Over the years with Eilidh, he'd adjusted to the fae way of thinking. Where would Koen fit into their lives?

Munro understood that she was a queen, and as such her role was bigger than her personal desires. They would never share a normal existence even by fae standards, much less human ones.

The landscaped whizzed by as he pondered and ran. Canton Dreich grew nearer by the second, and still he had no idea what he would say to her. A part of him was angry at her choice, but even more than that, he was shocked. She hadn't even paused to consider him or Griogair before she made such a monumental commitment.

Crossing through the last lush forest on his way to Eilidh's castle, he barely noticed the scenery or paused to relish their bond, as he often would when entering Caledonia. Instead, his mind buzzed with *what ifs* and *whys*.

Her presence nestled in his thoughts, and his feet pointed straight to her. The longer they shared the rare and ancient fae-human bond, the more naturally he sensed her responses. At the moment, varying emotions flooded her mind at once: worry, annoyance, exhaustion, and exasperation. Beneath it all, however, an undercurrent of her love for him surged into his awareness. Without that frequent reminder, their relationship might not have endured as well or as long as it had. He recognised that no matter what else happened, she loved him deeply, and that knowledge made so many things bearable.

His internal compass led him to a formal reception room on the third level of the castle. He nodded to the saluting Watchers he passed and tried not to notice the servants who melted out of view as soon as he approached.

Without pausing to be announced, Munro strode into the room, past the courtiers and attendants, past the twenty-four members of the joint conclave. He nodded to Prince Koen and his father and walked directly to Eilidh, who sat frowning on a wide, carved wooden throne. Prince Griogair stood behind her, leaning languidly with his hand resting on the high back of the throne. His swirling violet eyes met Munro's, and the prince gave the druid an almost conspiratorial tilt of the head.

"Your Majesty," Munro said with a respectful bow.

Eilidh's stiff posture reflected the rigidity in her thoughts. She had avoided Munro's gaze until he spoke, instead listening to the conclave, who chattered hurriedly to one another. Finally, she turned to Munro. "My lord druid," she replied. "I didn't expect you today."

He smiled, hoping to break the tension. "Surprise," he said quietly.

Although she didn't return his smile, a ripple of silent laughter moved through their bond. She often said she loved his distinctly human nature.

"I thought I'd come meet this lad you're planning to marry," he said, careful to keep his tone light, even though she would detect his inner conflict.

She nodded and gestured to her other side, and Munro moved to a position opposite Griogair's but a pace forward. After all, as a druid, he technically outranked her. Still, that tradition was ancient and hadn't been observed for years, so Munro took care not to push the boundaries of propriety too far.

"I present Princes Koen and Estobar, formerly of Andena," she said to Munro, then turned her attention to the two men before her. "I introduce you to Lord Druid Quinton Munro."

They both nodded to Munro with respect, but Koen's expression revealed his unmasked curiosity. His aqua eyes evaluated everything about Munro, taking in his appearance, his clothing, his closeness to Eilidh, and the glance he gave Griogair. Munro couldn't decide if his immediate dislike for the prince was rooted in the lad's manner or the too-pretty, long dark lashes and full lips.

Estobar's appraisal of Munro appeared equally calculating, but at least he was much more subtle.

Then, as though they had noticed his presence, the members of the joint conclave also acknowledged Munro and spoke quiet words of greeting.

The scene struck Munro as a strange one. Considering how odd he still found fae politics, that was saying something.

"Prince Koen," Eilidh said pointedly to Munro, "wishes to establish himself in his own castle, along with his father and attendants and Watchers who are formerly of Andena."

The announcement surprised Munro. "But surely it's better for the Andenans to integrate into Caledonian society fully. By keeping themselves apart, wouldn't it appear Koen wanted to set up a kingdom within a kingdom?"

The two princes gasped and the others stayed silent, but Griogair chuckled. "My friend," he said. "You have hit on the truth immediately." He smiled at the two princes. "Of course our queen's new subjects will not wish to appear to desire the destabilisation of her reign. I'm sure they will agree they must stand shoulder-to-shoulder with Caledonians."

"This is outrageous," Prince Estobar interjected. "To suggest anything untoward about our request is an appalling insult."

The atmosphere in the room grew tense and silent. Eilidh gripped the arms of her throne. "I insult you?

I have offered your son the protection of my bloodline."

"Which we all know you were forced to do," Estobar countered, "or risk losing the Andenan gates to Queen Konstanze." He shrugged slightly. "There is no reason not to speak the truth."

"The truth?" Griogair asked.

"In fact, I suspect if our negotiations fail, the Stone might choose to send our people to Konstanze even now."

Suddenly, Munro understood. Estobar was jockeying to use the situation to get as much influence and power in Caledonia as he could scrape together. Munro felt Eilidh's fury ripple through their bond. The uncomfortable silence stretched as Eilidh worked to collect herself.

Munro turned to Koen. "Did you know the Source Stone was druid made?" He kept the question light, but he held the attention of every faerie in the room.

"No," the prince said. "I hadn't realised. Your people have achieved more than many suspected possible," he said slowly, as though choosing his words with care.

"Do you understand how it works?" Munro asked. "How it determines when to shift and to whom?"

"No," Koen said again. He glanced at his father, then back to Munro expectantly.

Rather than answer, Munro nodded. "No, I thought not." He said nothing more, but left the implication hanging. Doubt played across Estobar's angular features.

"Of course," Estobar interjected. "We would much rather ally with Caledonia than Ashkyne."

"Ally?" Eilidh said, sitting forward on her throne. "You imply we are equals and that you are more than refugees, subjects of a queen murdered by her own people for her greed and incompetence."

Prince Koen paled and stepped back a half-pace as though Eilidh had slapped him.

Eilidh softened her tone. "Caledonia has offered you refuge, Prince Koen, despite the crimes your mother committed, and our offer stands. However, your father's words indicate you may harbour second thoughts. If you do not wish to become my mate, third to Prince Griogair and Lord Druid Quinton Munro, I will not force you. You may stay in Caledonia as any of my subjects or find a place in another kingdom. Surely some queen will agree to take you in, despite your reckless treatment of Caledonia's offer. No matter what you choose, remember this: the portal has closed. The gates will not shift again today."

Koen looked back to his father, but Munro shouted, "Boy!" The startled young Prince met his harsh glare. "The queen is talking to you. Are you a child? Do not show her disrespect by turning away. Speak for yourself and let your answer be your own."

With effort, Koen tore his gaze away from Munro and met Eilidh's eyes again. "Of course, Your Majesty. I'm honoured by your offer and will, as I pledged, become your mate." He placed his hand over his heart and bowed at the waist.

"Very well," Eilidh said. "You shall take your place in Canton Dreich with me and my first mate, Griogair. The joint-conclave will see to your people. Former Andenans are now Caledonians and will be treated with the same heart as any in my kingdom."

Prince Estobar once more interrupted. "Your Majesty," he said. "I'm delighted all will be as you have promised. I would ask one small request, to seal the formality."

"Yes?" she said, her voice tight and her patience clearly wearing thin.

"I ask that the bonding to my son happen right away. Tomorrow or tonight even. My son and I have little need for a large, lavish ceremony as you might undoubtedly wish to hold. However, we are content for you to simply keep your word and to become your subjects. My son would find it unbearable to go any extended amount of time outside the embrace of your bloodline. I might even suggest that when you visit the new gates Andena added to your kingdom, you and Koen will be able to cement your pledge by offering a sacrifice to the Mother of the Earth together as mates."

Munro had to credit the guy's audacity. First he wanted basically his own fiefdom within Caledonia, and when that didn't work, he tried to make his son

Eilidh's second mate, not her third. The real topper, though, was him suggesting Koen should have an immediate opportunity to give her a child.

"As you are surely aware, I am taking Lord Druid Quinton Munro as my second mate in less than a week," Eilidh said.

"Of course!" Estobar said. "We are aware of your intention to take a human mate. I would never suggest you alter those momentous plans."

"I will wed your son at the Festival of Meir in thirteen moons' time." She paused a beat. "And, Prince Estobar, when I choose to visit the borderlands with my mates is a private matter and not open for discussion."

"Of course, Your Majesty," Prince Estobar said, giving no indication of frustration or disappointment in her refusal. "As a gesture of good faith, I will inform you now, the gate that leads to the borderlands the humans know as Belgium is unstable. Queen—" He paused and corrected himself. "Vinye had forbidden its use and did her best to ward and seal it."

Eilidh tilted her head, considering. "Do you know what is amiss with the gate?" she asked.

Estobar shook his head. "No, Your Majesty. I bring it up because with Vinye gone, her protective wards will have failed. I am sure you will know what to do to safeguard Caledonians from harm by using this unstable borderlands entrance."

"Thank you for informing me. Now, I am certain you wish to get settled," Eilidh said. Her face went momentarily vacant as it did when she was communicating telepathically. "Our head steward is on his way. He will show you and your son to your rooms." She stood and turned to Griogair and Munro. "Shall we retire so we can speak privately?"

"Your Majesty?" Estobar said, somewhat more tentatively than before. "If you are going to have a conference with your mate and bonded druid, perhaps Koen should also attend?"

Eilidh laughed, startling the older faerie. "Good morn, Prince Estobar. I hope you and your son will find your transition comfortable. The sun is rising, and we are all tired. Take the day to rest. I will speak with you both after the first evening meal." Without giving him further opportunity to reply, she quickly departed through the back archway. Munro and Griogair stepped after her.

She didn't slow her pace until she'd reached her private rooms. As soon as the three of them were alone in the cosy chamber none would dare enter without an invitation, she sighed. "I'm so sorry," she said. "I'm so very sorry."

"Hey," Munro said, and pulled her into an embrace. "None of that. You did the right thing." Just a half hour before, he'd felt annoyed and conflicted. After seeing how Estobar tried to manipulate her, he had an idea of what she was up against. She must dread the thought of taking Koen as a mate.

She melted into his arms with the kind of vulnerability she only ever showed to these two. She tilted her chin up and looked into Munro's eyes. "I sensed how angry you were when I proposed to him."

"Not angry. Surprised."

She turned to Griogair. "And you. I can't sense your thoughts, but I know you well enough, my mate. My decision didn't please you either." She slid out of Munro's arms and sank into a long, low seat and kicked her slippers off.

Griogair sat beside her and slipped an arm around her, kissing her on the cheek. "You are a queen. You made a difficult decision. I have never been more proud to be your mate as I was today."

"Besides," Munro said, "this Koen kid is a lightweight. If he gets out of hand, Griogair and I can take him, easy."

A tired smile crept over Eilidh's face. "It would be better if you took him under your wing. He will need help and guidance. Estobar has too much sway over Koen and will meddle at every turn."

Munro made a face. "I'm not sure you want the kid learning from me. I'm not a good influence."

Griogair chuckled. "We'll do what we can. Won't we, Munro?"

"Oh, all right," he said in a mock long-suffering tone.

"Quinton," Eilidh said, quickly becoming serious. "Why did the Stone choose me? Of all the queens, why me? Geography? That's never been the primary reason in the past, although most queens' borderlands are somewhat close in the human realm."

"I don't know," he said. "None of us understands the Stone, but I'll make it my priority to learn what I can. It's so overwhelming to be near the thing. We haven't been able to study it with any objectivity, but I'll try. I'm sure the keepers will help."

Griogair stroked her hand. "Do you have further need of me today, my love?" he asked. "If not, I will take my leave."

Munro silently thanked him. The arrangement worked in no small part due to Griogair's tact and consideration. Munro wondered once more how Koen would fit in to their strange little family.

"Good day, Griogair. I hope to see you at the first evening meal, if you have no other arrangements to attend to." She hesitated. "I need to speak with both of you before I depart to inspect the new gates and welcome our new citizens."

Munro glanced at Griogair. It was plain from the prince's expression he had no idea why she would make such a request.

"Of course," Griogair replied. "At moonrise." He stood with grace and leaned over to kiss her on the cheek. Nodding to Munro, he departed through the archway.

Eilidh rose and went to her dressing room. After a few moments, a flurry of attendants entered. Fabric bustled as they helped her remove her ornate dress.

Although he could have attendants help him undress, take away his laundry, and prepare new clothing for him to wear come nightfall, Munro preferred to do things himself. He made his way to Eilidh's bed chamber and sat on the edge of the swing bed. He removed his shoes one at a time, the same as he'd done when he was a beat cop in Scotland. Thinking of his old home for the first time in a long time, of the life, friends, and family he'd left behind, he glanced around the lush surroundings. He struggled to imagine himself walking into his aunt's sitting room and having tea and cakes like he did so long ago, or being out on patrol with his old partner, PC Getty, or taking orders from Sergeant Hallward. Would they be waiting if he walked through the door?

The fleeting fantasy vanished from his mind when Eilidh swept into the bedroom, naked except for a long, sheer robe. Even with the trials and worries of her first years on the Caledonian throne, she'd bloomed since returning from exile. Although she still had the lithe frame of her race, she appeared softer, her hips slightly fuller. Living in hiding for decades had made her lean, but now she'd come into the fullness of maturity. She'd never looked lovelier.

"What were you thinking just now?" she asked as she approached. He noticed a flutter of unusual energy about her aura, but the moment passed quickly and he dismissed the distraction as a trick of his mind.

Munro shook his head and reached out to take her hand. "I was in another world." Without missing a beat, he added, "You're beautiful."

The early morning sunlight streamed towards them from the outer chamber. "Liar. I'm exhausted," she replied, and they curled up on the swing bed together. After a long, languid moment, she said, "I didn't think you'd come."

"Why?" he asked, genuinely surprised.

"You've been distant of late. I know my choice to take Koen didn't please you."

"I've been giving you and Griogair the opportunity to be together without tripping over me. Besides, it's been hard work establishing the Druid Hall."

Her expression turned serious. "Griogair asked you to stay away?"

"No, of course not," he reassured her. "But he is your mate, and you love him. You deserve time alone with him."

"I need *you*," she said. "When you are across the portal from me, I feel empty. Will you return to live in Caledonia? Perhaps after we are mated?" Something in her expression and the quiver of their bond told Munro she was holding back. This was the most vulnerable he'd seen her in some time.

"I can spend more time here if that's what you need." He kissed her temple and she nestled into him. "We've had an interesting development at the Druid Hall," he said. "Huck thinks he's found a female druid."

"Really?" she asked.

"We can't be sure until we talk to her, but he said she read some runes."

"That's an unusual gift, even among the fae. She must be well developed. Where is she?"

"Amsterdam," he said. "A city outside the Ashkyne borderlands. Konstanze has been giving him pretty much free reign to visit the human realm through her gates."

"He's travelled into our borderlands as well. My Watchers tell me he makes a few trips a month through our gates."

"I think Huck is restless."

"Maybe he wishes to visit his own homeland. Where is he from?"

"America," Munro said. When Eilidh gave him a blank expression, he added, "It's over the ocean from Scotland."

"North?" she asked. "To the frozen lands?"

"West. Beyond a large ocean we call the Atlantic."

Eilidh sat up in the bed, making it sway sharply. "He's from The Bleak? Why did you never tell me this? I knew he was not from the area around my own borderlands, but I always assumed…" Her voice trailed off.

"What's wrong with him being from America?" The fae gave strange names to human places, calling large cities *wastelands*. It didn't surprise him that she didn't know the human names for cities outside her own borderlands. She even referred to cities in Scotland by their ancient fae names rather than the common English names.

"We don't talk about The Bleak." She shuddered as though someone had just walked over her grave.

"Who is queen of those gates?"

"No one," she said. "The Bleak is a wild place, full of dangers. The fae were driven out millennia ago, the queens killed, and the gates severed." After a pause, she added, "I never considered there might be druids there. I'm glad Huck Webster escaped such a horrific existence as he must have experienced in those desolate lands."

Munro searched for a way to bridge the gap in their understanding to gently ask what she thought Huck had escaped *from*. The druid had been working for a Texas oil company that did business in Aberdeen when Flùranach and Rory found him. Munro wondered how many abandoned gates might still exist, connecting somehow to the American landscape.

Eilidh shivered. After the stressful day she'd had, Munro decided not to press her merely to satisfy his own curiosity. "Rory is planning to seek out Flùranach. He thinks he knows where she might be hiding. Our only hope of finding more druids is with the aid of someone like her."

"It is a brave choice," Eilidh said.

"He's stronger than anyone realises."

The conversation trailed off, and they lay together in the morning light. Eilidh's breathing slowed and she drifted towards sleep, her head resting on his bare chest. Her voice flitted into his mind. *I love you.*

"I love you too," he whispered and closed his eyes. Such a simple thing, to lie with her and talk about their days, their worries, their plans. But he never took it for granted. Their world was too changeable, and he never knew what each moment might bring. For now, he pushed Koen and this mysterious druid of Huck's out of his mind. Instead, he thought about being with the woman he loved. He wished the moment would last forever, but in the morning she'd rush off to do whatever her kingdom required, to plan her third wedding. He'd return to the Halls of Mist and talk to the keepers about the Source Stone, hoping to unlock its ancient secrets.

It seemed like only moments later when Eilidh woke him with a light kiss, but the daylight had already dimmed. Her eyes shone in the darkness.

A smile played across his lips. He'd missed her. He realised how much he looked forward to the time they would spend alone together after their wedding. Of course, that time would include travelling, feasts, and galas at which he would be formally introduced to Caledonian society as her mate. Some of the time, however, they would be completely alone, and the idea pleased him.

"Good evening," he said and returned her kiss.

Her smile was marred by an expression of worry.

"What's wrong?" he asked.

"I am planning to ask Griogair to travel to the Andenan borderlands with me." Her words came out in a rush. "I need to greet the Andenan people and on such an occasion, it is customary to visit the altars and speak with the Andenan Watchers. If my wen-lei finds them to be suitable, they will be integrated into our own force. I will also have to quietly learn if Estobar is telling the truth about the broken gate in the Andenan lands. This entire process will involve such upheaval."

"I'm glad Griogair will be going with you. He's a lot better at politicking than I could dream of being."

Her smile brightened. "You don't mind?"

"Of course not," he said, slightly confused at her worry. It wasn't like this was the first time she and her mate had travelled without him. Perhaps she was anxious because of the upcoming wedding. "People respect me because I'm with you, or because of this Druid Lord title. But I'm just a guy from Perth who fell in love with someone who became a queen. When it comes to the serious or formal stuff, Griogair is your man, not me. I'm not jealous of your relationship with him. I'm surprised you think I would be."

"Thank you, Quinton," she said and wrapped her arms around him. She kissed him fiercely, and he returned her passion in equal measure.

"We have a little time before you need to leave, don't we?" he said, now wide awake and fully aware of her intimate touch and writhing movements.

"I'm their queen," she said. "They'll not leave without me."

∞

Huck and Rory left the Ashkyne Hall, the last of the places they intended to search for Flùranach. The pair spent the early part of the evening visiting every Hall, ostensibly requesting permanent access to the borderlands to facilitate their search for other druids. Huck did most of the talking while Rory concentrated on searching for Flùranach's presence.

Depressed and dejected after long hours of no luck, Rory wanted to scream in frustration. "I'm certain I felt her the other day. I would swear to it," he said as they descended from the Hall into the courtyard.

"I know," Huck said. Rory appreciated the support, even though the other druid had no way to really be sure if Rory was telling the truth or losing his mind.

"She might have mixed in with the crowd and left right afterwards. A lot of them did."

Rory nodded, staring at the immense blue orb and considering each of the kingdoms it led to. "If only the portal could tell us where it sends people. I mean, how does it choose which kingdom someone goes to?"

"I dunno," Huck said. "I guess I never thought about it. I step through, and I always end up where I want to go."

"What if you don't know where you want to go?" Rory asked, more thinking aloud than expecting an answer. He approached the blue glow and gazed into it.

Without warning, Huck moved into the portal and disappeared. Rory stood and stared for a moment, uncertain what the other druid was up to. But Huck was like that, always jumping in without questioning or thinking his actions through.

A few minutes later, Huck reappeared. "Ashkyne," he said.

"Interesting." Rory scratched the thick, short red hairs of his beard. "I wonder if it would do the same for me. It makes sense you would go to Ashkyne. That's how you'd get to your druid-girl. But me, I don't have an attachment to any kingdom. I suppose if any, it would send me to Caledonia."

Huck nodded. "Only one way to find out for sure. What harm can it do to try?"

Rory chuckled. "Well, if I don't have a clear destination in mind, the Stone might trap me in there forever or send me someplace that didn't exist up until I stepped through. For all we know, it could chuck me anywhere in the human realm with no way back without walking five hundred miles."

"You sound like Munro," Huck said.

"All it takes is one serious magical accident to make you cautious. Flùranach was eight years old when she encountered the time stream by linking with Tràth. She came out looking twenty-five, by human standards, and thinking like she was a thousand. When I touched the Source Stone, I have never faced anything before or since that made me feel like more of an insignificant speck."

Huck shifted uncomfortably. "We could ask the keepers."

"I'm not sure they know any more about the Source Stone than we do, and the Stone controls this portal." Bracing himself, he thought about Flùranach and passed into the blue glow. He expected to detect the difference in the air as he moved into one of the kingdoms, but nothing changed. Before long, he realised he'd simply moved straight through the glow of the portal to the other side. He looked at Huck through the dazzling light and moved into the orb once more. Again, nothing happened.

"So if you don't want to go anywhere, you don't?" Huck asked, furrowing his dark eyebrows together.

"But I do want to go somewhere. I want find Flùranach."

"That's *who*, though, not *where*. Maybe the portal isn't smart enough to find a person."

"It alters entire kingdoms and controls the gates, for god's sake."

They both stared as two faeries came through the portal. Rory didn't know either of them, but they nodded to him as they passed and went about their business.

"Maybe it's leading you here because she's still around and we missed her," Huck said.

"We went to every Hall. They aren't *that* big. I would have known if she'd been close."

"Maybe she's not in a Hall. We didn't check the library."

Rory looked towards the library entrance. Beyond the runed pillars, a stairway wound deep below their feet. Housed within was the Source Stone itself, directly under the portal. He hadn't been inside the library since he touched the artefact six months before. The event affected him differently than the others, maybe because of his magical injury. Connecting with the Stone strengthened the positive and powerful within him but also intensified his nightmares. He wasn't in any hurry to relive the experience.

"Can't hurt to check," Huck prodded him.

"What's our excuse though? With the queens, we asked for access to their gates."

Huck shrugged. "We're druid lords. Do we need an excuse?"

"We'll say we're looking for Munro. He spends half his life in there." Rory wasn't sure why he hesitated. Like Huck said, they weren't likely to be questioned, but cold dread filled his stomach. With great effort, he pushed past his fear. "Okay," he said.

With focused willpower, he followed Huck to the library entrance. He silently commanded his feet to move one in front of the other, down step after step, until they reached the vast foyer below. Black pillars held mounted runestones dotted within like a museum display. The druids' steps echoed off the high, stone walls and ceiling. It felt like a tomb.

Keeper Oszlár shuffled in, as he tended to do, bent from extreme old age. He straightened his back and met Rory's eyes. He looked sad. "You're not ready," he said.

Rory approached the old faerie. "What?" He thought he hadn't heard the keeper right.

"And neither is she, for that matter."

"She's here?" Huck asked.

Oszlár tilted his head noncommittally.

"How long?" Rory said, rapidly becoming angry. "How long have you been hiding her?"

"Why?" Oszlár asked. "Why do you want to know? Do you seek revenge? Justice, even?"

"I need her help."

"You aren't ready."

Rory fumed. "What gives you the right to decide when I'm ready?" he shouted. "I want to see her."

"Are you still having nightmares?" Oszlár asked.

Rory flushed. The question caught him off guard. "How do you know about that?"

"I saw within you when you touched the Source Stone. Her actions damaged you. Deeply."

"Yeah, well, I'm over it." Rory didn't believe the bravado he forced into his voice. Still, he bloody well wasn't going to be told how he felt by someone who saw a vision in a rock, even one as powerful and strange as the Source Stone.

"Ah, but she isn't."

The statement only made things worse. What did *she* need to get over? She attacked him, ripped off his clothes, and forced her way into his mind. His bond was shattered by what she did. He felt as though he would never be able to love anyone or anything again. And *she* was upset?

"I thought a druid's word was law," Huck said.

"Some things," Oszlár said, "are more important than tradition. You will see her again, but not before you're both healed." His eyes grew sharp and keen. "It is vital that she join you. If anything gets in the way of that coming to pass, the consequences for the entire fae race are far worse than you can imagine."

The keeper's words struck Rory as both ominous and peculiar. "You're claiming you know the future?" he asked.

"I know a few things," Oszlár replied, his previously harsh tone melting into wry humour.

"Flùranach is important to the future of your race?"

"She is the key to our survival."

Rory sighed. "I'm not going to hurt her. I just want to talk to her."

A soft voice spoke from a side entrance. "Rory."

All three turned. Flùranach stood fifty feet away near a darkened archway. She looked changed, more mature, possibly. Like the difference between a woman of twenty-five and the same woman at thirty. Her skin was the palest, most delicate pink, and strands of dark red hair wisped from beneath a hooded robe. Her green eyes swirled with magic, but still held that haunted look he'd seen in them the last time they met.

"I didn't notice you there," Rory said.

"I've been learning to mask my essence," she told him.

"I sensed you at the shifting of the gates."

"I faltered," she said and looked away as though ashamed.

Oszlár stepped towards Flùranach. "I can't allow this."

"I need you," Rory said, and Flùranach's face lit up.

"I will do anything you ask," she said. "Have you forgiven me?"

"I..." He was trapped. If he said no, Oszlár would make things difficult. But he didn't want to lie. This moment felt too important to tarnish it with falsehood. "I want to."

"I forbid you to leave," Oszlár said to the girl. "Go to your room."

Flùranach bowed her head in a submissive manner unlike any Rory had seen her demonstrate before. He almost didn't recognise her. "If a druid lord commands me to go with him, I cannot refuse. I don't wish to defy you, but I have little choice."

"I heard no command," Oszlár said. "He wishes to speak with you, and I'm telling you that you aren't ready. This is too important for us all, child. Don't be selfish, as is your habit. Remember, your wilful selfishness initiated the whole of your misfortune."

"I command you to come with me, Flùranach," Rory said. The authority in his voice sounded strange and foreign even to his own ears. "You will serve the Druid Hall."

She bowed her head low, as a servant would do. "As you wish, my lord druid." She kept her eyes down and didn't meet Oszlár's glare as she walked around him.

"You are willing to take responsibility for her, are you?" Oszlár said. "You don't even know what has happened to her, where she has been, or what she's endured. You haven't forgiven her for her last catastrophic mistake. What happens when she makes another? What will you do if she breaks another druid and you realise you might have prevented the disaster by leaving her to train with me?"

The keeper's words stung. The last thing Rory wanted was for Aaron or Huck or some future druid to go through what he had. The Flùranach standing in front of him didn't look like the same impetuous young woman who had attacked him. But was he prepared to challenge Oszlár? Why did the keeper's insistence on keeping them apart grate so much? Why didn't he just leave her behind? They could talk to this girl of Huck's without Flùranach. Sure, her talents would make life easier by confirming what they suspected, but they weren't against a wall...yet.

"I will take responsibility for her," Rory said, staring into Flùranach's downcast eyes. "She won't hurt anyone else."

Oszlár gazed at Rory searchingly, then nodded. "I will give my blessing on one condition." He turned to Flùranach. "Return here every fourth day so we might continue your training. If I sense you are becoming unstable, you will return here permanently without argument."

"Thank you," Flùranach said and bowed to the keeper. She turned to Rory and waited for his next command.

Every eye in the room was on him. *Jesus*, he thought. *What have I done?* "Fine," he said. "Let's go."

CHAPTER 6

HUCK ASCENDED THE STAIRS with Rory and Flùranach behind him. The tension stretched between them as they walked in silence. Everything about Flùranach exuded regret. She didn't seem dangerous. In fact, her behaviour came across as eerily submissive, in stark contrast to the eager, brash young woman who'd approached Huck six months before with wild claims about him being a druid. But Huck hadn't seen her since, so he was hardly an expert.

He turned as they arrived at the portal. He opened his mouth to speak but froze when Rory turned to Flùranach. "Stop it," Rory said. "Or I send you to Oszlár right now. Got it?"

She nodded and blushed. Huck didn't know what she did that bothered Rory and wasn't going to ask.

Rory asked Huck, "Are you ready? If we leave now, do you think we'll get through Ashkyne and to the German gate before daybreak?"

Huck nodded. "The run to Amsterdam isn't bad. We'll arrive in good time. How does Flùranach's thing work, exactly?" He didn't understand why he was asking Rory instead of her. Something about her seemed off, as though she was a shadow of her former self.

"When we found you, she sensed your presence from outside the building. So we can go, check out the house, then come straight back and talk to the others. We should be able to find out what we need to and return before the gates close at dawn."

"If she's a druid, I want to speak with her," Huck said. "Aren't we planning to invite her here like you two did with me?"

Rory hesitated. "We can't take a strange human through the German gate without Konstanze's permission, not unless we want to battle a bunch of her Watchers, which we don't. We can see how much time we have, but we can't bring her with us today. Besides, we've always said we should give someone time to make the decision. Learning about the Otherworld is a lot to take in."

"When I found out, I wanted to join you instantly."

"She might be different. It won't hurt to give her time to consider her options."

Rory was right, but Huck felt an inexplicable sense of urgency. Maybe his reaction was partly motivated by the attraction he had for her, but he believed that pull was more than just physical. There was something special about her and he wanted, no *needed*, to get to know her. "Okay," he said. "I can always stay behind and spend the day in Amsterdam and return when the gates reopen at nightfall." Rory cast a glance at Flùranach, and Huck wondered if the other druid was afraid to be alone with her. Maybe Huck should come back with them after all. "We'll play it by ear."

"Let's go," Rory said, and they went through the portal. On the other side, they had a little bit of a hold-up when the Watchers routinely challenged Flùranach. She pulled out an identity token bearing the sigil of the keepers, and they let her pass. The druids had created their own tokens for those who lived in and served the Druid Hall. Huck made a comment that they'd have to make one for Flùranach, but Rory said nothing. His wary expression spoke volumes. He watched her as though she was a dangerous animal.

When they arrived at the gate to the German borderlands, Flùranach asked, "Shall I cast the illusions now?"

"Sure," Rory said. Flùr would definitely stand out, and with those pointed ears and shining eyes, Rory couldn't pass for human anymore. Only Huck still appeared completely human, although he had noticed his hair looked thicker and glossier and his skin had an almost unnaturally healthy sheen.

"No pink hair this time?" she asked softly.

A smile flickered across Rory's lips but was quickly replaced by an anguished expression. "No," he said, his voice almost choked.

Again, the pangs of regret played across her troubled eyes, and she nodded. With a scant whisper, she gestured at Rory, adding minute flaws to his skin, rounding his ears, dulling his hair, and changing his eye colour. She did the same to herself and added the additional illusion of jeans and a t-shirt. Rory and Huck's clothes were simple enough to pass for human attire, so she left them as they were.

Rory nodded, and his expression softened. "Thank you." With a glance at the tall, glowing gate, he added, "We should go."

The scant praise made Flùr flush with happiness, but Rory had already passed through the gate and hadn't noticed. Huck let Flùranach go second, and he went last. They immediately turned and made their way through the countryside. The Watchers on the human side of the gates didn't show themselves. They encountered no other people until they came to Dutch cities. The trio rushed through without slowing, keeping to smaller, less populated roads. Even still, they moved so fast that anyone who saw them would assume their eyes were playing tricks on them.

Once in Amsterdam, the three travellers had to be more careful. The city never went completely silent, even at this late hour. They had to dodge vehicles on the road and avoid people who hung about here and there, especially as they passed through the tourist parts of town. *It must be a weekend*, Huck thought, but he couldn't be sure. Faeries didn't operate on a

Monday-through-Friday, nine-to-five work week, so neither had he for quite some time.

When they approached the right street, they stopped. Huck didn't need to say a word. Flùranach immediately focused on one house, her gaze travelling to the highest level. "I was right, wasn't I?" he asked. "You can sense her power?"

"Yes, I think so." Flùranach said, but she frowned and shook her head as though trying to deflect a bee buzzing around her ear.

"What's wrong?" Rory asked, concern etched on his human-looking features. Huck found it strange to see him without the usual glowing blue eyes and pointed ears.

"Her power feels strange to me, but the house has been warded," she said, "which interferes with my perception. This doesn't feel like any ward I've encountered before, and yet the impact is strong. If I did not feel drawn to the druid presence inside, I would experience an urge to pass this place by, my mind not wanting to accept it."

"Could a druid create a ward?" Huck asked, looking from Flùranach to Rory.

"I don't know," they both said at once.

"I'm going to knock," Huck said.

"At this hour?" Rory reasoned. "We should wait until morning."

"Rory," Flùranach said, her attention still fixed on the top floor. "I believe she is not alone. I'm not sure. The ward is confusing my senses."

Huck stopped short. He'd not even considered the woman might not occupy the house alone. Was she living with a husband or boyfriend? Could that person be another druid or an outcast faerie in hiding? His gut twisted when he contemplated the possibility. He'd only seen her the once, but he didn't enjoy the idea that she may be spoken for.

"I'm going in," he said. "If there's a faerie inside, there's a good chance they're awake anyway, with the way faeries stay up all night and sleep during the day." He turned to Rory. "Coming with me?" he asked.

Rory glanced up and then at Flùranach. "Can you enter a warded building?"

She furrowed her brow. "If you take my hand, I will try. But without your touch to guide me, my mind will quickly send me in the wrong direction. This enchantment is peculiar and powerful." Considering Flùranach was an astral faerie with strong mental powers, that was saying something.

With a reluctant nod, Rory held out his hand and Flùranach took it.

"Okay," Huck said. He walked across the street to the house, and with a glance back at Flùr and Rory, he pushed the doorbell.

A muted ringing sounded inside the quiet house. He pressed again and waited. After the second chime sounded, a set of light footfalls padded towards the front of the house. Someone paused near the door. She was probably watching him through the peephole, Huck thought. There was no motion for a long time, and he wondered if she was hoping he'd go away. But if she could see him, she knew he wasn't alone. Would the presence of others frighten or reassure her?

He'd stand there punching the bell until daybreak if he had to. He lifted his hand and pressed again, ringing for a third time. Finally, several sliding latches made a scraping sound as someone unfastened them. The door opened as wide as the thick chain lock would allow. Her small face peered at him in the darkness. "What do you want?" she asked. Her accent was deep and throaty.

"I need to talk to you," he said, uncertain what he should say. The plan had seemed so reasonable in his head, but now he wasn't sure.

"I don't know you. Go away." She sounded scared.

"I know you're a druid," he told her. "So am I. So is he," he said, pointing to Rory, who stood behind him. With a gesture to Flùranach, he said, "And she's fae."

The woman paled. She slammed the door but didn't move away.

"Please," he called as loudly as he dared. The last thing he wanted was for a neighbour to summon the police. "We're not here to hurt you. We only want to talk."

"Who sent you?" she replied.

"No one. We're from the Druid Hall."

"The what?" She sounded genuinely surprised.

"The Druid Hall. We live and work together in the Halls of Mist." When she didn't speak for a few moments, he added, "We've come to offer you a place with us." Huck held his breath and listened hard.

"How did you find me?" she asked so softly he almost didn't hear.

"I followed you from the coffee shop," he said. "I recognised what you were when you read my runes."

He waited a long few moments, then the chains slid in their locks. She opened the door again. "How do I know you are what you say?" She peered through into the darkened entryway at Flùranach. "She does not look fae."

He gave Flùranach a nod, and she momentarily dropped the illusions on herself and Rory. The woman in the doorway sucked in her breath but didn't back away. "Can we come in?" Rory asked gently. "I swear we aren't here to hurt you."

She gave a fearful glance over her shoulder.

"Is there someone else here?" Huck asked.

She nodded and opened the door a little wider. "Come in, but please keep quiet. I don't want to wake my family."

Huck's hopes fell. She had a family. He'd just met her. The news shouldn't bother him. With a mental kick to his determination, he reminded himself he had a job to do. He stepped into the gap, but turned when the other two didn't follow him.

Flùranach had gone bone-white. She gripped Rory's hand for all she was worth. "I can't cross the threshold," she said, swallowing uncomfortably. "Some druid magic is making me sick."

The woman inside seemed pleased. "We are warded against the fae," she said. "The stronger you are, the more adversely you'd be affected."

Huck looked at her. "Can you remove it? Just temporarily?"

She knitted her dark eyebrows together. "I have to protect my family," she said.

"Not from us," he told her. "We mean you no harm. We just want to invite to you the Druid Hall."

"You may enter if she waits outside," she said. "I have no reason to trust the fae."

"She serves the Druid Hall," Rory said. Huck knew Rory didn't want to send him inside alone, but neither did he trust Flùranach outside on her own. "She will do as we command."

The woman's eyes widened. "A faerie serves a druid?" Her tone was sceptical.

"Yes," Flùranach answered without hesitation. "I serve the druids unequivocally."

The woman watched for a moment, then she bent and picked up a stone hidden amongst some shoes inside the front door. "Come in," she said, opening the door all the way. She was wearing pyjamas: dark purple patterned bottoms with a soft, grey long-sleeved top.

Flùranach was able to follow her inside, although she still appeared somewhat strained. When they all reached a small seating area at the top of a flight of stairs, the woman put the stone near the corridor leading deeper into the house. So she would let them enter this one room only. His curiosity brimmed. Why was she so cautious? Why was she afraid of faeries, and who was she trying to protect?

"Sit, please," she said in a voice barely above a whisper.

"I'm Huck Webster," he said. "This is Rory and Flùranach." The visitors sat with their backs to the large window.

"I am Demi Hartmann," she told them and took a place in a soft, beige armchair opposite them. "Tell me about the Druid Hall," she said. "I have never heard of this place."

"You know of the Otherworld?" he asked.

"Yes." She shivered and tugged on her sleeves until they covered all but her fingertips.

He told her about the Halls of Mist and how it connected the fae kingdoms by a magical portal. Then he described the Druid Hall, the druids' place in fae society, and their goals of discovery and creation.

Flùranach asked, "Who unlocked your powers, Demi?"

Again the veil of fear returned to Demi's features. "What do you mean?"

"Druidic powers lie dormant until the human has contact with a faerie, either one with a compatible bond, which is rare, or someone like me. I sense the talents of all druids."

"It was a long time ago," Demi said. "Several years."

Her resistance bothered Huck. Nearly all the faeries he'd met were respectful and happy to know druids. Why would she be afraid of one? Unless what had happened to Rory had also happened to her. His mind reeled, but he didn't want to jump to conclusions.

"Why do you need such a powerful talisman to keep the fae away?" he asked gently. When she sat in silence, tugging at her pyjama sleeves, he added, "We can protect you."

She glanced up. "Can you?"

"In the Otherworld, a druid lord's word is law. Come with us. No one can hurt you if you're under our protection."

"Mama?" a tiny voice came from the corridor. At first, Demi's chair blocked their view of the new arrival. Then a small boy with wild black hair sticking up in every direction scrambled around and climbed into her lap. He eyed the strangers cautiously and hid himself in his mother's arms.

"Jago," she said softly. "What are you doing out of bed?"

"I heard talking," he said in a sleepy voice.

"Come on," she said, standing with the boy in her arms. "Little boys shouldn't be out of bed so early." She walked into the corridor beyond, but not before Huck saw the fear on her face had amplified. She hadn't wanted them to know about the child.

"Rory," Flùranach hissed as soon as the pair had disappeared from sight. "The child is fae."

"Are you sure?"

She cast a glare in his direction, more of her old spirit showing through. "I know a faerie when I sense one. The child is not human."

"Why didn't you tell us before?" Rory asked, his tone sharp. "This changes everything."

"It explains why she would ward the house, but why don't the wards affect the child?" Huck asked.

Flùranach replied, "The only way I can imagine is if he helped make them."

"Can you detect another faerie in the house?" Rory asked.

"It's the ward stones," Flùranach said. "My senses are muddled. Even your own druidic presence feels peculiar to me."

A few minutes later, Demi came back. She sat in front of them and said nothing at first. She appeared deep in thought, and Huck didn't want to interrupt. Finally, she said, "If you will protect me and my family, I will go with you."

Why the sudden change of heart? Huck wondered. There was so much more she wasn't telling them.

When they hesitated, she said, "Was this not what you offered?"

"The boy is fae," Flùranach said.

"Half-fae," Demi corrected. "He is my son."

"Who is his father?" she asked.

Demi's eyes flared with anger. "What does it matter? He is *my* son."

"Demi," Rory said. "We want to help you. We want to offer you protection, but we need to know from whom. The father is the one you're hiding from, isn't he? He's the one you're afraid of?"

She looked away, then nodded. "He is a fae royal, or so he claimed." She sighed. "I met him five years ago in Germany. He was so beautiful," she said, but her words were angry, not wistful. "He awoke these senses in me, and we were attracted to each other in a way I had never experienced with a man before."

"But something went wrong," Huck said.

"He quickly became cruel. He liked...he liked to humiliate me." Her cheeks flushed. "Many times, he hurt and punished me if I didn't do as he demanded. My mind was so entranced that I didn't resist, no matter how he had begun to repulse me. Then one day, he told me some words had come to him, words I must say to bond myself to him forever. He tried but could not compel me to say them." Tears slid down Demi's cheeks and dripped onto her grey shirt, leaving wet marks. The room felt close and uncomfortable. Bring forced to bond to a faerie they didn't want was every druid's nightmare. Only someone like Flùranach, someone with an affinity for all druids, had the power to force a bond.

"How did you escape?" Flùranach asked, breaking the silence.

"Jago saved me. Within four months of falling under the spell of this man, I became pregnant. I knew the instant the seed of magic awoke within me. Jago's life force gave me resistance. I grew stronger. Jago's magic coursed through me as though it was my own. For the first time, I could stand against this man. His power lost its hold over me.

"My reprieve wouldn't last. I feared the protection Jago gave me would disappear when I gave birth. I had to run. I went to my grandmother, who had some money, and begged for her help. I thought she would think me insane. She listened without judgement and agreed to help, even demanding to come with me as I escaped. You see, I inherited my abilities from her side of the family. We have a long tradition of strange powers popping up every few generations. There is even a Hartmann storybook, full of faerie stories. In our family, we have passed these tales down to our children. I think this was why I fell for Ulrich so easily. When I first met him, I realised those stories were real."

"Ulrich?" Huck asked in disbelief.

"Yes," she said. "Ulrich is the name of Jago's father."

Huck turned to Rory. "There is a royal named Ulrich."

Rory blinked, as though trying to remember why the name sounded so familiar.

"Konstanze's brother," Huck whispered. "We'll have to take her through Eilidh's gates. We can't risk moving her through Germany."

"When can we leave?" Demi asked. She stole another glance towards her son's bedroom. "We've had to run many times when he's found us before. I don't know how he found out about Jago, but he became obsessed. I'd thought maybe we would be safe here a little longer, but now that you've discovered me, we must leave soon. Word will find its way to him."

"We would never tell him where you lived," Huck said.

She smiled sadly. "We've been running from Ulrich for years. He will find us. Either we will go with you to this Druid Hall, or we will leave Amsterdam and never return. Either way, we leave today."

Ah, Huck thought. That was why she agreed to go with them. From the moment he followed her from the coffee shop, he'd doomed her to run again. "We have to get permission from the queen before we can take you through the gates." When he saw her expression, he said, "Not Konstanze, don't worry. We know the queen of Caledonia, and we can bring you into her territory. She's no friend of Konstanze. We'll have to travel to Belgium to reach her gates."

Flùranach tensed but said nothing. After only a fractional hesitation, she gave a nod.

Huck turned to Demi. "Give us this one day. We'll get permission from Queen Eilidh, then we'll come back to get you."

"All of us? You will give shelter to my grandmother and Jago as well, yes?"

"Yes," Huck said. Rory opened his mouth to say something, but he shook his head as though he thought better of it.

"And we will be safe in this Druid Hall?"

Huck nodded. "In the Otherworld, druids are revered. He could never hurt you as long as you're with me." He hadn't meant to say it like that. He'd meant to say "with us." The others looked at him, but he couldn't correct himself now.

"We have to go," Rory said. "The gates will close at daybreak. If we don't leave now, we'll have to wait until night falls again."

She nodded. "I will wait one day."

"I could stay with you," Huck said. "Flùranach and Rory have to go, because she casts the illusions that make them appear human, but I don't have the same problem."

A small smile flitted across her face. "No," she said. "I must tell Omi and Jago we are to leave again, and I need to do that alone. In truth, I think she has been preparing ever since she saw you in the street below our window."

Huck was reluctant to leave her, afraid she would bolt the second they were out of sight. But there was nothing he could do. "Okay," he said. "We'll be back as quickly as we can after nightfall."

"We will be ready," Demi said.

CHAPTER 7

MUNRO CONVINCED EILIDH TO STAY in bed longer than usual, and he suspected she wanted to soothe any unspoken jealousy about her trip with Griogair. Once they rose and dressed, they shared their first meal of the evening with Griogair. Over fruit and cream, Eilidh asked the prince to join her in visiting the gates and altars. The three of them met with Prince Koen and his father, who seemed perturbed to hear Griogair was going along. Eilidh mollified them by asking them to be a part of the welcoming entourage on the journey. For some reason, the news that Munro wouldn't be taking the journey pleased the princes.

The ridiculous wrangling made Munro chuckle. If the new guy thought he might be able to displace Munro in any way, it showed how little most of the fae still understood the nature of the bond. To be fair, though, Eilidh and Munro were one of two bonded pairs known to exist, all the others having died out thousands of years ago.

Even though Munro had planned to stay in Caledonia a while, Eilidh's departure changed his plans. Leaving his future wife to deal with the domestic mess the Source Stone had thrust upon her, he headed back to the Halls of Mist. He arrived in the early evening, when activity was at its greatest around the portal, with scholars and fae from all kingdoms travelling back and forth. Shortly after Munro came through the portal, a passel of young faeries was herded to the library by their mentors to learn about rune study. He had to check himself for a moment. He recognised their youth and thought of them as children, as all faeries would. But some of them were likely fifty years older than him. How easily he'd slipped into the fae way of thinking.

Some of the youths stared at him, but he pretended not to notice. Instead, he gave a cordial nod to their teachers, who returned the gesture of respect with a quiet, "My lord druid." He waited until they descended into the library, gave them a few minutes, then followed. Rory and Huck would still be in Amsterdam, and nobody expected him back. Now seemed like a good time to talk to Oszlár about the Source Stone.

At the bottom of the stairs in the library entrance hall, one of the keepers' assistants divided the students into smaller groups. Munro slipped through the crowd, back towards the keepers' private study chambers. The keepers lived like monks, with none of the trappings their exalted status among the fae could give them.

He located Oszlár in his office. The fae didn't use traditional desks and chairs like he might have found in a human-built room used for the same purpose. They had different attitudes towards rank and status. When they built to impress, the intent often went over his head.

Munro paused in the archway, his keen vision finding Oszlár, despite the lack of light in the room. The old keeper dozed, holding a thin rune slate in one hand and a stylus in the other. He looked even more ancient while sleeping, his face retaining none of the sharpness that made him so formidable.

"You can't be here," came a voice behind Munro.

He turned and faced one of the other keepers, a round-faced male faerie with wispy grey hair, who rushed up behind him. When the keeper recognised him, he paused. "Oh, my lord druid. I didn't realise it was you." Although faeries could usually sense the difference between a human's presence and a druid's, after he'd touched the Source Stone, he *felt* like a faerie to them.

"I didn't realise he was asleep," Munro said. "I'll come back later."

"I'm not asleep," Oszlár said, adjusting himself in the low chair. "I was meditating. Come in, Lord Druid Munro." He waved a hand at the other keeper, shooing him out. Keepers were never shooed, except by Oszlár. As the oldest faerie alive, the others permitted him some eccentricity.

"I wish you'd call me Munro. Or Quinton even," he said. "All this Lord Druid stuff can get to be a bit much."

Oszlár nodded. "I understand, but I'm afraid I can't do that. You see, this *Lord Druid stuff* may save your life." He gestured to the chair opposite him and put his tablet and stylus aside.

"Save my life? From whom?"

"You and your brother druids' powers and positions are still in an embryonic stage. What if the queens decided they didn't want humans to wield *any* power in the Halls of Mist? Can you defend yourselves? Can you live without the gifts and assistance of the queens? Could you even return to the human realm if they decided to cut off your access to their lands?"

"Eilidh would never isolate us," Munro said.

"No," Oszlár said. "You're right." He settled back in his chair and smiled. "What brings you to the library today? We've not read together for some weeks. I always enjoy learning from your translations." Fae runes did not symbolise any alphabet, but instead represented concepts and the magically imbued intent of the rune creator. Therefore, every reader might interpret a rune in a different way. Munro had discovered the druids' talent for using runes, although none of the others had the ability to read as widely as he did. He had the ability to translate entire stories, even the oldest and most complex. The others seemed to find an affinity with a few runes that spoke to them, but struggled with anything more.

"I'd like to study the Source Stone," Munro said.

Oszlár's eyes narrowed. "Why?"

"It's the most interesting artefact here."

"And the most powerful. Are you not content with the changes it brought about already, through mere moments of contact?"

"Content?" Munro asked, surprised. "I don't want anything from the Stone. I only want to understand it."

A smile spread across Oszlár's face, and he laughed. "My dear friend, I have studied the Source Stone for thirteen centuries, and *I* do not fully grasp its mysteries."

"That artefact changed me fundamentally," Munro said. "Every alteration to my body, to my mind, maybe even my understanding of the runes came about because of this rock. Even faeries can't tell what I am anymore. It choses queens." He leaned forward, growing excited. "How can any stone choose a queen? How does it know who should rule? Who has the best mind, the best heart?"

Oszlár watched him closely, but didn't answer.

"I remember when I read the Killbourne Wall, when we learned that the first druids, the draoidh sorcerers, may have created the fae. The interpretation rang true. Essentially, we are creators. I knew the ancient runemakers were those same druids. They had to be. The fae have the ability, but it's limited to a shadow of what I can do." He stood and paced, unable to contain his energy. "So, yes, if the ancient druids can make a faerie, a magnificent, sentient being who can think, grow, perform magic, love, live, die, why not make a stone that can reason? But how?"

"You think if you can understand the Stone, you can create another?"

"No. Maybe. I don't know. There aren't enough of us. We have missing pieces. I can make stone objects move, sometimes even in a lifelike way, but they're just rocks."

"Why has Lord Druid Huck Webster not come to touch the stone?" Oszlár asked him, his swirling gaze penetrating through Munro's musing.

The druid paused and considered. "I think he isn't in a hurry to change. He was eager to join us in the beginning. Now he spends much of his time in the human realm. He isn't prepared to let go. Someday he will. When he's ready."

"And you? Are you in a hurry to change?"

"You think I'll change even more if I touch the Stone again?" Munro asked, surprised. The idea hadn't occurred to him. What further changes might happen to him? But then, what *couldn't* the Stone do? He had no idea of its powers or limitations. All the more reason to learn as much as possible.

"I'm not certain," Oszlár admitted. "We possess no written records of the draoidh interacting with the Stone. I would, however, advise caution. Our people depend on the Stone. Yes, it may change you, but there is also the chance *you* may change *it*. Without the Stone, the fae will die."

"I've already touched it once, like most of the others. You weren't worried then."

"You are more powerful now than you were in the beginning," Oszlár said.

Munro considered. Was he? He'd felt like a god right after encountering the Stone, but the mood faded. Now he considered himself a mostly normal guy with a few enhanced natural abilities. "I'd like to visit the chamber, at least. Do you think that's all right?"

Oszlár agreed and led Munro into the lower area where only the keepers themselves and the druids were permitted to go. Unlike last time, the pair went alone. The round room bore a hard chill, and the runes covering the walls remained silent, at least for the moment.

On both of his previous visits, all the keepers had been there. They had raised the Source Stone from the floor with a rhythmic chant. Now, Oszlár stood alone on the opposite side of the round chamber, watching Munro closely. Power emanated from the Stone's resting place. The air in the chamber felt heavy and thick.

Munro turned his attention to the rune-covered walls. When he'd last entered, he'd ignored the symbols carved around him. "Who made these?" he asked the keeper, running his hand over the cool, stone surface.

"Many hands," Oszlár replied.

Munro nodded and moved towards the centre of the room. The Stone rested, embedded into the floor. With careful steps, he paced around it, probing as he did when he read runes, but none of its secrets were revealed. The artefact eluded him, as though it contained no runes at all.

"What is the meaning of the chant you use when you raise the stone?" Munro asked.

Oszlár thought for a moment. "In your language, roughly, 'Awake and listen. Receive our sacrifice. Accept our offering.'"

Munro frowned. He wondered if he would interpret their invocation differently. "Would you write down the runes for the chant?"

"No," Oszlár said. "We hold the words sacred. Our oaths forbid us from teaching them to anyone other than an initiated keeper. To inscribe them would provide too great a risk."

"Of course," Munro said. He understood. If someone else learned how to raise the Stone, that might prove disastrous. "Thank you for telling me." He did wonder why Oszlár had. Perhaps he believed it would do no harm, considering the druids had already heard the words, even if they didn't understand the fae tongue.

Munro looked around the room one last time. The magic in the air was thick, but not overwhelming. "I'm no closer to understanding how the artefact works," he said, disappointed that nothing had come to him. He'd thought for sure if he came here again, especially now that he'd learned more about runes, something would have made sense.

Oszlár shook his head with a smile. "You are so young," he said under his breath.

Munro flushed with embarrassment. Of course if the fae hadn't unlocked the Stone's secrets over thousands of years, he was unlikely to work it out in fifteen minutes. "Perhaps we can come back another time," he said.

The aged keeper gestured to the door. They walked up the long, winding stairs together. "I wonder if we should begin with something less...complex. There are other objects of power. Ancient ones. I will consult with the keepers, and you and I can work with them together, if you like."

Munro nodded. "I recall in one story, we read about enchanted weapons." He avoided mentioning the scholar, Ríona, who'd first showed him the tale. She'd died horrifically because of her association with him. His gut churned at the unwelcome memory.

"Ah yes. The Andenan artefact. I remember." Thankfully, Oszlár didn't mention her either, but his expression suggested the story would now always remind him of her.

"Do any of these weapons still exist?"

"Do you believe you need a weapon?"

They reached the entrance of the library, and Munro laughed. Oszlár had an annoying way of answering questions with questions. "I have no interest in weapons, only in enchantments. An enchanted peanut would be as interesting to me as a sword."

Oszlár chuckled. "Lord Druid Quinton Munro," he said and bowed formally. "You grace us with your presence as always. I will research your request about the Andenan runes. May the Mother favour your path."

Only then did Munro realise the room was not empty. He wished he understood why Oszlár was so determined to put on these formal performances when anyone else was around. Was the druids' position really so precarious? "Thank you. I'll see you again soon, Keeper Oszlár." He bowed his head and left. Climbing the stairs two at a time, he set off for the Druid Hall.

∞

Rory watched Huck jogging ahead of him and Flùranach as they raced through the Ashkyne Otherworld. The American druid seemed lost in his own thoughts, excited on one hand, but angry and spoiling for a fight on the other. Rory hoped the run would calm him down. They'd need to keep their heads when talking to Eilidh. She was a friend, but she was also a queen. He'd have to find a way to frame their request with care. Naturally, they'd talk to Munro first, but Eilidh would probably want to speak with them all to get the full story. From what Rory had learned about the balance of power between the queens, sneaking a druid out of the Ashkyne borderlands and through Eilidh's territory would be no small thing. And how would they explain to the fae world about Demi's child with Konstanze's brother? What a mess.

Flùranach loped beside Rory with ease. She glanced over, her hair catching the early morning rays of the Otherworld sun. "I would like to speak with you alone," she said.

He had mixed feelings. How could he ignore the bad things she'd done? On the other hand, he hadn't forgotten the good times either.

"I know what you're thinking," she said. "You don't trust me yet."

Her words made him falter, and Huck raced even farther ahead. Rory didn't try to catch up. He didn't particularly want Huck to witness this conversation. Nothing about this situation would be comfortable for anyone, so the fewer people involved, the better. "I wish you wouldn't do that," he said. When Flùranach said she knew what he was thinking, she meant it literally. If people voiced their contemplations internally, she had the ability to hear the words as though they'd said them aloud.

She matched his pace. "This is what I am. I can't change my magic any more than you can change yours."

He didn't answer, but kept his attention on the path. The grassy hill below their feet became white and sandy as they approached a beach. The sunrise over the green-tinged ocean was like nothing he'd seen on the beaches of Scotland. The light here was so much truer, the colours brighter. The deep sand slowed them further. He could just make out Huck ahead, his feet splashing as he ran at the edge of the incoming tide.

"I'm sorry I disappeared. I heard there was an extensive search for me," she said.

"You don't owe me an explanation." He hadn't been involved in the search nor asked for updates. Of course, he wondered from time to time where she'd gone, but how could he not?

"I owe you so much more than that."

Rory's bones ached with weariness. As usual, they'd been up all night, and he wanted to crawl into bed for a few hours. He needed less sleep than he used to, especially since touching the Source Stone, but the events of the last day and finding Flùr again had exhausted him. "Look, let's put the bonding thing in the past, okay? I want to move on."

"Do you mean that?" She sounded hopeful.

"I've said from the start that we need you. Things went much smoother tonight because you were there. I'm not sure what would have happened if you hadn't been there. We wouldn't have discovered the boy was half-fae, for one. She certainly wasn't eager to tell us."

"I'm happy to aid the Druid Hall. I've always loved you all." She watched him closely, and he felt the weight of her stare.

He remembered how their lives had been in the beginning. But she'd been a little girl then, and everything had changed since. Even after the time stream transformed her into a young woman, though, they'd had some nice days together. He'd been so attracted to her, so confused by it all. "Why did the keepers hide you?" he asked.

Only then did her intense look waver. She glanced away. "I'm not supposed to talk about such things."

"Why did Oszlár say you were the key to saving us all? Did he mean faeries, druids, or both?"

She kept silent for a long time. Her expression told him she was torn. "I'm not supposed to talk about such things," she repeated.

He stopped dead and grabbed her arm, spinning her so they stood toe-to-toe. "You serve the Druid Hall!"

"I do." She met his eyes and held his gaze. "I will serve you always." That *you* was so much more personal than a simple statement of where she was employed.

"So tell me the truth!" he shouted.

"If you command me to break my vow to the keepers, I will," she whispered.

She stood there, her red lips slightly parted, her fiery hair whipping in the ocean breeze, and he wanted to kiss her. He wanted to slap her. He wanted to shake her and beat her, but mostly he wanted to kiss her. Only willpower held him in place.

She knows, he thought. *She knows I want to strangle her and that I want to take her.* He imagined her willing him to do one or the other...or both.

He let go of her arm, shattering the intensity of the moment. "No," he said roughly. "I don't want you to break your vow."

Tears glistened in her eyes as he stepped back from her. "Rory," she said. "I will do anything for you. I'm yours."

"No," he said. "You were never mine."

"I could make you forget the bad things."

He stood and stared at her, shocked and repulsed. Did she believe he would let her into his mind, allow her to rummage and tinker with his deepest memories and fears? "No," he said sharply. "Never that."

"I would never touch your mind if you didn't ask me to," she said quickly. "I only want to ease your pain."

"You can't fix what's wrong with me, Flùranach." He softened his tone. "Look, I know you didn't mean to, but we both know neither of us can ever bond again because of what you did. You might make me forget being your prisoner, but I'll never have what all druids want more than anything—a bonded faerie." *You took that from me*, he thought.

"What if you could?" she asked, her eyes searching his.

His insides went cold. He didn't have room for false hope. "Each druid can only make one bond in his life."

"It's true we will never be able to bond with anyone but each other," she said, watching him as though waiting for a reaction.

"Then…" Understanding hit him square in the chest. He would never bond another faerie, a faerie naturally compatible with him. However, she implied he could bond with *her* again, a faerie who'd used a rare talent to force an unnatural pairing. "Never," he said. Those few days as her slave, he'd been more like a zombie than a man. He'd endured a living hell. He'd wanted to die. He still bore faint scars on his wrists to prove it, despite the attention of talented faerie healers.

She quickly backed off. "I shouldn't have said anything. It's too soon. We aren't ready."

She sounded very much like Oszlár. What did the old keeper know about this?

Fumbling over her words as though desperate to smooth over her blunder, she went on. "But now that I have told you, you must know I would say the words first. You would never be in danger of what went wrong before."

What went wrong? That made the incident sound like an honest mistake. What she'd done had been anything but. "It won't happen. Get the idea out of your head. I mean it." Anger flooded through him anew.

"I will earn your trust again." She actually sounded convinced she would someday change his mind. If he hadn't been so angry, he might've pitied her.

She looked beautiful in the morning light, her hair whipping about her face, but looks weren't everything. Rory turned away. "Come on," he said. "We've lost sight of Huck." He broke into a run again and heard her do the same a few paces behind. She stayed just out of his line of sight. For that, at least, he was grateful. His mind spun and her expectant eyes filled his thoughts. She'd broken him. Magically, mentally, emotionally. Didn't she understand? She'd broken him, and now she wanted not only his forgiveness, but his trust. He couldn't trust her any more than he could love again. He'd work with her, be responsible for her, and make sure she kept her word to Oszlár. No matter what, though, he wouldn't hit her or take advantage of her desperation, but most of all, he wouldn't be her slave *ever* again.

CHAPTER 8

WHEN RORY AND FLÙRANACH ARRIVED at the Druid Hall mid-morning, the corridors stood empty. The Hall's head steward, Hon, greeted them at the entry arch.

"Hi," Rory said as the steward bowed. He squirmed when they acted subservient. "Flùranach will be staying at the Druid Hall. We have a room somewhere, don't we?"

"Of course, my lord druid. She is...your guest?"

Rory stopped short. The steward was politely inquiring if she was to be put with the druids or in the servants' hall. Rory didn't quite know what to do with her either. She wasn't a cook or a cleaner, but he didn't want her bunking with him.

"I serve the druids," Flùranach said. "I will happily stay wherever there is room...perhaps near the kitchens or the washing halls."

"Of course," Hon said.

Now Rory felt bad. Although even the men who washed the floors were as haughty as any faeries he'd ever met, putting her with them didn't seem right. He opened his mouth to suggest one of the rooms set aside for visiting scholars would be more appropriate, but Flùranach didn't give him a chance.

"Thank you," she said to Hon. "If you will show me to the kitchens, I haven't eaten all night. I will prepare a small meal before I take my rest for the morning." She turned to Rory. "My lord druid, at what hour will we leave for Caledonia?"

"I'm not sure," Rory said. "Perhaps an hour before nightfall. Depends where Eilidh and Munro are staying. If they're at Canton Dreich, we could arrive shortly after their first evening meal."

"If I may," Hon said. "Lord Druid Munro returned last night. He is taking his morning's rest."

Rory raised an eyebrow. He hoped nothing was wrong. He'd expected Munro to be gone longer than one night. "Well, that makes things easier," he said, but niggling worry ate at him.

Flùranach lowered her head into a bow. "I will wait for you to send for me, my lord druid."

Rory watched the steward lead her away. He went to his room upstairs and found a plate of food waiting for him. The Hall's servants always seemed to anticipate what he needed before he asked. They provided whatever without him noticing their presence most of the time. Convenient, but slightly creepy. He ate and lay on his bed, which he'd asked to be modelled more after the human style, four legs and on solid ground. He still hadn't grown used to those swing things the fae slept in.

Thoughts of Flùranach filled his brain and danced around frantically. He couldn't relax, even though exhaustion weighed him down. He'd never felt so mixed up in his life. Long ago, he'd given up the idea of bonding with a faerie and all the benefits that would bring, like longer life and access to deeper levels of magic. He was stronger and faster than a normal human, sure, but he wouldn't reach his potential without a faerie partner. Over time, he'd come to terms with the loss. Now *she* came back and reminded him of what would never be…without *her*.

Flùranach had manipulated him too many times, coercing him with her astral talents. She'd thrown him to the floor and ripped his clothing like tissue. In all his years, he would never forget the wild, animalistic hunger in her eyes when she'd attacked him. Her features contorted into something primal and terrifying. He'd been paralysed, unable to resist when she compelled him to say the words that locked him into bondage. Even his mind hadn't been his own. She knew his thoughts. He hadn't even been able to pretend. Her face hovered over his and she held him down with unnatural strength. He responded as she demanded, in spite of his fear, even as his mind screamed *no* over and over.

Rory sat up with a sudden shout, his chest covered in sweat and tears streaming down his face. Had he fallen asleep? His heart hammered against his ribcage, and his hands shook.

HIs nightmares hadn't been so bad in a long time. Oszlár was right. He wasn't ready. Why hadn't he listened?

He staggered into the small room just off his bed chamber. Stripping off the clothes he'd fallen asleep in, he lowered himself into the round marble bathing tub inset into the floor. Scrubbing himself with the sparkling crystals provided, he let the gentle fizz wash away the bad dreams.

The dark memories retreated into their hiding place by the time he descended to the druids' workshop. He found Huck and Munro already there, chatting. How long had he slept? It only seemed like seconds.

"What time is it?" he asked.

"It'll be dusk in Caledonia in about two hours," Munro said.

Rory sank heavily into a sturdy armchair, yet another replica of a human design.

"Rough day?" Huck asked.

When Rory didn't answer, Munro said quietly, "Huck told me about your trip to Amsterdam...and Flùranach. Is everything okay?"

She wants me to bond with her again. "Yeah, I'm fine. So, you think Eilidh will help? We can't take Demi through the German borderlands if she's running from Konstanze's brother, so we'll need to go through Belgium."

"You'd need to travel to England, not Belgium. The Belgian gate is unstable, according to Prince Estobar. It's not worth the risk, at least until we verify his claims. I think Eilidh will help, though. We'll need to find her before to get her official permission, though. She's gone to visit the Andenan altars with Griogair."

"She what?" Rory said, sitting up. "They're trying to have a kid?"

"What? No," Munro said. "No," he repeated. "They didn't go to make a sacrifice. They're checking out the new borderlands, to see the new territory and greet the fae who are part of her kingdom now."

"Oh, okay," Rory said, glancing at Huck. "Sorry. I didn't know faeries ever went to altars except when they wanted a baby."

Huck sighed. "How long will it take to find her? We promised Demi we'd only be one day. She won't wait around."

"Eilidh's a queen," Munro said. "She can hardly eat a fig without a thousand people hearing about it. Besides, I can locate her through our bond." An uncomfortable look stretched across his face. Rory suspected he was imagining walking in on her and Griogair unannounced. What if they *were* trying to have a baby? It was none of Rory's business, of course, but he was curious about the three-sided arrangement. Once, Aaron had asked Rory if he thought all three of them ever *got it on,* to use Aaron's expression. Sometimes he wondered. Their situation wasn't exactly traditional. Aaron joked that Griogair would be up for anything if Munro was, but then, Aaron had a juvenile sense of humour.

"There's ferries every day from Holland to England," Rory said.

"I'll go with Demi," Huck said. "Once you talk to Eilidh, meet up with us on the other side of the Channel. Even if it takes you a few days to get to Eilidh, Demi will be much happier if we get her out of Amsterdam right away."

Rory nodded. "I'll tag along with Munro," he said "but Flùranach should go with you. She can disguise Demi and her family, assist if there's any trouble at the border, plus she can help you find us at the meet-up spot."

"Which is where exactly?" Huck asked.

"If you take a train from Amsterdam down the coast from The Hague, you can catch a ferry to England at the Hook of Holland. It lands about fifty miles north of London, in Essex. There's a hotel right next to the port," Munro said. "With any luck, we'll meet you there before you even have to stay a night."

"The trip will be slower with a kid and a grandma in tow," Huck said. "I don't know how fast any of them can move."

"They'll be fine," Munro said. "If she's successfully evaded a fae prince for four years, she's a smart one. If she can make wards as powerful as you've suggested, she knows things even we don't." He paused and scrubbed his hand through his hair as he contemplated. "Did you ask about her sphere of power? Or the kid's?"

Huck frowned. "I didn't think to ask. Does it matter?"

"No," Munro replied. "I was just thinking that with my stone, your fire, and all the others being water, would be nice to meet an air druid. Would round out the set. Get us closer."

"To what?" Huck asked.

Munro shook his head and chuckled. "I don't know."

∞

Huck walked back and forth in the workshop, going over the plan in his mind. Rory sent Hon for Flùranach, and Munro went to grab a few things. The sun would set in the Netherlands soon, and Demi would be waiting. She'd insisted she wouldn't stay more than one day, and he believed her. He admired everything about her, from her fierce determination and loyalty to her family to the courage she showed in defying one of the fae.

"Would you stop pacing?" Rory said.

"I can't," Huck replied. "We need to leave...now. I wish we hadn't stopped to sleep. We should have taken her to England right away."

"You heard her," Rory said. "She wasn't going to leave right that second anyway. She needed time to pack her things and get her family together."

"She was stalling. If her grandmother really had been anticipating the move, I'd bet they were ready in an hour. I should've stuck around."

"Seriously, mate, she didn't want you there."

"What if something happens to her?"

"Ulrich doesn't know where she is, and even if he did, she has wards to protect her. If Flùranach couldn't get past them, I doubt any faerie could. Demi will be fine. You have to let her do things her way. She's scared, and rightly so."

Huck stopped his striding and looked at Rory. Was he actually afraid? Was that why he was so rude to Flùranach? Everything that happened between them was before Huck's time, and he didn't really understand. If a faerie like Flùr wanted to bond with Huck, he'd say yes in a heartbeat. Things had gone wrong when Flùr and Rory bonded before, but she apologised and was willing to try again. How could Rory not even think about it, especially considering he could never bond with anyone else? Huck's Otherworld-enhanced hearing had picked up a lot of their conversation on the way through the Ashkyne territory the night before. She'd practically been begging. That girl shouldn't beg any man for anything. Huck had sped up when the other two stopped to argue, relieved when he'd finally gotten out of earshot.

"What took you so long?" Rory snapped when Flùranach entered the room.

Her eyes widened, but she masked her surprise quickly. "Forgive me, my lord druid," she said, dropping her gaze to the floor.

A look of shame and disgust crept over Rory's face. Was he angry at her or at himself? "Forget it," he said. "Are you ready to leave?"

She nodded with a frown.

"What's wrong?" Huck asked her.

"I'll admit I'm not eager to return to Caledonia. Queen Eilidh may have a few words for me. I may even face trial for my crimes."

"Don't worry about that. I want you with Huck," Rory said. "I'll talk to Eilidh about you. If she won't grant you passage, you can return to the German gates. I don't see any reason why Konstanze's Watchers would stop you if you're on your own."

Flùranach looked alarmed, but at that moment, Munro entered with a small travelling pack slung over his shoulder.

"I really do need your assistance," Huck told Flùranach quietly. "Your illusions may prove useful." He added, "If you have to return to the Halls of Mist by way of German borderlands, I'll go with you. Rory and Munro can take Demi through Caledonia."

"You would?" she asked.

"The journey would only take a few hours. I think Munro and Rory can manage that long without me."

In truth, he didn't like the idea of leaving Demi, but once she crossed into the Caledonian borderlands, she'd be safe.

They were all heading towards the door when Aaron entered. His eyes went immediately to Flùranach, then he shot an accusing glare at Rory. "What's *she* doing here?"

Munro held up a hand. "We talked about this. She's working with us. We've already located two new druids because of her."

"She's dangerous to any unbonded druid." Aaron backed towards the door. "I'm out of here."

Rory looked torn, as though he wanted to argue with Aaron but couldn't. "You don't have to go," he said. "We're leaving." He nodded towards Huck, who touched Flùranach lightly on the arm.

"Come on," Huck said. "It's time."

The four of them walked the short distance to the portal together. Munro and Rory entered first, leaving without another word.

Once the other druids had disappeared into the blue glow, Huck turned to Flùranach. "You ready?"

"Yes, my lord druid," she said.

"You can call me Huck." He wanted to be kind to her. Someone should. Despite anything she might've done, they did need her, and treating her like something they'd scraped off their shoes wouldn't help.

She smiled but didn't reply.

They took the same route back to the German borderlands as they had the morning before. Huck looked at her as they ran. "You're in love with him?" he asked. He didn't know why he asked. Their relationship wasn't any of his business.

"Yes," she said.

"Do you mind if I offer some advice?"

She glanced over, uncertainty playing over her pale features. Her green eyes swirled with astral magic as she considered him. "No, I do not mind."

"Give him some room. And maybe don't be so subservient."

"He needs to understand that I'm not a threat."

"You're a threat to him simply by what you are. All the bowing and scraping makes him feel guilty. Just relax. Maybe don't focus on him quite so hard."

She didn't say anything for a while. "I will try," she finally replied. "Are you in love with the druid Demi?"

"I just met her," he said quickly.

With a smile, Flùranach replied, "That wasn't what I asked you."

"I think I could be. It's complicated. I don't know her very well, but there's something special about her."

"You're very intense," she said.

"What do you mean?"

"It's difficult to explain. When you looked at her, every particle in the room vibrated with your aura."

Huck was glad the light had grown dim. His cheeks warmed. Had he been that obvious?

"Perhaps you should relax a little. Maybe don't focus on her quite so hard." Flùranach's voice had a definite lilt of humour as she repeated his advice back to him. To make matters worse, Huck suspected she was right.

They didn't talk much more on the remainder of the run, both of them lost in their thoughts. By the time they passed through the Otherworld gates and made their way to the outskirts of Amsterdam, the sky was fully dark. They danced through the shadows and sped towards Demi's street.

Suddenly Flùranach stopped. She whipped her head around and grabbed Huck's arm, putting her finger to her lips. They crouched in the darkness in a tight alleyway. The smell emanating from a nearby garbage bin assaulted his nose.

"What?" he whispered.

She shook her head, signalling for him not to talk. They waited long minutes in the darkness, and he itched with worry. Suddenly a cry rang out, but was quickly muffled.

"That's Demi," he said and stood.

Flùranach grabbed his arm and pulled him back. "Be silent. I'm listening to their thoughts."

"Who is it?"

"Faeries. At least ten. Ulrich's men."

"They took Demi?" Before she could answer, a second cry sounded, this time a scream. "I'm going," he said.

He took off, and Flùranach ran beside him as he raced to Demi's house. The street was utterly silent and unnaturally dark. The front door stood ajar. "How many are in there?" he said to Flùranach.

"I can't tell," she said. "The wards confuse my senses." She glanced down the street. "But many fae went that way."

"Let's go after them," he said. "They might have Demi."

"Or she may be inside and in need of help. I will pursue the fae. I am faster without you, and you have no magic to defend or attack."

He hated to admit she was right, but had no choice. "Go," he said.

Without any further prompting, Flùranach sped through the flickering lamplight at the corner of the street and disappeared. Huck rushed to the open door and peered inside. With a slow movement, he budged the door all the way open. The house stood eerily silent. He glanced back towards the street, sorry that he hadn't gone with Flùr, but he'd never be able to find her now. He sighed and stepped inside. The door banged against the doorjamb, no longer fitting properly into the squint frame.

He made his way up the stairs to the room where they'd first talked with Demi. Moving towards the window, he looked down into the street. A neighbour across the way peered through the curtains, but she quickly drew back when she saw Huck. "Shit," Huck said, worried someone had called the police. He didn't want to be hanging around if the cops showed up.

When he turned back to the darkened room, his perfect night vision caught a dark stain on the living room floor. He crouched beside the stain and touched it. Fresh blood. His heart tightened. Demi? But if so, where was her body? Would Ulrich have killed her and stolen her body? *Maybe she's still alive*, he thought. But taking the measure of the blood on the floor, someone had bled too much to be walking around. He glanced towards the window. Either way, Ulrich had Jago. Of that he was certain.

A flash of movement came from over his left shoulder. Huck dropped to the floor and rolled out of the way to keep the knife slicing through the air from landing in his neck. When he looked up again, the figure dove at him once more. Only his Otherworldly strength prevented the woman from succeeding in her furious attack.

"Omi?" he called out.

The old woman blinked and hesitated, giving Huck the advantage. She had fury and adrenaline on her side, but he was young and much stronger. He gripped her bony wrist hard, and the knife fell to the carpet beside his ear.

"I'm not here to hurt you," he said. "I came to help you."

The old woman spat in his face but ended her struggle. "Because of you, she is gone. She and my beautiful grandson are gone." She winced at his grip, which he warily released, pushing her gently so she had to let him up. Blood from the carpet had seeped through his shirt at his shoulder.

"Ulrich killed them?" His stomach tightened.

She shook her head. "Ulrich is dead."

A wave of relief spread over Huck. He lowered himself into the chair, taking an involuntary glance towards the window. "Someone took them and the body? Who?"

The old woman shrugged. "His soldiers, I suppose."

A siren sounded a few blocks away. "We need to get out of here," Huck said. "Did you finish packing before they came?"

"We packed the most important things," she said.

"Okay." Huck couldn't think. He wanted to go after Demi and Jago, but he had no clue where to start. Besides, Flùr was on their trail. If there was any hope of finding them, Flùr would do it. "Okay," he repeated. "We leave now. For England. The Belgian route won't work. Flùr will get Demi and Jago and catch up with us." He sounded surer than he felt. "They'll be okay."

The old woman didn't look convinced, or like she trusted him even a little, but she stood and showed him where their bags were. She picked up a rucksack and threw it over her thin shoulders. He grabbed the larger pack as well as a small one with superheroes printed on the side and a large stuffed bear. "Huck Webster," he said.

She eyed him for a moment. "Lisle Hartmann."

"Let's get out of here before the police arrive, Lisle."

She nodded, stopping only to move the ward stone to its proper place by the front door. The gesture saddened him. The faerie she'd needed protection from was already gone.

He waited as patiently as he could manage, but urged her to hurry. A few moments later, he led the way into the darkness. By the time they reached the end of the street, the sirens had arrived at the house. Fortunately, no one paid attention to a bent old woman and a man carrying a teddy bear.

CHAPTER 9

As soon as Munro and Rory stepped into the Caledonian kingdom, Eilidh's emotions rushed over Munro. She was, without a doubt, engaged in intimate and pleasurable activities. Always before, he'd fought the rare flashes of jealousy, but this time he allowed himself a moment of annoyance. She planned to marry Munro in less than a week. Would she really try to get pregnant with another man's baby? *Now*, of all times?

They'd never talked about children. He'd assumed they'd have hundreds of years before they thought about babies, considering the extended lifetime provided him by their magical bond.

On the other hand, before he knew Demi had a half-fae child with Ulrich, he wasn't certain he and Eilidh *could* have children together. The fae only reproduced after venturing through the Otherworld gates to make sacrifices to the Mother of the Earth. He'd never worked out what was special about those altars. Their necessity prevented the fae from cutting themselves off from the human realm and explained why the queen who controlled the most gates had the most power.

He tried to push his mistrust aside. Eilidh would have her reasons for her decisions. She wasn't a careless or frivolous woman.

The laughter and pleasure that had rippled from his connection to Eilidh stopped abruptly. Shame suffused his thoughts at the perverse satisfaction he felt in interrupting Eilidh and Griogair's lovemaking. *I'm such a tool.*

"Which way?" Rory asked as they descended from the glowing portal.

Eilidh's bond pointed Munro somewhere east of the portal. So she wasn't at Canton Dreich. Munro gestured towards her presence.

He stepped towards the Watchers that guarded the portal, and a quick conversation told him they wouldn't find any major roads going that way. The shifting of the gates had added a massive new swath of land, including a major Andenan city. Munro thanked them and led Rory across the eastern plain with confidence. His bond wouldn't steer him wrong.

"How does this new territory thing work?" Rory asked as they ran.

"I've wondered before what was at the edge of the kingdoms' borders. I mean, the kingdoms don't intersect, except at the Halls of Mist or in the human world. So how far does each kingdom go? Are they infinite? Or is there a wall? Is every kingdom an island? I really don't know."

"So how does the Stone add new lands? Is there like an earthquake?"

"We'll need to ask Eilidh. Seems like everyone is happy, so I can't imagine the shifting was violent or dangerous, but who can say with faeries," Munro said.

Eilidh's emotional turns flooded his mind. She had started sending him telepathic messages, beginning with, *Why are you in Caledonia?* She knew he couldn't reply, so why ask? Obviously, his sudden appearance wasn't welcome. Her essence radiated impatience with him. Of course, she'd told him she would take Griogair to the gates. Now he understood her surprise at his acceptance of her decision.

They ran on in silence until Rory interrupted his musing. "Something wrong?"

Munro grumbled to himself. He wished he had more skill at keeping his thoughts to himself. "Eilidh," he said, hoping Rory wouldn't ask too many questions.

"Flùr wants to bond again," Rory spat out, sounding bitter. The resentment didn't surprise Munro. He'd never forget the night he stopped Flùr's attack on Rory and the guilt that still plagued him at having arrived too late. If only he'd made it to that hotel room five minutes earlier.

That she would make such a request *did* stun Munro. "Seriously?"

"Yeah," Rory said. "She said neither of us could bond with anyone else, but we might bond with each other again."

Munro scowled. The bond had been unnatural. Only by using her rare talent for druidic affinity had Flùranach been able to circumvent the usual magical order and seize Rory's bond. The magical assault had been a selfish and violent act. "What did you tell her?"

"I said no." The hesitation in Rory's voice told Munro there was more going on. "I don't see how I can trust her."

The previous day, Munro had heard Rory shouting in his sleep. The terrors were nothing new, but over the past few months, his restless and haunted dreams had become less frequent. Now Munro understood why the nightmares had returned. "If she's going to be a problem, send her back to Oszlár. She can stay with the keepers and join us when we need her. There's no reason she has to live at the Hall."

"We need her all the time," Rory said. He sounded tired. "We should be searching for more druids every night. Even if she slept at the keepers' place, I can't avoid dealing with her."

The decision was up to Rory, but Munro didn't like seeing his friend so torn up like this. He didn't respond. They started travelling over more uneven ground, and the conversation slowed as they picked their way more carefully.

After a while, Rory spoke again as though they'd never even paused. "I almost hit her last night."

The admission made Munro falter for a second, but he recovered quickly. Where was this going? "Listen, mate," he said, but Rory cut him off.

"I wouldn't. She caught me off guard. I'm still so mad. I'm having trouble sorting everything out."

"I'm sending her back to Oszlár," Munro said. He couldn't let Flùranach hurt Rory, but he wouldn't stand by while Rory smacked her around, either. This situation was a disaster waiting to happen.

"When you bonded with Eilidh, did she say the words first?" Rory asked.

Munro looked at his friend. Would he actually consider bonding with Flùr? "No, I did."

"And did the magic make you...do what she said?"

"No," Munro said. "Nothing changed until she said the words too."

"I guess the process works differently when you're naturally compatible." Rory fixed his gaze on the horizon. The huge Otherworld moon shone blue in the eastern sky. "Do you think if Flùr said the words first, I'd be safe? She couldn't control me if she submitted before me, right?"

Munro reflected on the idea. None of them really understood the ancient bonding magic. What Flùr and Rory were considering was a perversion of the ritual. No one could predict what might happen. "I don't know. But what if the reversal meant you had the power to control her?"

"What do you mean?" Rory asked.

"What if going through with her proposal meant she would be forced to obey you, had no choice but to agree with you, and the bond compelled her to please you? You admitted your impulse to hit her. Do you trust yourself not to abuse that power the same way she did?" This whole plan sounded like a bad idea.

"I won't hurt her," Rory said.

"Why are you considering this?" Munro said. "Yes, we need her. We all accept that. Well, everyone but Aaron does. But your bond isn't required to obtain her help."

Rory kept silent for some time, but after a while he said, "I'll never have what you and Eilidh do. I'll never bond naturally. This may be my only chance to reach my potential, to live more than a natural human lifespan, to achieve the magical competency you take for granted."

"Look," Munro said. "You need to understand. Even my bond with Eilidh isn't always wonderful. Having someone in your mind all the time is a pain. I sense her whims and disappointments. I accept that she has the power to end me with a simple thought. Our bond demands ultimate trust. Something deep drove us to make that commitment."

"Are you saying you had no choice?"

"I probably had a choice in the beginning, but I didn't understand what I was getting into. The pull was primal and nearly impossible to resist. For you and Flùr to bond again, I'm assuming she'd manipulate your magic like before to force the link." He changed direction to lead them around a hill. Towering pine trees loomed overhead. A dense forest threatened to slow them even further.

"I hadn't thought of that," Rory said.

"Do you think she's manipulating you with her astral talent? She's capable of it."

"I don't think so," Rory said.

"But you aren't certain." Munro knew he couldn't be positive. Humans weren't capable of detecting fae magic, especially mental manipulations. "Huck told me what he overheard of your conversation with her." Rory flushed, but Munro didn't know the reaction came from anger or embarrassment. "I can't tell if you're trying to talk yourself *into* or *out of* bonding with her."

"I'm not sure either," Rory admitted. "I hate that we're at their mercy. Sometimes I think we shouldn't have left Caledonia. At least there, we had Eilidh's protection."

The same thing had crossed Munro's mind. But the druids made the decision to leave because they needed to establish themselves and not be beholden to any one queen. They took a risk in doing so, but the Halls of Mist was sacred to the fae. No one would attack them there. "Staying with Eilidh might have been easier," Munro said. "But we need the queens' respect. Plus, living at the Halls of Mist, we are granted access to most kingdoms' gates. That'll be important as we search for druids. If the queens considered us part of Caledonia, there's no way we'd get free rein."

"I wish we had our own gate to the human realm, like a back door. If things did go south, at least we would have a way home."

"The other day, I talked to Oszlár about the Source Stone. He asked if we were thinking about making our own." Munro repeated the conversation and recalled his failure to discover anything of use.

"Maybe the thing to do is to make an Otherworld gate. They seem less complicated than the portal."

Munro couldn't think of a reason not to try. There were no gates directly from the Halls of Mist to the human realm, but he didn't know why not. "When we cross through with Demi, we should look at the borderlands gate more closely."

On the rest of the journey, their talk moved towards Demi and what her talents might add to the knowledge the druids had gained over the past year. Then they drifted into mundane chatter about their latest efforts to create new talismans. Both men shared their frustrations that their capabilities hadn't grown faster. Their techniques had refined, but too much of their time had been spent getting set up, arranging for servants and supplies and the day-to-day running of the Hall. At least Munro and Rory didn't have to see to the fae who came from all over, hoping to be compatible with the only unbonded druids, Aaron and Huck. Of the two, Huck put less into making himself available for that. Munro wasn't quite sure what pull the human realm had on the American. He still returned repeatedly, as though looking for something. Did Huck even understand why he went back so often?

Over the next hill, Munro stopped abruptly. A large, beautiful faerie city spread out before him, a castle dominating the far side. Eilidh called him from inside like a beacon in his soul. No matter what difficulties they had, the communication problems or the cultural clashes, being close to her felt like coming home.

∞

Getting Lisle Hartmann to *Centraal Station* took longer than Huck would have liked. Although pretty spritely for her age, she couldn't move like a druid who'd been breathing Otherworld air for six months. Even worse, she kept arguing that she should've stayed.

"I must go home in case they come back," she said.

Huck urged her on and bought two tickets to Hook of Holland. They had to be on the next train if they wanted to catch the last ferry to Essex. "If they're in the human realm, Flùr will find them and meet up with us," he said in a low voice. "Nobody will be returning to that house for a while." As an afterthought, he added, "I'm sorry."

"Everything is your fault," she said. Her words rang clearly despite her thick German accent. "You led Ulrich to us."

Huck led her down to the right platform, and they waited for the train. The whine of electric train engines as they whizzed by in the darkness combined with the rumble of them moving over steel tracks. Had he led the prince right to Demi's front door? Had Ulrich or one of his men followed him over the German border into the Netherlands? He didn't know for certain, but he had difficulty imagining that was the case. Surely he would have had an inkling someone was following him. Besides, there was that strange figure outside Demi's house that first night. Whoever it was, they'd been there before him. Still, if he'd moved more quickly, he should have gotten to Demi before Ulrich had the chance.

"How did he get in?" Huck asked. "I thought your wards would keep him away. Flùr couldn't get past them."

"Again! Your fault!" she spat.

Huck looked at her. He couldn't deny it, even if he hoped her accusation wasn't true. A train came to rest in front of them. They stood aside as passengers streamed out of an open door. At the first opportunity, he led her inside, guiding her gently by the elbow. "I wasn't even there," he said as they made their way to a four-person section with two seats facing each other, separated by a table.

The old lady parked herself by the window, clutching her knapsack to her chest. Huck took the aisle seat facing her and chucked Demi and Jago's packs down next to him. He watched Mrs Hartmann closely. She was like iron, sitting rigidly, glaring towards the platform. When the train began to pull away from the station, she looked at him. "She moved the ward for you, to let your faerie in."

Dread and guilt filled Huck's stomach. Demi must have forgotten to put the stone near the door again. Such a small thing would've been easy to overlook, he supposed. With everything going on, the upcoming move. Especially if she couldn't detect the wards magically. She probably took their presence for granted. But still, Mrs Hartmann was right. Everything was his fault. If he'd stayed away, Demi would be safe.

No words of apology came, although remorse washed over him. What could he say to make any of it all right? "We'll get them back."

She resumed staring out the window, her expression hard and tinged with grief. Clearly, she didn't believe a word he said.

The rest of the journey passed as though they were strangers who happened to share the same destination, which, he supposed, was the case. In many ways, her willingness to travel with him in the first place surprised him. Maybe she did have some hope he'd find Demi.

After a tedious couple of train changes, they finally arrived at *Hoek van Holland* railway station. Huck looked at his watch. They had cut the timing close. Fortunately the train station was next to the ferry terminal, so they hurried over to book their passage. He bought tickets for five, reserving a family cabin for Lisle, Demi, and Jago and a standard, two-person cabin for himself and Flùranach. He handed Demi's and Jago's tickets to Lisle. She accepted them in silence.

They waited as long as possible to board the ferry. He was worried she might refuse to board without Demi and Jago, but she followed without protest. Her gaze, however, never left the entrance. When the doors shut and the boat pulled away, her face fell as hope crumbled within.

Huck wanted to tell her not to give up, but the reassurance sounded stupid, even in his head. His hopes now rested on... "Flùranach," he said aloud, catching a glimpse of her familiar red hair. Her fae traits had been disguised, but he recognised her easily.

She wove towards them through a group of standing passengers. His gut clenched when he realised she'd come alone.

"I tracked them to the German gates," she said when she got close enough. "I would have pursued them, but the Ashkyne Watchers would not allow me through, even with my keepers' token." She stole a glance at Lisle. "Forgive me, elder," she said. "I did not think I should fight them. They were many more than usual. They claimed Prince Ulrich had been killed and told me the gates were closed to all."

"You did all you could." Huck said.

"I'm sorry," Flùranach said to Lisle, but the old lady sat in stony silence, staring at nothing as though a light had extinguished within.

The expression on Flùranach's face changed as she considered the old woman. "You are a druid," she said.

Still, Lisle didn't respond.

Flùranach looked at Huck with surprise. He hadn't realised, either, and Demi hadn't told him. At least this explained why Lisle had been so accepting of Demi's story about Ulrich. What Huck didn't know was if the woman's powers were unlocked. If the old woman's abilities had never initiated, they would after contact with Flùranach. Assuming, of course, she ever roused from her grief-stricken trance.

Huck's thoughts turned to Demi as they journeyed across the North Sea. Where was she? Why had Ulrich's men grabbed her, and what would they do with her and Jago? He assumed they'd be taken to Konstanze. He couldn't be sure how Konstanze would deal with them. Jago was her family, after all. He'd never heard of a half-human faerie before, so he didn't know how the boy would be regarded. Either way, they had a tricky path ahead. None of the possible outcomes passing through his mind struck him as good.

He glanced up to see Mrs Hartmann staring into his face. All he could do was bear her condemnation. "We should find our cabins," he said. "We have a long, eight-hour crossing ahead." He doubted any of them would sleep.

CHAPTER 10

HUCK, FLÙRANACH, AND LISLE met Munro and Rory in Essex and explained about Demi and Jago's kidnapping. The subsequent travel from Caledonia to the Halls of Mist took an excruciating twenty-four hours. Eilidh granted all of them passage, including Flùranach, although Munro said the queen wasn't too thrilled about the entire situation. Of course, she wanted to help the druids. On the other hand, she didn't like crossing Konstanze and was displeased to learn Flùranach had hidden in the Halls of Mist for months. Eilidh only allowed her in Caledonia under the protection of the druids. This announcement surprised Lisle as much as it did Huck. It appeared to come as no shock to Flùranach, who was merely grateful for a way back since the gate in Germany had been closed.

Tràth and Douglas met up with the druids' party after the audience with Queen Eilidh. Surprising everyone, Douglas opted to join the group, offering no explanation other than to say he regretted not helping out more.

Naturally, Lisle couldn't run like the rest of them. She took the shock of the Otherworld air with her usual stoicism, but still moved at a snail's pace. So Eilidh arranged for her to be taken by cart, propelled by six Watchers rolling it along with air and earth magic. Even with their help, the journey passed slowly, and every mile pained Huck.

The Halls of Mist buzzed with rumours by the time they arrived. A human druid had been taken in the Ashkyne borderlands, people said, accused of the murder of Prince Ulrich. Lisle muttered denials, but her voice trembled. She appeared to have aged ten years in one day.

Druid Hall servants prepared a room for Lisle, and Huck made sure she got settled. All her toughness had evaporated when she learned about the charge of murder against Demi. Lisle wanted to be alone, even though he worried about her feeling neglected in this strange new place. She insisted, leaving him no choice. Before he left, he asked her, "Why didn't Ulrich's people take you too?"

"They didn't know about me. I was upstairs when they arrived. The ward stone masked my presence." She sat uncomfortably on the fae-made swing chair, clutching Jago's teddy bear to her chest. "I heard Ulrich and Demi fighting. They had woken Jago with their shouts, and he was crying." She looked away, sorrow making the deep lines in her face even more pronounced.

When she didn't say anything further, he said, "I'll have some food sent up. You are welcome to eat, sleep, whatever. Just...I wouldn't leave the Hall, if I were you."

She glanced up at him, looking pale and fragile. "Where would I go?"

Because he had no answer, he simply nodded and left her alone. He considered with dread that he'd ruined at least three lives by trying to bring Demi here.

When he arrived at the workshop, he realised the druids hadn't all been together in quite some time. Despite the circumstances, something about the reunion reassured him, as though his fellow druids had his back. Inside, he found the others already deep in conversation. Munro interrupted the chatter when he saw Huck. "How is she?"

"Tired, I think. Confused." No, that wasn't right. When she'd come to the Otherworld and the Halls of Mist, she'd appeared unimpressed, as though none of the wonders of the fae realm touched her. "Numb is maybe a better word."

"You're sure she's a druid?"

"Flùranach said so," Huck replied. Aaron gave a snort at the mention of the faerie's name, which earned him a glance from Rory.

Douglas, the youngest druid at only nineteen, sat forward. "I'm interested in these wards she uses. Did Lisle make them?"

"I didn't ask," Huck said. He sank into a chair.

Munro spoke up next. "Our first priority is Demi and Jago. We need to send a message to Queen Konstanze. Word is Demi's been arrested, but we don't know what Konstanze means to do. I have never heard anything about fae law regarding queens arresting humans."

"Too bad Eilidh wouldn't come back with us," Douglas said. "She'd know what to do."

Munro cast him a dark look. "She said she'd meet us later tonight if she can. In the meantime, I'm planning to talk to Oszlár," he said. "The keepers seem to be the ones who hold the kingdoms together, the only ones every queen respects."

Huck worried the druids were out of their depth. They'd never experienced a crisis like this or anything that put them directly at odds with a queen. He hoped the keepers would be amenable to assisting them.

Munro stood and went to the corridor and spoke to someone on the other side of the door. "Please send word to Keeper Oszlár. We need him urgently."

"Yes, my lord druid," came the reply. Footfalls sounded on the stone floor and moved away as Munro returned to the workshop.

"We can get her back, right?" Huck said. "I thought our word was supposed to be law."

Munro shook his head. "The commands of the draoidh *were* law. So far, we've stepped into some of the role those ancient druids had in fae society millennia ago, but we haven't determined how far that will get us in reality. The queens have supported the Hall up until now, but this will be our first real test."

Huck grumbled. A part of him had hoped they could order Konstanze to give up Demi and Jago.

Aaron shrugged. "They helped us build this Hall, their people make up our servants, they defer to us in every conversation, and pretty much grant us free passage in their kingdoms. I don't understand why this is going to be a problem. Perhaps Konstanze doesn't know Demi is a druid."

The head steward, Hon, entered the workshop and bowed. "A message from Ashkyne," he said.

Munro stood and took an envelope from Hon, then unfolded the parchment within. He glanced up at Huck. "She knows," he said.

Huck's chest tightened. "What does it say?"

"Thank you," Munro said to Hon. "When Keeper Oszlár arrives, please show him in here."

Huck stood. "Munro?"

"Queen Konstanze of Ashkyne has invited no more than two members of the Druid Hall to enter her kingdom under her protection. They may administer whatever death rites are appropriate to the druid Demi Hartmann."

"What?" Huck crossed the floor and snatched the letter out of Munro's hands. He read the last half aloud:

> The execution of the murderer Demi Hartmann, citizen of the Ashkyne borderlands, will take place on the Eve of Hainne.

> Queen Konstanze has decreed her nephew, the lethfae known as Jago, a ward of the crown. The child will be raised under the protection of the royal bloodline and suffer no consequences of his mother's crime.

A cold sweat broke out over Huck's skin. "She can't do that," he said. "Can she? Demi is one of us." He read the letter top to bottom again, as though the words on the page might change if he concentrated hard enough.

"We have two full nights from tonight before the Eve of Hainne," Munro said. "Which, coincidentally, is my wedding day."

"Konstanze would execute a druid on your wedding day?" With a chill, the blood drained from Huck's face, and he lowered himself into a chair. His hope withered.

"She's making a statement," Munro replied with a glower.

∞

Demi sat cross-legged in the centre of the bare, stone room, elbows on her knees and head in her hands. Her stomach churned. The power vibrating through the Otherworld air made her gut clench. She hadn't eaten since they brought her to this prison. Most of her misery, of course, came from worry about Jago. They'd been carried a long distance in a blur, and all the while Jago had cried for his mama.

Tears of frustration stung her eyes. She mustered all her willpower, commanding herself to stay still. She'd discovered her captors would not tolerate resistance. They would not hesitate to immobilise her again with their strong air flows.

The entire first day she'd been bound, and she didn't want to return to that state. She'd had enough of being tied up in the days when she was Ulrich's lover. She'd learned how to feign compliance when required to.

Over and over, she replayed the moment of his death. So painful and gruesome. Blood had spurted from his neck and across her face. The suddenness of it had stunned her, and she hadn't snapped out of her shock until Jago shrieked. Her sweet baby boy. Was he crying now? Was he frightened? Her mind went to dark places. A wailing moan built in her chest, but she stuffed it down and refused to let any sound escape her lips. She needed to be strong.

A whisper came to her ears. "Are you truly draoidh?" it asked in German. She looked around but saw no one. "I need to know. Are you of the Druid Hall?" The voice seemed to be carried on a breeze as though echoing from far away.

Her mind raced. Huck claimed druids were revered in the fae realm. Had he been telling the truth? Should she admit her lineage, or would this land her and Jago in worse trouble? She considered Huck. He'd seemed sincere. She'd wanted desperately to believe him, enough that she was willing to risk to moving her family with him. He'd promised them a safe place, safe even from the powerful fae. Were the druids enemies of the fae? He'd told her some fae served the druids, but judging from her current situation, not all feared his people. Doubts crept in. What power could humans hold to make the fae revere them? *None.*

She held her silence, waiting for the voice to say something more. It did not.

∞

"What do you think?" Munro asked Keeper Oszlár.

The ancient fae frowned as he studied the letter.

"It must have been self-defence," Huck said. "Demi told us Ulrich was abusive. That's why she was hiding Jago from him."

"The letter doesn't say anything about a trial or hearing. Surely someone will be allowed to speak for her," Munro said.

Oszlár returned the letter to Munro. "In Ashkyne, Queen Konstanze will do as she pleases. Her people expect strength and even ruthlessness from her. Did the lady confess?"

Munro turned to Huck with the unspoken question.

"All Lisle told me was that she heard Demi and Ulrich arguing."

The scowl never left the elder keeper's face. "I would like to speak to the newest member of your Hall, if I may."

A moment passed before Munro realised he meant Lisle. She was, he supposed, one of them now.

"I'll get her," Huck offered and slipped out of the workshop.

"How can we convince Konstanze to release Demi and Jago?" Munro asked.

"We will see what she wants. If her primary objective was to avenge her brother, Lady Druid Demi Hartmann would be dead already, and you would not have been invited to visit Ashkyne. The offer of death rites, while strictly adhering to protocol in the case of a condemned faerie, is clearly an excuse to negotiate with you."

"What about the boy?" Aaron asked.

"As the child's blood relative, Queen Konstanze is within her rights to take him under her protection. I'm surprised, however, considering he's lethfae."

"What does that mean?" Rory asked.

"Even I am shocked at the news Ulrich was azuri fae. Many rumours surrounded him, and he was known to be, shall we say, cold-blooded, but none suspected he followed the Path of Stars. Queen Konstanze's family did well to keep his talent secret.

A half-druid child recognised as part of the royal family will only remind the fae of Ulrich's clandestine visits to the human realm and what many still consider to be impure magic."

Munro opened his mouth to argue how much that perception had changed in the past year, but at that moment, Huck entered the workshop with Lisle Hartman. The old woman's eyes were bloodshot, with dark circles under them. "They are going to execute my granddaughter?" she asked. Although she looked exhausted, her voice sounded stronger than before.

"We'll try to stop them," Munro said. "This is Keeper Oszlár. He's advising us on how to proceed. He'd like to speak with you."

She eyed the ancient keeper warily and raised her chin. "What do you want to know?"

Munro admired her grit. Even though she was clearly distraught, she was still fighting with everything in her.

The keeper bowed to her. "My lady druid," he said. "If we are to help your granddaughter, I must know what you saw."

"Why don't we sit down?" Huck said, but nobody moved or spoke for an instant. Lisle seemed to be evaluating Oszlár.

After a long silence, she began speaking. "I put Jago to bed early. We planned to leave in the night, so we decided to rest after supper. I couldn't sleep, so I was awake when the front door opened. At first, I thought Demi had gone to the corner shop. She had mentioned that she planned to buy Jago some treats for the journey. But then I heard shouting." Lisle's eyes shone as she stared straight ahead as though watching events replay in front of her. "I got out of bed and went to check on Jago, but then I heard him crying downstairs. I rushed down, but as I came to the landing, Demi saw me and gestured for me to stay back. She looked frightened, so I did what she wanted."

"Where was the boy?" Oszlár asked.

"Clinging to Demi's leg."

"And where was Prince Ulrich?"

"Standing in the centre of the room."

Munro's instincts told him she was leaving something out. The idea niggled at him, though. Could she be lying? Or was she simply omitting certain facts? He wanted to jump in and ask, but he decided not to interrupt the keeper's questioning just yet.

Lisle went on. "Demi looked at me, and I knew by her expression he was attempting to weaken her."

"What do you mean?" Munro asked. "What was he doing?"

"I don't know." Lisle hesitated and touched her fingers to the side of her face. Munro could tell she once again was hiding something and had a suspicion what her secret might be. If she'd been a compatible bond with Ulrich as well, she may have felt an inexplicable attraction towards him. If that was the case, he may have begun to unlock her druidic talents in that short time. Such a pull towards the man who'd hurt her granddaughter would be confusing, not to mention mortifying. He had no evidence of such a connection, but the theory would explain some of her reticence. "Ulrich shouted," she continued. "I heard pain in his voice."

"What did you see?" Huck asked.

"Ulrich had been pacing as he ranted, and he had moved back and out of my sight. He was out of my view when he cried out, but I can tell you, Demi did not touch him."

"What about the child?" Oszlár asked.

"Jago?" Lisle narrowed her eyes. "He's only four years old, a baby. What could he do but cry for his mama? He did nothing to Ulrich. I swear on my life." Her words left no room for doubt. Fae children were not helpless in the same way a human child would be. On the other hand, Jago was only half-fae. He'd likely never met a faerie before, much less been trained to use whatever power he might possess.

"So if Demi didn't kill Ulrich, who else could have?" Aaron asked.

Lisle shrugged. "I cannot pretend to understand the ways of magic. Although my family has a long tradition of stories of the fae, I thought them to be no more than stories until Ulrich appeared. Might a faerie have been invisible or struck him from a distance or using a weapon I couldn't see? Is there no spell or enchantment that might kill?"

"I suppose it's possible." Munro looked to Oszlár. "Any ideas?"

The old keeper kept his focus on Lisle. "What manner of wounds did you detect on the prince?"

"His body was out of view, but I do know he did not die quickly. He was still living when his men rushed in."

"What happened next?" Huck asked her gently.

"I called out for Jago, but in the commotion, he didn't hear me. Demi pleaded with me. She said, 'Stay back, Omi.'" Lisle sighed. "I shouldn't have listened to her, but..." Her voice trailed off.

"They frightened you," Huck said.

She nodded. "They were dressed in black and very tall. Their eyes swirled and glowed. They moved like no one I'd ever seen. They blurred out of sight before I knew what happened. The next moment, they were gone, and they'd taken Ulrich and my grandchildren with them."

"So maybe he wasn't dead?" Aaron suggested.

Huck shook his head. "There was a huge pool of blood on the floor when I arrived. I don't imagine anyone who bled that much would survive."

"What do you think?" Munro asked Lisle. Time to test his theory that Lisle may have also possessed a compatible bond with Ulrich.

She appeared to be considering how to respond, but finally she nodded. "The moment was brief, but I believe he is dead. Despite his pain, his heart was still beating when his men arrived, but I would swear he died in that house. I am certain."

On one hand, Munro felt satisfied that he'd uncovered a big part of her deception. She might not even realise her powers had been unlocked by Ulrich. But her story had holes in it. Faerie didn't just drop dead. He also considered the initial shout and pain may not have been the time of the death blow. What if one of his men killed him, using the chaos as a cover? Munro wanted the theory to fit, but he didn't know what motive might a Watcher have or how he could strike a killing blow without the others noticing. Still, if astral magic or illusions were involved, eye-witness statements meant little. "What was Ulrich's sphere of magic?"

"Air," Lisle replied. "I remember Demi saying he used to bind her with air."

"No," Munro said, "I mean his primary talent. If he had the ability to bond with a druid, he must have been azuri. That means astral, which is the mental, blood magic, temporal magic, or spirit magic. We've never found anyone with spirit magic, though, so don't know how those talents would manifest."

She shook her head. "Demi only mentioned his use of air and some water talents, but never anything like those others."

Munro wasn't going to argue with her. Perhaps Ulrich only used his earth talents. When she had been an outcast, Eilidh fought her astral abilities for years.

Rory turned to Oszlár. "I'm guessing astral," he said. "Besides being the most common, Ulrich's attempts to control Demi fit with mental magic. Illusion would explain why Lisle didn't witness more specifics."

Oszlár nodded slowly. "Perhaps."

"I think you're right," Lisle said eagerly. "Demi often spoke of feeling as though she was heavily under his influence."

"You must accept Konstanze's invitation," Oszlár said. "Speak to the lady druid and learn what you can about the night of Ulrich's death. Your best hope to free her is to convince Konstanze of her innocence."

"What about this whole draoidh thing?" Huck asked. "I thought we were supposed to wield more influence than this."

"I had hoped," Oszlár began, "we might uncover more secrets to unlock the power of the draoidh of old before this test of belief came. Right now, tradition is the only weapon you possess, and

Konstanze knows this. You will be better off if the lady druid is innocent."

"What if I confess?" Lisle said. "If I say I killed Ulrich, they should release Demi and Jago."

Munro sighed, unhappy that their weakness in fae society would lead to this gloomy state of affairs. "They won't believe you any more than I do, and a confession wouldn't solve our problem."

"I doubt Konstanze will release the boy, no matter what else happens," Oszlár said.

"But my granddaughter would live."

The old keeper shook his head. "More likely, the Ashkyne queen would demand to execute you both. No, false confessions will help no one." He turned to Munro. "You must go to Konstanze. Whatever you do, do not back down or show fear."

"Come with us," Munro said. "I will need your advice."

"She will not admit even the keepers. The move is unprecedented, but she is within her rights. The queens' rule in their own kingdoms is absolute."

Munro nodded. "I'll leave in an hour," he said. Then, realising their dependence on the fae had the potential to take a nasty turn, he thought about his conversation with Rory. He'd not given the problem much thought when they spoke about wanting their own gate to the human realm. They'd be able to access Caledonia as long as he was bonded to Eilidh, but if anything ever happened to her, all bets were off. Munro didn't want his men stranded in the Halls of Mist forever. "Rory, you come along. I'd like to continue the chat we had on the way to Caledonia about gates."

"No," Huck said. "I'm going with you. Demi knows me. She trusts me more than she would anyone else. Munro, I need to do this." With a glance to Lisle, he added, "This is my fault. If everything goes wrong, I at least want the chance to tell her how sorry I am. Please."

Munro breathed in, then blew out the air in a rush. "Okay," he said. Events were changing too fast. He didn't have time to really think things through, so instinct would have to do.

"I know what you're talking about though, Munro," Rory said. "An idea came to me about our little problem. I'm on it." He glanced around at the others. "All of us are."

Aaron nodded. "Sure, I'm in. Whatever we need to do."

Douglas spoke up, reminding Munro for the first time he was in the room. "Count me in," he said.

Although prospects seemed bleak, the druids' willingness to work together and support each other buoyed Munro's spirits. Now he had to figure out what to say to Konstanze.

CHAPTER 11

THE MORE TIME PASSED, the more the walls closed in on Aaron at the Druid Hall. When his powers were unlocked by the blood faerie Cridhe, he'd felt like he was a part of something for the first time. After he learned Cridhe planned to kill them all, well, the news dampened his enthusiasm, to say the least. Later, Munro invited him to the Isle of Skye, then on to Caledonia. He'd swept along with the crowd, going the only places he believed his magic would ever truly belong.

But his best mate Phillip was murdered by Cadhla, the former queen of Caledonia, and Rory was permanently scarred by Flùranach. These events brought home to him that although the druids might not fit into the human realm, at least no one there was plotting their deaths. Now another queen had them in the crosshairs. As long as their magic was so underdeveloped, the druids were sitting ducks.

Worse yet, Flùranach had come back from who knows where and was living under the same roof.

Aaron had heard she was scheming to bond with Rory again, but Rory turned her down flat. What happened when she wouldn't take no for an answer? What if she set her sights on Aaron? He and Huck were the only two unbonded druids. Unless, he supposed, they counted Lisle and Demi. But Demi probably wouldn't leave Ashkyne alive, and Lisle had to be eighty if she was a day. What were the chances of them finding the old lady a compatible faerie before she croaked of natural causes?

Aaron stood to leave the workshop. He had decisions to make before it was too late. His gut told him the Halls of Mist weren't safe as long as they didn't have a way out that wasn't dependent on a queen. All their food, their supplies, and their servants came from the kingdoms. If the queens refused the druids permission to access their gates, the druids would be in serious trouble.

Hon stepped into the doorway, blocking Aaron's exit. "Queen Eilidh of Caledonia," he announced.

Aaron didn't trust Eilidh, truth be told. She was messing Munro about. What sort of woman wants to marry three guys? She claimed to love Munro, but hers wasn't any kind of love Aaron understood. Why Munro put up with her taking a third husband, Aaron didn't know. He figured being bonded made it near impossible to object, another reason bonding didn't appeal to Aaron much. He didn't want to fall for some faerie, just to get treated like Munro and Rory did. The others didn't appear to mind, but nobody would put a leash on Aaron's neck. Even Douglas had changed since he'd bonded with Tràth, almost never leaving the prince's side. Aaron had known Douglas before, and he hadn't seemed gay. But with all the stuff Douglas claimed he and Tràth got up to at these wild parties, it sounded like Douglas had gotten into the swing of things, so to speak. If bonding with a guy would make Aaron gay, he would say *no thanks*. Not interested.

After a moment, Eilidh followed the steward into the workshop. The druids wouldn't receive most royals in the workshop, but with her, most of the usual protocol didn't apply. "My lords and lady," she said with a tilt of her head. Aaron choked on a laugh. She never would act so formal if Oszlár hadn't been around. "Keeper," she said to the old faerie.

"Your Majesty," Oszlár said. "I hadn't thought to find you away from Caledonia with the transitions your kingdom has undergone in recent days, not to mention your upcoming wedding."

Was there a criticism in the statement? Aaron raised an eyebrow at Rory, but Rory shrugged. He didn't know either.

"I consider the needs of the Druid Hall a priority. Quinton believed I may be able to assist with Queen Konstanze," she explained.

"Naturally," the keeper said.

Rory stood and greeted Eilidh. "Sorry, Eilidh. Munro left not ten minutes ago. Konstanze sent a message inviting two druids to speak with her." He glanced at Lisle with some discomfort, clearly not wanting to discuss Demi's execution in front of her. "Will you excuse me? I'm going to escort Lisle to her suite."

"Of course," Eilidh said, watching the old lady carefully. Aaron would give his eye teeth to know what she was thinking.

Rory guided Lisle out, leaving Aaron and Douglas as the only two druids in the workshop.

"What was Konstanze's message?" Eilidh asked Oszlár.

He handed the parchment to her. Eilidh read through the document, glanced up at him, then looked to the other druids. With a sigh, she returned the parchment to him. "This isn't good," she muttered, then straightened herself as though she'd made a decision. "Keeper, might I have a word with you? I'd be happy to walk back to the library with you so as not to take more of your valuable time than necessary."

Curious, Aaron thought. What did she want to tell him that she wouldn't say in front of the druids?

"Of course, Your Majesty," Oszlár said. He turned to the others. "I suspect we may be forced to wait some time before the others return from Ashkyne. Please send word upon their return, and I will offer whatever assistance I can." He handed Konstanze's letter to Aaron.

"Sure," Aaron said. The whole thing struck him as odd. Just before Eilidh arrived, Oszlár said he planned to wait at the Druid Hall. Why would Eilidh's request change his mind?

Oszlár and Eilidh left the workshop together, strolling down the path towards the entry hall. Aaron turned to Douglas. "I'll be right back. I want to find out what they're up to."

He peered around the stone arch that led to the corridor. The pair walked ahead, and his keen hearing picked up their murmuring voices. Keeping his steps light, he followed. Words floated to his ears, but he had trouble catching everything. Interestingly, they were talking about Demi's boy.

Eilidh stopped in the courtyard, and Aaron hovered behind a stone column. If someone walked up from the other direction, he'd look a bit odd lurking there, but the Druid Hall wasn't exactly bustling with activity.

"I'd not expected this," Eilidh said to Oszlár. Her brow creased into a frown.

"Children are a gift from the Mother," Oszlár said.

"But a lethfae child? What place would a half-blood have in our society? How would that child be regarded? Not having the full magic of a faerie, but not draoidh either."

"Or perhaps the best of both?" Oszlár said. "In millennia past, when draoidh lived and worked among us, lethfae children, although not common, did exist."

"I've never heard of them," she admitted.

"None of us had realised the draoidh had human origins until recently. Why would we think their children as anything other than fae?"

"As you well know, times were different then. Our attitudes towards humans have changed over millennia. Only a few years ago, any of us would consider bedding a human unthinkable, much less contemplate taking one as a mate. These customs are doubtlessly why Ulrich kept his visits to the borderlands secret. I wonder if he even knew Demi was a druid when he began their relationship," Eilidh said. "When I met Quinton, I didn't understand the magic pulling us together."

"Your concern for this woman's child is admirable," Oszlár said.

Aaron moved so he could see Eilidh's face. Why *was* she so intent to ask about Jago? Did she know more about this than the druids realised?

"If I may ask, Your Majesty, why are you concealing your aura?" Oszlár asked.

The sudden change of topic startled Aaron. Faeries didn't typically go about with their presence masked, from what he understood, unless they had something to hide. She was adept at illusion. Aaron had the half-baked notion maybe the person he spied on wasn't Eilidh at all. A chill swept over him.

"Ah, I do apologise. I'm practising my focus," she said.

"Admirable," he said and paused. "I heard you and your mate visited the new Caledonian altars to make sacrifices."

"Yes," she said.

"A surprise to everyone, but we all pray the Mother blesses your union."

So she *was* trying to get pregnant with Griogair. Aaron grumbled to himself. Munro couldn't be happy about this. Why would she do this just days before the wedding?

"A surprise?" Eilidh asked, a hint of annoyance ringing in her voice. Aaron had to hand it to the old guy. Nobody else would have the balls to question a queen like this.

"You are taking another mate in a couple of days."

She gave a laugh, but her humour sounded forced. "Even Quinton did not question me so rigidly when we discussed my intent. If our arrangement doesn't bother him, why should it worry anyone else? I chose to honour Griogair and seek the blessing of the Mother. Isn't this cause for celebration?"

"All children are cause for celebration," the keeper said. "All unions are worthy of honour." His tone softened, and he took the queen's hand. She seemed surprised but didn't pull away. Neither of the faeries spoke for a moment.

Eilidh glanced up suddenly. Aaron held his breath and stepped back, hoping she hadn't seen him. He felt like a right idiot, eavesdropping like this, but if Eilidh had something to hide, or if there was a chance this might be an imposter, he wanted to know what was going on.

Unfortunately, the pair turned and continued their walk out of the Druid Hall, towards the library. There would be nothing for Aaron to hide behind on the path. He followed them as far as the entrance to the Druid Hall, and he watched them in the distance.

"What are you doing?" Rory's voice came from behind him.

Aaron jumped. "Jesus. You gave me a fright," he said, turning around to find the red-haired Scot standing in the courtyard. Wanting to change the subject, he asked, "How's Lisle?"

"I don't think she's eaten or slept since we left Amsterdam," he said.

"Do you think Munro and Huck have any chance of getting her family back?"

"If our so-called status means anything, yes. But that's the big question, isn't it?"

"I've been thinking about that," Aaron said. "I don't like the fae having so much power over us." He didn't mention Flùranach. Judging by the look on Rory's face, his mind had already gone to the same place.

"It's weird you bring up the queens' control. Me and Munro talked about that on the trip through

Caledonia. I have some ideas. Want to help me muck about with a gate? Douglas said he'd help too."

"Where? Caledonia?" Caledonia was the only kingdom where they had unrestricted access. Considering what he'd just overheard, though, Aaron was uneasy about visiting just now.

"No. Right here. I got an idea of how to start our own gate when Munro and I chatted about his visit to the Source Stone." He gestured towards the workshop. "I'll show you."

Eilidh's strange conversation with the keeper forgotten, Aaron followed Rory, relieved to learn he wasn't the only one who'd been concerned with maintaining a safe way out.

∞

"I don't like this," Munro said. He and Huck stood outside an audience hall in Drokstul Castle, waiting for Konstanze to receive them.

"What's wrong?" Huck asked. He shifted his weight uncomfortably.

A few minutes before, Munro had told him to stop pacing. Now he almost wished he hadn't, because the American's fidgeting irritated him more than the striding back and forth had.

Munro gave a quick shake of his head. Faeries' hearing was even sharper than the druids', and that didn't even take magic into account. With any number of unfriendly ears listening, they had to act with caution. His mind spun as he considered the situation. He should have negotiated for a bigger contingent of representatives from the Druid Hall rather than showing up like a couple of supplicants. If a queen had answered the same missive, she would have demanded an honour guard plus at least an advisor or two. No way would she walk into hostile territory alone.

On the other hand, he hoped accepting Konstanze's terms would show they weren't worried or intimidated. That, of course, couldn't have been further from the truth, but several times in the past, his ignorance of social rules had worked to his benefit.

Footfalls echoed down a wooden floor, drawing near the door. Munro turned to Huck and met his eyes. "Poker face," he said, his voice low, hoping none of the fae would understand the reference even if the comment was overheard.

Huck nodded. "Got it," he said. To his credit, he did school his features by the time a faerie stood before them and gave a barely courteous nod in their direction.

"Queen Konstanze will see you now," the faerie said. He wore all black, as did most of her servants. His uniform was devoid of any ornament and struck Munro as appropriate to wear to a funeral. Perhaps the hard, utilitarian edge to the castle's structure contributed to the association. This place had none of the light, open design of Caledonian architecture. Every detail, from the people to the stonework, seemed a deliberate effort to intimidate.

Instead of taking them into the large hall, however, the faerie led them to an immense wooden doorway. He grabbed a wrought-iron handle and pulled. Munro frowned. Very few entrances in Caledonia even had doors, and they'd copied that form in the Druid Hall. He'd grown accustomed to the unrestricted character of the buildings, so this structure felt closed in.

Their guide stood back and gestured for them to enter. Munro stepped inside without mentioning the lack of courtesy in the faerie's manner, even though his conduct didn't bode well. If a servant felt secure being disrespectful to a druid lord, what did that say about Konstanze's attitude?

The queen lounged on a long, elegantly curved wooden chair from which she read over a parchment without acknowledging their approach. Munro quietly surveyed the room. There were no windows and no obvious exits other than the one behind him. He assumed there was a hidden door somewhere on the far side, since he thought it unlikely Konstanze would let him block the only entrance. Behind Konstanze stood three faeries, all elders. Members of her conclave, he guessed. They watched the druids warily, which told Munro her insouciant demeanour was a careful performance. Whatever she had in mind, the conclave hadn't been wholeheartedly convinced of its wisdom. Another worrying sign.

Huck shifted his weight again, and Munro shot him a look. "We're holding a two-seven off-suit," he said quietly. The worst possible poker hand out of the draw. He forced himself to smile and hoped he was convincing. He had to keep Konstanze off balance. The druids might be in a bad position, but he had no intention of confirming they had nothing to bargain with.

Questions played across Huck's face, but he merely nodded. "Time for the flop," he whispered back. Of course, if any of the faeries nearby had ever played poker, their code would prove useless.

Queen Konstanze, on the other hand, watched the exchange with irritation, clearly not understanding what passed between the two men. She placed her scroll on a low wooden table. "I think it's time," she said, "we stop pretending." She lifted her gaze to meet Munro's.

"I wasn't aware we'd been doing anything of the sort," Munro said, focusing on maintaining a calm tone. "You've arrested and sentenced a member of the Druid Hall without trial. We've come to secure her release and that of her child as well."

Munro noticed the clench of her jaw and flick of her eyes before she hid her concerns behind a cool mask. "The human woman had never been to the Otherworld before her arrest. How could she be a member of your Hall? She is merely a citizen of the Ashkyne borderlands."

"Lady Druid Demi Hartmann was under our protection and a member of the Druid Hall the moment she struck an agreement with us. Humans are not ruled by faerie queens," Munro said. "You had no right to take her."

"No right?" Konstanze shouted, all pretence of serenity evaporated. "She murdered my brother!"

"Did she?" Munro said. "I have a witness who claims Demi Hartmann didn't touch Ulrich."

"Ridiculous," Konstanze spat. "I have personally spoken to every one of Ulrich's men. I am certain you can't say the same."

"Ulrich's men weren't the only people there. There was another druid in the house. Beyond the wards. Someone your men missed."

Konstanze turned her head slightly, as though watching the faeries behind her out of the corner of her eye. They glanced at one another but said nothing. "Then produce your witness. Bring him here, and I will hear what he has to say."

"Here?" Huck muttered, "You've got to be joking."

Munro held up a hand, hoping to stop the other druid from giving anything away. "What about the boy? You acknowledged in your letter he bears no responsibility. Why hold him? Surely the fae do not imprison children."

Konstanze looked startled. "He is not a prisoner. I want him trained by the best royal tutors, his talents fostered and enriched. The child is the one remaining remnant of my brother's bloodline. I assure you, he will be as well cared for as any fae infant."

Munro nodded. The explanation gave him some peace of mind. Fae children were rare, by comparison, and therefore protected fiercely. He sensed from Konstanze's reaction she was surprised he would suspect ill intentions towards the boy. "Thank you," he said. "I would be most grateful if we could see Jago when we visit his mother."

"He is naturally distressed by the recent transition," Konstanze said carefully. "I would not wish to upset him further. However, we will arrange for you to view the boy from a distance, to assure you if you doubt my word."

The last part was uttered with such contempt, Munro thought it unwise to push further. "I request a public trial for Demi Hartmann, to be ruled on in the Halls of Mist by impartial judges. We will call our witness there, where we can be assured of her safety."

Anger flashed in Konstanze's eyes. "You are in no position to make demands, *druid lord*," she said, spitting the title with disdain. "The human murdered my brother. She is not fae. There will be no trial."

"She is a druid!" he shouted. "She is under my protection, and I will not stand by while you kill an innocent woman."

Konstanze's lips curled into a sneer. "Will you not?" She glanced towards her advisors again, then lifted her eyes to meet Munro's. "And what will you do to stop me?"

Munro cursed silently. He'd forgotten his warning to Huck. They were holding losing cards and had nothing to bargain with. He groped for a way to back-peddle. He never should have voiced even an implied threat.

"You will do nothing," Konstanze said with quiet menace. "You will do nothing because you *can* do nothing. Any authority the Druid Hall has amassed is based on fear and lies."

He wanted to argue that they'd never told a single lie, but he knew that's what she expected. He held himself perfectly still and hoped Huck would do the same. "Is that so?" he said.

"You humans parade around, and those weak-minded queens bow to you. To *you*," she repeated incredulously. "Based on what? A few runes on an old wall and long-forgotten tales. What power do you possess? What right do you have? None." Her eyes narrowed in a predatory stare as she considered the pair in front of her.

"The keepers back our position," Munro said.

"The keepers?" Konstanze laughed. "That's your winning argument? That a cloister of academics support your claim?"

"So your challenge against the Druid Hall is actually a challenge against the keepers?" Munro asked.

The faeries behind the queen adjusted their posture minutely. This was likely the part of her strategy they felt the least comfortable with. The keepers had, according to Eilidh, always been revered, even though they were often not magically powerful themselves. They gathered and protected the whole of fae knowledge, lore and priceless artefacts, including the Source Stone. For that reason alone, none dared cross them.

Munro went on, "We spoke to the head keeper just moments before leaving for Ashkyne. If you have no respect for the Druid Hall, then no doubt he would be happy to call for a trial himself." He added carefully, "Unless you fear what public proceedings might reveal about your brother and his secrets. After all, no one suspected your brother was azuri, did they?"

"Ulrich was a gifted faerie, blessed with equal measure of water and air talents. Our family bears not a single drop of azuri blood," she spat.

"And yet, he was compatible with a druid, sought desperately to bond with her. Everyone knows only the azuri can initiate such a union. The bond requires higher magic. Interesting that you would deny he had such a powerful gift."

"I know what you're trying to do," Konstanze said. "That silly child queen you're bonded to has clearly taught you some of her manipulative tricks. She might be able to fool the keepers with her ways, but you lack her astral talent."

Munro struggled to keep his racing thoughts from showing on his face. Was this about Eilidh taking Queen Vinye's lands when Konstanze expected them to come to her? Was Konstanze trying to undermine the druids because she feared the power they added to Caledonia? Eilidh never talked about Konstanze as a rival or Ashkyne as a threat to Caledonia, but the Source Stone's choice may have put Eilidh into Konstanze's sights. Before this, the druids had an open agreement with Konstanze. Her brother's death and losing Andena must have hit her hard to force this turnaround.

One of Konstanze's advisors leaned forward and whispered into her ear. He must have used a gust of air talent to diminish his voice, because Munro couldn't catch so much as a murmur. She nodded and waved him back.

"There is a solution," she said. "I harbour no desire to combat the keepers, and you wish to save face after failing the girl under your protection." She tapped her fingertip on the table as she considered. "I am prepared to release the human to you now." She glanced up and met Munro's eyes.

"What do you want?" he said. Her demand would be huge after she'd been clear that she had every intention of executing Demi and maintained he was powerless to stop her.

"Leave the Halls of Mist," she said.

"What?" Huck and Munro said together.

"Oh, don't pretend the Druid Hall is anything more than a building, mostly constructed by the fae of other kingdoms. You would be more comfortable in Caledonia, near Queen Eilidh, whom you intend to join formally in only a couple of days' time. I understand being separated from someone with whom you share a bond is most unpleasant. Surely you would rather be close to her. You can rebuild your residence in Caledonian lands."

"Why?" Huck asked.

"Because you are not the draoidh of old, and I am sickened at the way you pretend you are. They were masters of magic. Trained. Powerful. Legendary. And most of all, they were *fae*. You craft trinkets and imbue rocks with trickery to cause them to appear lifelike, but what use is that? No doubt you possess talents that may be valuable to the fae someday, but to see my people bow to you as though you were masters of ancient lore disgusts me."

Munro was stunned into silence. On one hand, she was offering a decent deal. Their status in society was fragile at best. And their workshop didn't have to be in the Halls of Mist. Moving wouldn't change their work. Deep down, he almost agreed with her. He'd always felt like a pretender. Oszlár's urging had been mostly at the heart of the establishment of the Druid Hall. Without that, Munro might not have thought to move in the first place. He'd never wanted the glory or the deference many of the fae gave them.

"And you would be willing to give up the opportunity for any Ashkynen fae to bond with a druid?" Munro asked.

"There are no azuri in my kingdom," she said flatly. "So your *opportunity* means nothing."

Before Ulrich died, she'd appeared friendly to the druids. He'd had no idea she harboured such resentment. But losing her brother after having the portal choose Eilidh to assimilate the new gates had clearly unhinged her. He paused. He had to take this to Oszlár. "I would like to see Demi Hartmann," he said. "That is, after all, why we're here. I will consider your offer."

"I will hear your decision before you leave Ashkyne," she said.

"I'm afraid that's impossible. I'm not a king. Our decisions are made collectively, as a conclave might make them. I could agree to move back to Caledonia, but my choice wouldn't bind the other druids to do the same. If you want the Hall gone, I must discuss your terms with them."

For the first time, she radiated uncertainty. She glanced down, as though resisting the need to confer with her conclave. "Fine," she said. "You may visit the human prisoner."

"And the boy," Munro reminded her.

She pressed her lips together. "And the boy."

CHAPTER 12

HUCK'S GUT CLENCHED WITH WORRY. He had to find a way to convince Munro to move the Druid Hall, but he suspected the former cop would never go for it. Too much pride. Too rigid. Acted more like a faerie than a human these days. With his gold-tinged skin and pointed ears, he looked more like them too. He told Konstanze he wasn't a king, but he sure as hell acted like one. When he'd told Huck off for selling his crystals, he laid down the law. Huck hadn't argued with him. As the least experienced of the druids, Huck had no clout. Because he still hadn't touched the Source Stone, he was the least powerful as well.

On their way to visit Demi, they followed the same faerie who'd taken them to Konstanze, but this time six Watchers tagged along. Huck turned to say something, but Munro shut him down immediately. "Not here," he said.

Yeah, Huck thought. *Not a king.*

Their guards led them outside the castle to a low building attached to the smooth outer wall. The stonework inside was the same, grey, but with none of the imperfections of a human-built structure. The eerie precision seemed sterile, like they were entering a high-tech laboratory instead of a prison.

Down two flights of stairs, they arrived at a closed door. Their guide spoke to the Watcher on guard. "Visitors for the condemned."

The Watcher rose and started to bow, but stopped when he received a sharp look from the steward. "Through the door," the guard said. "I've removed the barriers."

"Thank you," Munro said and inclined his head, acknowledging the unfinished bow. He paused before entering and asked, "She is well?"

"Yes, my lord druid," the guard answered, then winced. He'd clearly been instructed not to show deference to the druids. "Yes," he repeated.

Munro nodded, and he and Huck went through the door.

Demi sat cross-legged in the centre of the seamless floor, surrounded by a faint glow, which was the only light in the room. The room's inside appeared much like the outside: grey, cold, and without ornament or flaw. She did not open her eyes when they approached, not until Huck said her name.

Munro closed the door behind them. "Are you all right?" he asked.

She glanced up with red-rimmed eyes.

Huck went and sat across from her. "I'm sorry I wasn't there," he said. "I came as soon as I could." Guilt welled within him. He should have stayed with her. They shouldn't have rested during the day. If he'd run a little faster, taken less time to prepare, five minutes even, none of this would have happened.

"You couldn't have stopped them," Demi said at last. "Where is Jago? Is he all right?"

Munro stood behind Huck, between the seated pair and the door. "The queen agreed to let us check on him. I don't believe they'll hurt him. The fae protect children fiercely."

"*Their* children perhaps," she said. "I don't trust them."

Huck took one of Demi's hands. "I'll make sure he's all right," he said. "I promise."

"He must be confused and frightened," she said, choking back a sob.

"Your hands are freezing," Huck muttered and reached for his fire energy. Without a talisman or focus, the process proved difficult, but he managed to create a well of warmth. He rubbed his palms over her fingers.

"What have they told you?" Munro asked.

"Nothing," Demi replied. "I was separated from Jago and brought here. You are my first visitors." She smirked, but the expression faded into a smile when she met Huck's eyes. "Thank you," she said, her voice soft.

"They plan to execute you in a couple of days for Ulrich's murder," Munro said.

"Jesus." Huck found Munro's lack of tact stunning.

Demi paled. "No," she said. "I must protect Jago." She glanced at the door behind Huck. "You have to get me out. I have to see him." Her eyes widened, wild with panic.

"Calm down," Munro said sharply. Then he softened his tone. "Jago will be fine. We're doing everything we can, but no matter what happens, they won't hurt him. He's half fae and the queen's nephew."

She shook her head and withdrew her hands from Huck's. Pressing her eyes closed, she rocked back and forth, hugging herself.

Huck turned to Munro, "Will you lighten up? Can't you understand that she's upset?"

Munro shifted his gaze to Huck, then looked back at Demi. "I need you to stay focused, Demi. We may have a chance to get you out of here, but for our plan to work, you must tell us exactly what happened in Amsterdam. Lisle told us her story, but she claims she couldn't see from where she was hiding."

Demi froze. "You talked to my grandmother?"

"She's with us in the Halls of Mist," Huck told her. "She's safe."

Demi exhaled slowly and straightened her posture. "Thank God. I told her to stay hidden. I didn't know what Ulrich would do to her if he discovered she was there."

"What happened in Amsterdam, Demi?" Munro asked again. "Lisle said she heard you fight with Ulrich. She saw you when he collapsed, but said you were nowhere near him."

"I killed him," Demi said flatly, her gaze distant. "He threatened me and swore he would kill me and take Jago. I had no choice."

Munro continued the unrelenting interrogation. "How did you kill him?"

"What does it matter?" Demi asked.

"The truth matters," Munro said. "I intend to push for a trial. The fae will recognise even a human has a right to defend herself. Did he touch you? Or just threaten to?"

"I don't remember," Demi said. "That night is a blur in my mind. So much happened at once. He insisted I give Jago to him. He held me with air bonds, but I fought his influence as much as possible."

"Air?" Munro asked. "Your grandmother and Queen Konstanze both said air was his primary talent. That can't be. Only azuri fae can bond druids as far as we know, and you said he tried to compel you to say the bonding words, right?"

"Yes," Demi said, confused. "Soon after we came to spend time together, he said we would bond if I recited these words he'd learned. He attempted to coerce me again the night he died. This time, he seemed even more excited. He claimed he'd learned of other bonded pairs, but they were different from us."

"Different how?" Munro asked.

Huck had a bad feeling. What difference did any of this make? Demi had defended herself. But no matter the circumstances, Konstanze said she would let Demi go. Why put her through all this? If they'd been alone, he would have challenged Munro, but Huck didn't want to tell Demi about the offer. What if he couldn't convince Munro and the others to accept the deal?

"He said the other bonded fae had some kind of corrupting magic, but his was pure. I had never seen him so fevered."

"Did you ever witness him performing any kind of mental magic? Could he create illusions?"

"No," she said.

"What about blood? Could he heal himself? Or time. Did he ever mention losing time?" Munro stepped forward, towering over Demi and Huck.

"No," she repeated, shifting uncomfortably. "I only saw him use air and water."

Huck glanced up at Munro. What was he playing at?

"How did Ulrich die?" Munro asked. "There was a lot of blood on the ground."

"I...I stabbed him," she said.

He barrelled the next question without delay. "Where's the knife?"

"I don't know. I must have dropped it."

Munro turned to Huck. "Did you find a knife?"

"Lisle had a knife," he said. "She came at me when I went inside the flat."

"Did it have blood on it?" Munro asked.

Huck thought back. "No," he said, watching Demi. "The blade was clean."

"So she washed it," Demi said impatiently.

"In the two minutes between when the fae took you and my arrival?" Huck didn't want to disbelieve her, but her story didn't fit.

"What's your primary element?" Munro asked, suddenly switching tack.

"What?"

"You've had your abilities unlocked for what, five years? You must know, especially if your talents are defined enough to craft a ward able to keep Flùranach out."

"I didn't make those. My grandmother gave them to me. The lore has been in our family for centuries."

"What is Jago's primary element? Surely you have some idea."

"No," Demi said firmly. "I've seen no trace of magic about him." She raised her chin. "He's just a baby."

The pair maintained eye contact for so long, Huck would have thought they were having a telepathic conversation. Demi looked defiant, and Munro appeared as though he was struggling to reach into her mind and yank out the truth. Finally, he nodded. "All right," he said. "Time for us to return to the Hall."

Huck wanted to touch Demi's hand, to offer her reassurance, but she held her arms tightly around her body. "We're going to do everything we can to get you out. We're negotiating with Konstanze to arrange a fair trial at the Halls of Mist." He stood. "Try not to worry. Do you need anything?"

Demi shook her head. "Tell Jago I love him."

"Definitely." Huck smiled and tried to look confident.

"Let's go," Munro said and headed for the exit.

"Thank you," Demi said softly as they departed. The tears in her voice made Huck's heart clench.

Once outside the door, he turned on Munro. "What the hell was that about?"

"Not here," Munro said, nodding towards the Watchers near the building's exit.

Frustration and anger bit at Huck. No matter his reasons, Munro didn't have to be such an ass, did he? "Fine," he said.

Before they left, Munro stopped and spoke with the guard. "Would you provide her with some blankets? She's cold."

"Yes, my lord druid," the Watcher said quietly.

"Thank you," Munro responded with a polite nod. Then to Huck he said, "We've wasted too much time. Let's go."

∞

Douglas watched Rory work with a wooden ring and stylus. Guilt weighed on him. He should have been here practicing and studying over the past few months. No way would Prince Tràth want to move to the Halls of Mist, though, and Douglas didn't like being away from his bonded faerie. Not that he *couldn't* leave Tràth alone. He just thought he *shouldn't.*

And, if he was honest with himself, he liked the rock-star lifestyle he and the prince enjoyed. They ate when they wanted, slept when, where, and with whom they pleased. They travelled, had an entourage, and what parties they went to! Tràth introduced him to a type of smoke that didn't make him sick the way alcohol did. The herb heightened Douglas' senses, making every experience more vivid. And the women. Douglas usually stayed quiet around women, but his bond with Tràth changed everything. The prince had enough confidence for both of them and shared his secret through their new link.

Faeries had a different attitude towards sex. These perfect, gorgeous people would walk around naked with no shame, approach anyone they pleased, and suggest things he'd never had the nerve to consider before. Douglas figured he'd spent more time with his clothes off than on these past six months. He's seen and done things he never would have imagined. No amount of exposure to internet porn could prepare a person for what happened when an ordinary orgy went magical, not that he'd been invited to orgies before.

The thing that amazed Douglas, and perhaps the only thing keeping him from feeling overly guilty, was somehow it helped Tràth. Maybe the benefit came from the smoke, or perhaps the constant distraction did the trick. The prince's lapses and struggles with the temporal magic that haunted him, and by virtue of their bond plagued Douglas as well, had lessened over the past months. Tràth seemed stronger, more solid somehow. If the medicine he needed was drugs, sex, good food, travel, and wild parties, who was Douglas to complain?

Perhaps the distractions helped Douglas too. Although he'd not been attacked by that blood faerie like Munro, Douglas had trusted Cridhe. His life before meeting Cridhe had been a hollow mess. Never good at much of anything, he hadn't felt needed or important. When the faerie unlocked Douglas' magic, suddenly the world made sense.

Cridhe's betrayal devastated him, but meeting Tràth erased the pain. When the pair bonded, a better, smarter, more confident, deeply magical part of Douglas was unleashed.

Douglas fought self-reproach as Rory and Aaron worked together on a cross-section of an enormous oak. As water druids, the three of them had more affinity with wood than stone. With a stroke of his stylus, Rory's magic sculpted a rune into the wooden surface. The glyph wasn't one Douglas knew. He should stay here more, be more helpful. With a bit of convincing, Tràth might come with him sometimes. Despite not recognising the marks, Douglas easily read Rory's intent. *Portal.*

"How can a slab of wood make an entrance?" Douglas asked. "Don't we need to make something gate-shaped?"

Aaron rolled his eyes. "Is the Source Stone portal-shaped?"

"Prat," Douglas muttered.

Rory ignored them and ran his hand over the rough-hewn surface, muttering something unintelligible. After a few moments, he said, "He's right."

"What?" Aaron and Douglas said at once.

"There's something missing. Maybe the problem *is* the shape. The rune responds, but I can't break through."

Douglas considered the little he understood about runes. He'd not studied much beyond being shown the Killbourne Wall. That rune grouping had led Munro to understand where druids came from. They knew druids were great sorcerers in ancient times. One interpretation said they'd created the entire faerie realm, but Douglas had trouble imagining it. Of course, he hadn't made *anything* in a long time. His thoughts kept returning to that one artefact. "We sweated into wood," he murmured.

"What the hell are you on about, kid?" Aaron asked. "Sweated into wood?"

Rory's face lit up as recognition hit. "A quote from the Killbourne Wall," he said. "I don't remember the whole thing though. I only saw the artefact once."

Douglas nodded. His bond with a temporal faerie gave him excellent recall. Sadly, the talent went unused most of the time. What did he encounter that was honestly worth remembering? The realisation made him cringe. Was he wasting his life? He pushed the worry aside and recited the section:

> *We bled into stone. We sweated into wood. We wept into water. We sang into air. Those of time formed the web. Those of blood shaped the flesh. Those of the stars cast the thought. Those of spirit invited the soul.*

"That's the section about creating the portal to the Otherworld," he reminded them. "They also said they had to sacrifice something."

When we finished the foundation, the clan appointed me as scribe, so I laid the words of power given by each of my brothers and sisters. Each one imparted their most dear wish and sacrificed their self.

"What in the world does that mean?" Aaron asked.

"You know how the runes work," Rory said, "That was Munro's interpretation of the author's intent. When he said scribe, he probably meant the person who created the runes. So each of the druids that made the first portal contributed a word of power, perhaps a rune."

"But what about the part with the sweat and blood?" Douglas asked.

"Maybe it's like our expression when you put blood, sweat, and tears into something, in other words, working hard. They took more than a year to create their portal," Aaron said.

Rory shook his head. "I don't think so. Faeries don't use figures of speech as much as we do, and runes are never metaphorical."

"So, what, you want us to sweat on the wood?" Aaron chuckled. Douglas glared at him until he stopped.

"I don't see why not," Douglas said.

"Might as well try. Too bad the Halls of Mist are so bloody cold all the time," Rory said.

"If Huck was here, he could light a fire and get us in a sweat," Douglas joked.

"Or Tràth," Aaron muttered under his breath.

Douglas studied the other druid. What the hell was that supposed to mean? Before he could ask, he realised Rory had decided not to wait. He spit into hand and wiped the thick glob onto the wood.

Aaron groaned. "That's disgusting, mate."

Rory gave him a sharp glance. "Would you rather I piss on it?"

Before Aaron could muster a retort, a crackling noise silenced them. "What was that?" Douglas asked.

"I don't know," Rory told him. He smeared the spit on the surface of the wood. "Something is enhancing the rune. I can feel it."

Aaron brightened. "Could be the kid came up with a decent idea for once," he said. "Let's try each adding runes like they said on the Killbourne Wall."

Rory handed him the stylus. "Knock yourself out," he said.

With an anticipatory gleam in his eye, Aaron accepted the stylus. Considering his options, he focused a few moments before sinking the stylus into the wood. He carved another rune Douglas didn't know, but the meaning emanated. *Connection*. Copying Rory's movement, he spit onto the surface of the wood and rubbed the saliva in.

Nothing happened, but the intent behind the rune flowed around and mingled with the meaning of the first, altering it minutely. "Strange," Rory said, then asked Douglas, "You want to give it a go?"

"Sure," the younger druid replied. Because of his lack of practice with runes, he didn't have any faith in his abilities. He wished Tràth was here with his extra portion of confidence. He took the wood and stylus from Aaron. If Douglas wrote *portal* and Aaron added *connection*, what could he contribute to the mix? He supposed a portal had to link *to* something. But what? A place, of course. Hijacking a gateway that already existed might be easiest. The lone gate he'd travelled through went to The Isle of Skye, but what was the rune for Skye?

He closed his eyes. When Munro first created runes, he'd said he didn't know the lines to draw either, so perhaps Douglas just needed to focus. Unbidden, the Gaelic name came to his mind, the same name the fae used for Skye: *Eilean a' Cheò*. He moved his hand and let the thought carry him. The shape didn't come easily or flow as he might have liked, but he held the determination in his mind, focusing relentlessly on the words. When he opened his eyes, he saw a series of shapes formed an arc over Rory's inscription. A bead of sweat flowed from Douglas' forehead and dropped onto the wooden surface. The shimmering perspiration sparked when he touched it.

He glanced up at the other two druids, surprised to find them sitting back, talking quietly to each other. How had they moved without him noticing?

Rory met his eyes. "Welcome back," he said.

"Back?" Douglas asked, confused.

"You've been zoned in on that thing for over an hour," Aaron said, his tone teasing, but also tinged with respect. "You're gonna give Munro a run for his money in the rune department if you're not careful."

"Really?" Douglas couldn't believe it. He'd been working on this that long? A slight cramp shot through his right hand, and he flexed his fingers. Maybe the guys weren't just taking the piss out of him.

"You should work with us more often," Rory said.

That simple statement meant more to him than Douglas could express. "Yeah," he said, staring at the wood. "Too bad it doesn't do anything." He held the wooden slab out to Rory. When he did, the light shifted and a glimmer appeared over the piece. "Did you see that?" he asked.

 "Let me take a look," Rory said. He took the wood, tilting the slab back and forth. "Reminds me of seeing through water."

"We are water druids," Douglas said.

Aaron motioned for Rory to hand him the carving. He examined the wood closely. "Did you guys see green?" he asked. "Green and grey."

"Yeah," Douglas said, and Rory nodded. "I thought the colours were part of the distortion."

"I don't think so," he said. "Those look like pine trees to me." A smile spread across the druid's face. "Now we're cooking with gas."

Rory nodded. "Great work," he said to Douglas.

"It doesn't do anything though," Douglas said. His thoughts raced in spite of his underlying doubts. "I wonder if we need more types of magic. Do you think it would help if Munro added his stone magic and Huck his fire?"

"I'm not sure," Rory said, scratching the ginger stubble on his chin.

"The Killbourne Wall did say they used all eight spheres for them to make their portal," Aaron said.

"Sure," Rory said, "but they were creating a new world. We're just building a doorway."

"I think we should have started with a doorway," Douglas said. He waved his hand about four or five inches over the surface of the wood. When he did, his fingers appeared strangely bent, as though water refracted the light. He rose, wanting to show the others what he meant, but his legs wobbled underneath him and he plopped himself back down.

"You need to eat first," Rory said. "We made a good start, but this took a lot out of you. Let's grab some food and take another whack at it later."

"Okay," Douglas said eagerly. The success had bolstered his confidence, but Tràth's absence created an aching void. Being away from his bonded faerie made him more tired than usual. He wondered if Munro ever felt the same way. He'd make a point to ask the older druid's advice.

The trio went to make their way to the kitchens. Even though they had servants, they liked to rummage around in the food stores themselves, much to the dismay of the kitchen staff.

Their journey was interrupted. Just as they left the workshop, Munro and Huck rushed in from the courtyard. Munro said, "Good. You're here. We have a serious problem." He gestured back inside, and the other three didn't have much choice but to return the way they had come.

CHAPTER 13

MUNRO LED THE OTHERS into the workshop, but then turned with a thought. "Flùranach and Lisle should probably join us."

"Why?" Aaron scowled. Munro noticed he'd been doing that a lot lately.

Munro flopped down on a wide bench. "Because I think one of our next steps should be to go back to Amsterdam. Having Flùranach along allows the likes of you and me to go places where humans might see us. In case you hadn't noticed, she's the only astral faerie who's offered to work for us. If you've got another up your sleeve, one we can trust, then by all means." When Aaron didn't reply, Munro asked, "Rory? Do you mind seeing if they'll come down?"

"Sure," Rory said and left with quick, urgent steps.

Not wanting to tell the tale twice, Munro decided to wait before he and Huck launched into their story.

He noticed the runed wooden slab. It sparked his interest. "Whose is this?" he asked.

Aaron sat with his arms crossed, not saying a word. Douglas spoke up. "We were messing around with some ideas about how gates work while you guys were gone."

Munro picked the piece up and turned it. The area above the wood shimmered, but it appeared to be just a trick of the light. "The Isle of Skye?" He raised an eyebrow at Douglas, who nodded, looking pleased. Munro was glad to see him engaged.

"We were thinking we'd like to have our own way to the human realm," Douglas said quietly, even though no one was around to overhear. "I...we were gonna try the same technique on a door or something."

"Interesting," Munro said. He'd thought of attempting to manipulate the Source Stone, to fine-tune the artefact to allow a direct connection to the human realm, but this idea had a lot of merit. With this method, they might be able to make a gateway that bypassed the kingdoms.

Rory returned a few moments later, followed by Lisle. "Flùr left word she was over at the library checking in with Oszlár."

"No problem," Munro said. "I'll talk to her when I go see him later." He turned his attention to Demi's grandmother. She still looked pale, but her sharp expression told him she was in a lesser state of shock than when she'd arrived from her trip through Caledonia the previous day. "How are you feeling, Lisle?" he asked.

She hugged her light jacket around her thin shoulders. "Fine," she said. "Did you see Jago?"

"Yes," Munro said. "He's being well cared for. We weren't allowed to speak with him, but he appears healthy, if a little confused. He's not been mistreated."

She closed her eyes and pressed her lips together. "That is good," she said. Her thick German accent made the word sound like *goot*. She levelled her gaze at Munro. "And my granddaughter?"

"She's holding up," he said. When she looked puzzled at the expression, he added, "She's being quite brave."

"Brave," she repeated. "There have been times in my life I've needed to be *brave* too. Unfortunately, I know what that means."

Huck interrupted. "Queen Konstanze made an offer we should consider. She's willing to release Demi."

The old woman's eyes widened with hope. Munro wanted to smack Huck upside the head. "What offer?" Lisle asked.

"I don't think the proposal is one we can consider," he said with a warning glance to Huck. He knew the new druid had been chaffing at Munro's reluctance. As the newest and least enthusiastic about putting his efforts into the Druid Hall, Huck didn't see the full picture.

"Not even if it means saving Demi's life?" Huck shot back. Anger and frustration played across his strong features.

"What does Konstanze want?" Aaron asked.

Munro sat back on the bench. "She wants us to give up our claim to being draoidh and leave the Halls of Mist." He related everything that happened in Ashkyne.

Aaron whistled. "That's quite a play," he said.

"No shit," Rory said, then muttered, "Sorry," in Lisle's direction.

"I don't understand," Lisle said, her brow furrowed. "I do not know this word *draoidh*."

Munro gestured to the workshop. "That's the fae word for what we are: druids, creators, sorcerers. In ancient times, druids lived in the Otherworld and were revered for their powers. I don't know what happened. They must have died out, gone from the Otherworld until we arrived. At first, they didn't realise these ancient draoidh were humans like us, not until we proved it last year."

Huck argued, "Leaving the Halls of Mist won't change what we are. Why not give her what she wants and move back to Caledonia if it means saving Demi?"

Rory spoke slowly and thoughtfully. "What worries me is that this is only the beginning."

Munro nodded. "If we back down, no one will listen to us again. If we say, 'Oh, never mind. We aren't draoidh after all,' we'll never make up the ground we'll lose in every kingdom. Our power and influence will be diminished, not to mention the position of the keepers and every queen who supported us."

"So power is more important than Demi's life?" Huck spat.

Anger rumbled in Munro's chest, but he did his best to hold his emotions in check. Huck didn't seem to understand that Munro wasn't building an empire, but he *was* trying to change an ancient society. He resented the implication that he didn't care what happened to Demi. "I want to save her too," he said. "But this ultimatum of Konstanze's will put us under her thumb for the rest of our lives. No queen would let us have free rein in her kingdom after this, so we can forget searching for more of our kind. If we back down, then we're not just saying 'we're only human', we're confessing to running a con for the past year. Even Eilidh would find opposition in her own conclave to offering us public support." He sighed. "No, Konstanze plans to discredit us, Eilidh, and the keepers with this. Making the declaration Konstanze wants would affect the balance of power in the Halls of Mist. I'm not giving up on Demi, but we have to think about this from more than one angle." He ran his hand through his short hair as he considered the options. "But if push came to shove,

I'd do anything to save a human life, even if that means losing what we're working toward. I'm not cold, just hoping to avoid digging ourselves a deeper hole than the one we're already in."

Huck shifted uncomfortably in his chair and gave a reluctant nod.

"So what's our plan?" Rory asked.

"I've asked for a public and impartial trial for Demi. Konstanze has denied the request, but I'm going to find out what Oszlár thinks he can do. There might be some precedent we're not aware of. Some of us should return to Amsterdam to look at the scene again. We might get lucky and find evidence. Because here's the thing..." He glanced at Lisle. "I'm not convinced Demi killed Ulrich."

"What?" Several voices spoke the question together, including Huck's.

"She confessed," he said, looking bewildered.

"What makes you think she didn't do it?" Douglas asked.

Munro watched Lisle. She didn't appear surprised at his declaration. He didn't want to lay out his theory in front of her though. He didn't think he'd get her cooperation if she knew the direction his suspicions had taken him. The old lady turned her face away and blinked a few times, refusing to meet his gaze. "Just a hunch," he said. He turned to the others. "I'll go, see if I remember how to search a crime scene. Flùranach can use her illusions to help us stay hidden and alert us if anyone approaches."

"I'm in," Huck said. Munro didn't like the idea. The American was too emotionally invested. On the other hand, he seemed to have more motivation to exonerate Demi than anyone. Besides, Munro doubted he could stop him from joining in.

"I'll go," Rory said.

His volunteering didn't surprise Munro either. Ever since Flùranach came to the Druid Hall, Rory kept an eye on her every move. It also didn't surprise him that Aaron and Douglas didn't offer to come along. Aaron stayed as far away from Flùranach as possible, and Douglas showed little interest in returning to the human realm.

"I will also accompany you," Lisle said.

Her blue eyes glinted with determination, but Munro stood firm. "We'll move ten times faster without you," he said. "We can run almost as fast as a car and go virtually unseen. I appreciate your desire to help, but you should stay here." He hesitated for a moment. "Besides, we need to keep you safe until this blows over."

She narrowed her eyes. "And will it? Blow over? Will my granddaughter's life *blow over*?"

He suddenly felt like a cop again, talking to a bereaved family member who wanted to know why a crime hadn't been solved yet. "We'll do everything possible for Demi. I can promise you that." He held her gaze until she nodded.

"The trip will take several days," he said. "Time we don't have. We can't go through Ashkyne and the Belgian gate is supposedly unstable, so we're stuck using a gate in England and going over the channel. And, well, I have an appointment in a couple of days' time I can't miss." Eilidh would kill him if he was late for their wedding. The way he figured, they'd get back with enough evidence to cast doubt as to what really happened the night of Ulrich's death. If they could manage that, they might persuade Konstanze to at least delay the execution. He also put a lot of stock in the keepers' ability to convince her that executing a druid on his and Eilidh's wedding day was unnecessarily provocative.

"Maybe we'll get this doorway idea to work," Douglas said. "Surely we can take an hour or so to try. We couldn't use it to return, I don't think, but if our idea works, we'd cut the travel time in half."

Munro nodded, even though he was sceptical. They'd made a few talismans and all of them had learned to carve runes to some degree, but none had crated anything as complex as a portal. "I need to speak with Oszlár and Eilidh before we leave anyway, so you have your hour. We should plan to arrive in Amsterdam during the day, to allow time to speak to any witnesses."

"Humans?" Rory asked.

Huck cut in. "Some neighbours were peering through the windows that night. Maybe someone saw something."

"We'll ask around," Munro said. "But we'll need to be cautious. We have no idea if Konstanze has people watching the house."

∞

Since Huck and the other druid visited, Demi noticed a marked change in the treatment she received. A quiet, black-uniformed guard with dark blue-tinged skin and long, spiralled ears brought her blankets. Not once, however, did his swirling violet eyes meet hers.

Later, the same guard brought her a plate of fruit. Beside it on the tray lay a lone yellow flower. The kind gesture nearly made her weep. After he took her dirty dishes away, he carried in a large ceramic pitcher of water and a low, empty basin. She used them to wash and relieve herself, then put the items near the door, hoping she'd guessed their purpose correctly.

The entire time, a pale glow remained in the centre of the room. Occasionally the light disappeared, but she noticed the glow always dimmed when she heard voices outside. Someone, the blue-skinned guard, presumably, offered light and a few small comforts but wanted his actions kept secret. Was he the one who asked if she was a druid?

Again, the guard entered and removed the used objects. He glanced towards her, but didn't speak as he went about his duties.

"I need to know," she said in German. "Is my boy well? Please." She'd tried but failed to keep her voice steady.

He peered towards the open doorway, holding the pitcher of water in his hand. He made a slight gesture that may have been a nod.

Her mind raced. What else could she ask? This faerie shown her kindness, but how far could she push him? "Thank you for the flower. Was it your voice I heard when I first arrived?"

"You did not answer." His voice fell dead in the air as though they were in a soundproof room. He must have been shielding their voices from outsiders. The easy use of power rattled her. She'd long ago lost her wonder of fae magic. Ulrich had taught her magic was a thing to fear.

"I was afraid," she said. When she saw the minute frown crease his brow, she added, "for my child. He is everything to me, and I have a duty to protect him." Her amendment seemed to get through. The druid Munro had been right: the fae did revere children. Why would fear for herself surprise or disappoint him? Did he really believe the druids had more power than the fae? Huck told her druids were honoured in the Halls of Mist, but why?

"Prince Ulrich was the boy's father?" the faerie asked.

"Yes."

"You admitted killing him." A statement, not a question. Clearly he'd overheard the conversation with her two visitors.

"He threatened my son," she said. "Would you not do anything to protect your child?"

"How did you do it?" The guard asked the same question Munro had, but she noticed a difference in his tone. Where the druid wanted to know what weapon she used, the faerie seemed more awed, curious how she overpowered a faerie of Ulrich's strength.

What should she say? "There is magic that has been passed down through my family," she said.

He watched her, his expression unreadable. He wanted more, but she didn't know what to say. Should she lie? Tell the truth? He seemed to view druids as potent and fearless. What answer would convince him to help Jago? She needed to sound powerful. Raising her chin, she looked squarely at the guard who separated her from her son. "I turned his blood against him," she said.

He frowned slightly, then tilted his head to her in an apparent gesture of thanks, but she had no idea what he might be grateful for. She wanted to ask him for more information about Jago, but he left her alone again. "Hello?" she called. Switching English, she asked. "Are you there?" Panic welled in her chest. "Please. I need you to help my son. I don't care what happens to me."

After a brief silence, the air carried a voice to her ears. "He is well. The queen protects him."

No matter what she said or how she called, no more messages came. Those last words brought her no comfort, however. Jago needed to be protected *from* the queen. How could she possibly convince this guard to help her?

CHAPTER 14

LISLE WATCHED THE FOUR YOUNG MEN discuss the portal they intended to create. The goal was ambitious. Although she didn't want to speed them on their way to Amsterdam and the secrets they might uncover there, their innovation and excitement enticed her. For the first time in an age, curiosity sparked within her.

They were new to their power and lacked access to even the basic lore that had been passed down through her family. Still, they worked competently as a unit. She had difficulty piecing together their stories. Three of them spoke with thick Scottish brogues. The American, at least, had an accent she easily understood. Although she wouldn't want Huck to suspect, she felt kindly towards him because of his fierce determination to help Demi. If his resolve would stay as strong after he discovered the truth, Lisle wasn't certain. As she'd done so many times over the decades, she pushed her fear and worry aside and focused.

She'd given up thinking she would keep her secrets forever. She would be as strong as she had to be and hold out as long as possible. As always, family was everything.

∞

Munro didn't sense Eilidh's presence in the Halls of Mist, so she must have returned to Caledonia. Disappointment twisted in his gut. He missed her and wanted her advice on the problems at hand. Maybe he should step through the portal and send word for her to meet him here. He sighed. Even if he did, she probably couldn't arrive before they'd need to leave. Besides, they planned to travel through Caledonia anyway. He hoped she'd stayed nearby and wasn't at the furthest reaches of the kingdom, otherwise he couldn't justify a detour to see her before moving on to Amsterdam.

He walked quickly to the library, his steps turning into a jog. His rushing gait drew the attention of faeries in the streets, but at the moment, he didn't care about decorum. Someone had to stop Konstanze from this destructive madness. Three days. That was all the time they had to save Demi's life. A sinking feeling in his chest told him it wouldn't be enough.

Racing downward, he descended into the library. He stopped dead in his tracks when he reached the bottom and saw Eilidh, Oszlár, and Flùranach waiting for him.

"I sensed your anxiety as you approached," Eilidh said. What she didn't explain was why *he* didn't feel *her* emotions. Why had she erected a barrier between them? The last time she had done so, they were having a serious argument, back before she'd even become a queen.

Questions filled his thoughts, but for the moment, he had to stay focused. "Rory needs Flùranach," he said.

Flùranach bowed her head to him. "I'll go now," she said and flicked her eyes to Oszlár. When the old keeper nodded, she scurried to the stairs and left the three of them alone.

"We're planning another trip to the human realm. We don't have much time," Munro said.

"Come," Oszlár said. "Let us go into my study where we can enjoy some privacy. I can only assume Konstanze was less than reasonable."

They followed the elder faerie, who led them back into the private keepers' quarters. "It's worse than I thought possible," Munro told them. "She's trying to use this thing with Demi to destroy the Druid Hall." The trio sat in Oszlár's study, and Munro related the story, Konstanze's demands, and what little they learned from Demi.

"What do you hope to learn in Amsterdam?" Eilidh asked.

"Some proof of her innocence?" he said. "Both she and her grandmother are definitely hiding something. I just don't think Demi killed Ulrich. And there's no way Konstanze would execute her if we proved Demi's innocence. Finding evidence might be a way to dodge the whole mess."

Eilidh frowned. "Who do you believe did kill Ulrich?"

"That's the problem. If Demi confessed but didn't commit the murder, then we're left with two obvious possibilities: Lisle and Jago."

"The child?" Eilidh looked horrified. "He's a baby."

"Exactly. He's four years old. Even full-blooded fae children couldn't best an adult faerie as powerful as Ulrich. That leaves the grandmother. Who else would Demi give a false confession for? On the other hand, even if Demi suspects her grandmother and confessed on her behalf, we can't be certain she's right. We must consider whether one of Ulrich's men killed him, maybe on Konstanze's orders, and Demi is merely fearing the worst. The queen was adamant her brother wasn't azuri, even though he must have been. Perhaps his alignment and his having a lethfae child were more than Konstanze was prepared to deal with."

Eilidh met Oszlár's gaze, and Munro sensed something significant passing between them. Trying his best to ignore the exchange, he went on. "Even if we discover proof of Lisle's guilt, we'd be in a better position than we are now. She's safe with us. But as long as we find evidence Demi *wasn't* the one who murdered Ulrich, we have hope of getting her and her son back. To do that, we must return to Amsterdam."

"The girl is due to be executed in two nights. Without access to the Ashkyne gates, you will find it difficult to return by then," Oszlár said.

"That's why I need you to stall her. Besides, all the evidence in the world won't help if Konstanze refuses to listen. I asked her for a public trial in the Halls of Mist, but she shut me down. I hoped you would be able to persuade her."

Oszlár tilted his head to the side as he considered. "There is no body that has ever made such a judgement as the one you're requesting. The Halls are a place of utter neutrality. We wield no authority in the kingdoms."

Munro's hopes fell. "There's no precedent, even in the distant past?"

"I will speak to the other keepers," Oszlár said. "One thing is for certain: the Druid Hall must stand and grow stronger. The future of our race depends on your survival." The keeper's cryptic pronouncement wasn't the first of its kind. Judging by the grim, stubborn set to his mouth, the old faerie had no intention of explaining his insights into the future. "No matter what the fate of this one druid," he continued, "the Hall must stand."

"You're saying we should sacrifice one for the good of the whole," Munro said. His stomach churned. He hated the idea, but hadn't he made a similar argument to Huck? "We lose either way. If we back down, we're in a weakened position, but aren't we equally damaged if Konstanze executes one of us, proving we're powerless to stop her? Jesus. What if she's right? What claim do we have to power?"

"I will confer with the keepers and scholars to see if there is anything we can use to influence her decision," Oszlár said. "Konstanze is most displeased with us since the Source Stone chose Caledonia over Ashkyne."

"Surely she understands the keepers don't control the Stone," Munro said.

Oszlár shrugged. "The Stone has slept for a long time."

That was no kind of answer, but Munro knew better than to push the keeper when the old faerie was in a cryptic mood. In all their time working together, Oszlár never revealed anything he didn't want to. "Which reminds me," Munro said. "The guys are working on a portal of our own." At that announcement, Eilidh's eyes widened and the keeper looked up sharply. "I don't hold out much hope they'll produce a working gate before we need to leave for Amsterdam. Who the hell knows if it'll ever work? But...not all of us are going, so I'll send Douglas and Aaron over to study the Stone while we're gone. It's a long shot, but maybe they can learn something useful by reading the runes on and around the chamber downstairs."

"A working gate?" Eilidh said. "To which kingdom? Caledonia?"

"Directly to the human realm from the Halls of Mist. In their first attempt, they think they got a glimmer of the Isle of Skye. With a bit of work and experimentation, I suspect we'll do it, but I doubt the hour I gave them will be enough."

"You're trying to bypass the kingdoms to travel directly into our borderlands?" She sounded stunned and affronted. The news sent her reeling and her control slipped, giving Munro a glimpse of her emotional state. Her mind was in utter chaos. Everything about her energy felt wrong. But his insight lasted only seconds before she rebuilt the wall between them. Trying to figure out what he'd seen was like trying to remember a dream that slipped away upon waking.

"*Your* borderlands are *our* homeland. We have as much right to the human realm as you do to the Otherworld. We don't need anyone's permission." The statement came out angrier than he intended. He was just so damned tired of secrets and lies. Demi's, Lisle's, Oszlár's, and even Eilidh's.

"Of course not, my lord druid," she said. Her sudden capitulation sounded patronising, and her words annoyed him as much as if she'd picked a fight with him. At least if they argued, they'd be honest about what they were feeling.

Munro sighed. They were supposed to get married soon. This wasn't the way he planned to start their lives. Part of him did want to move back to Caledonia to be with her more. Had he spent too much time away? "Look," he said. "Our efforts are nothing against you or your authority in the kingdoms or even in the borderlands. But as long as we need a queen's permission to get to our own world, we're vulnerable. What if all the queens decided to cut us off completely? What if we lose the faeries who support us at the Druid Hall? Even our food comes from the kingdoms, unless you count a few rows of vegetables and a couple of fruit trees."

Her expression softened. "I would never do that, my love."

He took her hand, relieved the angry moment had passed. "I have to think about what happens after you and I are gone." Standing, he helped her to her feet as well. "Thank you, keeper," he said to Oszlár with a respectful nod. "I know you'll do everything you can. Douglas and Aaron will be here within the hour. Douglas appears to have a knack with the runes. I'm hopeful they'll learn something useful."

The keeper rose and gave a slight bow to both Eilidh and Munro. "Your Majesty. My lord druid."

∞

Rory's concentration fluttered as he inscribed a rune above the cupboard door frame. The others had helped him remove the door from its frame, but during the procedure, something intruded on his thoughts. Flùranach. He didn't catch what she was thinking or even exactly where she was, but she skittered on the edges of his focus. Doing his best to centre his mind, he tried to ignore her pulsating excitement and finish the job at hand. Runework didn't come as naturally to him as it did to Munro or Douglas. The younger druid's talent surprised Rory, but he was glad to discover another weapon in their arsenal. They needed every advantage they could find.

Rory's real talent was in shaping wood with the flows. Even as he ran the stylus over the frame, he detected the minute changes in the grain beneath his hand. He completed the rune for gate, much the same as he'd done on the slab earlier. This time he didn't hesitate to spit into his hand and rub the fluid over the surface. Much to his surprise, the wood became instantly malleable, curving with his touch. It creaked, answering his unspoken request. It would never fit the opening any more, as the once-square frame became a gracefully arched entrance.

"There," he said, stepping back. He turned to the others and caught Lisle staring intently at his work, an eager gleam in her eye. The old bat was cannier than she let on. Her expression reminded him of a storybook witch.

"Who's next?" Douglas asked.

"Not me," Huck said. "I want to help, but I'm afraid I can't control my fire magic enough. I might burn the whole thing down."

"I've got an idea," Aaron said. He pulled a small reed talisman from his pocket, one trinket of many they had crafted and carried around with them. The pen-shaped instrument fit Aaron's hand perfectly. When he touched the surface of the cupboard's doorframe with it, water spouted from the end. Rather than dripping onto the floor, however, Aaron guided the water into a flow of intricate rivulets. As the water wended over the surface, minerals crept along behind the receding trails and the wood slowly transformed.

The process ate up a chunk of their allotted hour, but the druids were too fascinated with his work to try to hurry him. When Aaron finished, Huck immediately ran his hand over the still-damp surface. "It's like stone," he said.

"Petrified," Aaron said. "It would take a long time to do the whole thing. Right now, the minerals only cover the surface. But it should be enough to prevent your flows from burning through."

Flùranach fluttered around upstairs. Rory could sense her looking on him. Usually his dim perception of her wasn't that strong, but right now she focused on him like a laser sight.

"That's amazing," Huck said. "Perfect. What rune should I write?"

Aaron thought for a moment. "We want to go to Amsterdam, right? You've spent more time there than the rest of us. So, you should inscribe the location, I think."

"Should I choose the nearest gate? The one in Germany? Or do we want to try to go someplace where a gate doesn't yet exist?" He looked to the others for input.

"We don't really understand how to make a two-way gate," Aaron said. "I have no clue if we need to build something on the other side and tune them together, or if the gate only exists in one place."

Douglas spoke up. "When I wrote the rune for the Isle of Skye, I'm pretty sure I connected to the gate already there. I couldn't swear to it, though. I didn't get a clear view."

"On the other hand," Rory began, "the borderland gates are patrolled on the human side by fae Watchers. We'll risk being seen by Konstanze's people."

"You must connect to an existing gate. The structure will already possess the strong energies you need to transport bodies so far," Lisle said. Everyone turned and looked at her, each face as stunned as the next.

"How do you know?" Aaron said, his expression fluctuating between excited and suspicious.

She shrugged. "I don't."

Rory didn't believe her. She knew something, all right. "It does seem the safest option," he said. "What about Eilidh's new gate in Belgium? If it's not working, it probably won't be guarded, and it's a lot closer to Holland than England would be. We'll need to rely on Flùranach to hide us from any Watchers we encounter in the borderlands."

Flùranach raced around upstairs, searching for Rory, pricking at his mind with her exuberance. She was driving him up a tree. "Will you excuse me?" he said to the group. No one replied. Their focus was firmly fixed on the stone-like frame of their new gate.

"Right." Huck took the stylus from Rory and picked a spot on the right-hand side to begin his inscription.

By the time Rory ducked out and headed to the main corridor, Flùranach had reached the large stone staircase leading down to the spot where the druids were working. He stepped to the landing just as she scampered down. Her swirling eyes lit up when she saw him. "Lord Druid Munro said you needed me." Her tone rang with hope.

Rory stifled a sigh. That's why she was so excited. She thought *he* needed her. "Let's sit down somewhere," he said, glancing around.

He led her into a side room, one of the many small reception rooms dotted around the Hall. They'd built the Hall to house hundreds, so with their current compliment, the vast structure seemed strangely deserted. A cold fireplace sat on the far wall, and they took a pair of chairs in front of it. Flùranach leaned forward in her seat. "I came the instant I heard."

"Thank you," he said, staring into the barren grate on the blackened stone. She was practically bouncing. What had her all aflutter? Surely the prospect of him taking her to the human realm again wouldn't cause so much excitement. For some reason, it filled him with dread. "Do you have some news?" he guessed.

She beamed. "Keeper Oszlár said I've handled the move to the Druid Hall better than expected."

"That's great, Flùr," Rory said. "Will you have to continue reporting to him?" Rory didn't know exactly what those meetings would entail.

"I don't mind," she said. "He told me something else." She bit her lip as though trying to decide whether to tell Rory or not.

"Oh?"

"He was...very encouraging. About us. About our bonding. And I understood his words meant you'd been considering what I said, that you had decided to forgive me and move forward." She radiated happiness. "I'd been afraid to hope." He opened his mouth to speak, wanting to slow her down. Where had Oszlár come up with all this?

Before Rory had a chance to say a word, she blurted out, "I love you so much, Rory. I always have." He knew what was coming next. The world moved in slow motion, and he felt like a crash victim whose life was flashing before his eyes. "*Dem'ontar-che*," she whispered. The ancient words, proclaiming her love and commitment to the bond. Her presence wormed towards him as she touched the warped stub of his scarred inner-self.

He hadn't heard those words since she'd forced him to say them when she'd attacked him six months before. He reeled and an energy pulsed between them as the force of her pledge blinded him.

Nothing could stop the horror coiling within. "What are you doing?" he said. "Sweet Jesus." He hadn't wanted to hurt her. He'd tried so hard to move beyond the injuries of the past, but once again, she put what she wanted ahead of what he needed.

"But..." For the first time, she seemed to grasp his reaction.

"For fuck's sake," he gasped, struggling to breathe as his heart pounded.

"But you told Lord Druid Munro you needed me." Echoes of her pain and confusion rippled towards him through the half-formed bond.

"I needed you to come to the human realm with us. To work. To use your illusions to protect us. Not this. You don't listen. You hear what you want, and you always have." Anger stormed in his chest. "You haven't changed a bit." He stood and stalked to the entryway. As furious as he was, he would be forced to deal with her. He refused to let his emotional state and Flùranach's selfishness endanger Demi's life. "Stay here until you're called," he commanded her. Meeting her eyes with intent, he added, "Don't say a word about this to anyone. Not a soul."

She nodded rapidly, her worry and fear playing across her face and into his mind.

He walked out of the room, wishing it had a door he could slam.

CHAPTER 15

"WHAT IS YOUR NAME?" Demi asked her guard when he brought her another tray of fruit.

He hesitated before tilting his head slightly. "Leocort."

"Do you have children?" she asked.

A flicker of surprise passed through his swirling violet eyes. "My daughter is a scholar," he said. "She lives at the Ashkyne Hall and has worked with the keepers on rune study for two hundred years."

Demi blinked. "I forget that faeries age differently," she said. "You must be proud of your daughter. My father was an archaeologist."

Leocort leaned in the entryway. "I do not know this word."

"He studied humanity's past by recovering and studying ancient artefacts, documents, and art."

"He is dead?" the faerie asked her.

The bluntness of his question startled her, but she nodded. "He had heart disease and died three weeks before his fiftieth birthday. When I was younger, I'd hoped to pursue the same kind of work."

"Why did you not?" Leocort asked.

She looked away. "Ulrich," she said quietly. "I was a student in Berlin when I met him. I'd gone to my family's home in the south of Germany for the winter holiday. My mother was still alive then." Demi had to fight the urge to lose herself in the memories. Leocort stared at her relentlessly, waiting for her to go on. "I think I fell in love with him the first time I saw him. He was so beautiful, so elegant. When he spoke, I felt light-headed. I couldn't stay away. He became like an addiction."

Leocort had gone perfectly still. The palpable silence tightened around Demi. She shivered, exposed and laid bare by his unwavering gaze. No matter how uncomfortable she felt, she had to go on. That she'd recently told the story to another stranger, Huck, made recounting the tale somewhat easier. But Huck had listened with sympathy and tenderness. Leocort stood in front of her, immobile and unreadable.

"My studies fell by the wayside, and I came more and more often to my mother's home so I could see him. No matter how she worried, I refused to stop seeing Ulrich, regardless of how cruel he'd become, the way he whipped and choked me and taunted my weakness. My mother died before I became pregnant with Jago. When Jago's life sprang up within me, Ulrich's domination was broken. My son's blood protected me. Only then did I realise how strange and tragic my mother's death had been. I think she died from anxiety over me. My grief and shame would have overwhelmed me, but for my son growing inside me.

"I had to get away while my son's soul shielded me from Ulrich's influence. He followed us to the North. Somehow he found us in Austria, then in Switzerland. We chose large cities. My grandmother told me the fae don't like cities, but eventually, he always found us. We stayed in Holland the longest." She paused, hating the light she cast on her actions, but she had to tell him if she wanted to gain his trust. "He promised he would kill me if I didn't give up Jago. How could I? How could any mother let a cruel, monster of a man take the light of her life?" She detected a glint of sympathy in Leocort's eyes. "I'm not a violent woman, but his blood is on my hands." She looked down at her palms, fingers outstretched. No matter what had happened that day, she carried the blame. Her hands dropped into her lap, and she met Leocort's eyes. "I had no choice," she said fiercely. "As you would do anything for your daughter, I did what I had to for my son."

The faerie guard said nothing, but he gave her a respectful bow. "My lady druid, thank you for sharing your story with me," he said and silently slipped out the door, leaving her alone with her tray of fruit.

Demi looked at the food and sighed. She wished he'd brought her a steak and potatoes instead of pomegranates and pears, that she didn't feel so weak and helpless, that she'd never met Prince Ulrich.

∞

The moment Munro and Eilidh were outside the library, he voiced his frustrations, careful to keep his voice low so passers-by wouldn't overhear. "When are you going to tell me why you're blocking our connection? Didn't Elder Oron tell you not to do that?" He was being unfair, bringing up her teacher and advisor and his warning not to disrespect their bond by keeping Munro out of her mind.

She turned towards the Druid Hall. "How does this new portal work?" she asked.

"What aren't you telling me? I touched your thoughts down there. You're a mess. Why won't you talk to me?"

"You are to become my mate in two nights' time," she said softly, nodding to a group of faeries who bowed as she passed.

"And meanwhile you're trying to get pregnant with Griogair's kid," he said, unable to keep the accusation out of his voice.

Despite her efforts to mask their connection, her surprise rippled through his thoughts. "You agreed when I told you about my intention. You said you didn't even understand why I would be worried." She slowed her pace and touched Munro's arm. "I took Griogair to the altars as a show of respect for him as my first mate. I thought you understood." She stopped, then glanced back towards the portal. "So much changed because of Vinye's death. I will take a third mate next year, a faerie I do not particularly like. He and his father push me constantly, always jockeying for position." She sighed. "I'm tired, Quinton."

Munro touched Eilidh's face and saw the way her eyes shone with unshed tears. "I love you," he said, not caring who heard him. The one thing his new position as a so-called *druid lord* afforded him was the position in society to officially become Eilidh's mate, to publicly declare his love for her, to touch her without creating a scandal.

She smiled with relief. "I love you too."

"Now," he said, "how about letting down that wall between us? I miss having your thoughts in my head."

She bit her lip, an endearing but uncertain gesture he'd never seen from her before. *Inside*, she sent to his thoughts.

He took her delicate hand in his, and she squeezed his fingers lightly. Whatever was bothering her had her trembling. He grew more worried with every step. *What didn't she want him to know so much that she didn't want him learning the truth where anyone would observe their conversation?*

Once in the Druid Hall's courtyard, she let go of his hand and stood opposite him. She furrowed her eyebrows a moment, as though considering. After a pause, she straightened her posture and looked him in the eye. As she did, she released the barrier between them.

A whirlwind of emotion made Munro catch his breath, but within seconds he understood why Eilidh had been masking her presence from him and everyone else. She wasn't alone. A tiny strand of foreign energy flowed through her aura like a ribbon of light through the night skies. "How…" he started, then cut himself off. How did this happen? Jesus. Dumb question. Eilidh and Griogair had just gone to make a sacrifice to the Mother to ask to be blessed with a child. He was surprised she knew so soon, but the spark of life within her was unmistakeable.

"I recognised her life the moment her magic awakened. It is so different from my own."

"Then she's not azuri?" Not that it mattered. He struggled to find something to say while his mind tried desperately to absorb the news.

"Her primary talent is of the earth, like her father's," she said. Munro knew fae parents didn't know a child's spheres from the start, but he supposed Eilidh's advanced astral abilities gave her unusual insight.

Most faeries tried for centuries, but she and Griogair had gotten lucky. Still, doubts plagued her. He sensed them as they rippled through her, clouding her happiness. "You'll be a fantastic mother, Eilidh. I'm happy for you and Griogair." He scrubbed his hand through his short, golden hair. "Before, the idea of you having a baby with him was abstract. Especially with us getting married so soon. But now that I sense her energy, now that she's real, it's different." How could he say otherwise? Sure, he felt conflicted and a tiny bit jealous, but Eilidh needed his support. He'd always sworn he'd be there for her, no matter what. She should be elated now, spending her energy taking care of herself and her baby.

"My daughter may be queen someday," Eilidh said, her voice quiet and her gaze distant, almost as though she was speaking to herself.

"May be?" Munro asked, honing in on the worry rippling through Eilidh's mind. "Why wouldn't she be?"

"Because," Eilidh said, smiling sadly at him. "I don't know how my people or the magic of the Source Stone will react to the idea of a lethfae queen."

"Lethfae? She's…"

"Yours," Eilidh finished for him.

"How?" *Jesus wept.* He'd gone stupid again.

Eilidh burst into laughter. "I will illustrate for you later if you'd like." She paused, her tone turning serious. "I have known for some weeks, and have been feeling uncertain how to tell you and Griogair. When her energy was only a flicker, I wasn't certain whose child she was. I was so surprised to conceive when I'd not visited the altars. Then, Griogair saw her strands when we went to Andena, and I had to begin hiding my aura. I wanted to tell you before it became public knowledge." She sighed. "So much is happening all at once. The first queen in an age to have multiple mates, and now a lethfae child."

"You think she'll be in danger?"

"Keeper Oszlár considers our child to be a gift."

"And you don't?" Her inner conflict worried him. Surely she couldn't be considering not having the baby. Now that he knew, now that he'd seen the bright light of *his* daughter's magic, losing her would be unthinkable.

Eilidh's eyes glistened. "I've never felt so complete." When she said the words, the chaos in her energy calmed somewhat, although her aura shone brighter than usual.

Munro pulled her into a bear-hug and held her tightly to his chest. He put his lips to her ear. "I love you," he said. "I love both of you." He felt like he might weep, and he wasn't really the type to break down.

They stood together for a long moment, but finally he released her. "I have to go," he said. "We must move quickly if I'm going to be back in time for the wedding."

Eilidh gave him a playful pinch. "Don't even think about arriving late." Her expression grew serious. "I have faith Oszlár will manage to stall Konstanze. She may wish to taunt me and put pressure on you with this promised execution, but I cannot believe she would tarnish such an important day," she said, then added with a frown, "Just in case, though, find the evidence you need."

"And if I can't?" he asked her. He didn't like to admit that he might fail, but there was every chance he would.

"In that case, I will stand beside you at her death rites. Our ceremony will wait if necessary." She paused, her expression dark. "But if Queen Konstanze thinks she can insult Caledonia, the Druid Hall and the Keepers of the Source, she'll learn a hard lesson. The wrong would not go unanswered."

Munro nodded, grateful for her willingness to put her life and happiness on hold to save a woman she'd never met. Postponing a royal wedding would be no small thing. If things escalated with Konstanze, months could pass before they'd manage to make their commitment official. An old-fashioned part of him wanted the ceremony to be sooner rather than later, now that they had a baby on the way. He kept the thought to himself. Eilidh would never understand why such a thing would matter.

Hand-in-hand, they made their way inside, stopping only to ask a steward where the other druids were working. When they arrived downstairs, the first voice they heard was Lisle's. "The seal should be in blood," she said. "Blood is the strongest."

"Seal?" one of the men asked.

Munro and Eilidh entered the cramped storage room where the druids were gathered around what looked like a pie safe. He would have laughed at their choice of places to make their first portal, but his voice died in his throat. A shimmer wavered in the space where the cupboard doors had once hung.

The old lady continued, "You must dedicate the magic."

Aaron noticed the new arrivals. "Hey," he said to Munro and Eilidh, his smile broad. "Good stuff, eh?" He cocked his thumb towards the shaky portal. It shone, then faded.

Munro nodded and stepped forward, running his hand over the wood. "It's not stable," he said.

Lisle glared at him. "Clearly," she said.

"You know how to fix it?" he asked her.

"I've been trying to tell these dunderheads," the old woman muttered with a snort.

"Show us," Munro said, gently coaxing her attention to the portal. This had to be the most incredible thing they'd ever made. The aura thrummed with chaotic energy.

"A knife," she said and quickly added, "A sharp one."

Huck slipped into the nearby kitchen and returned with a small paring knife. He handed the blade to Lisle. "Here ya go," he said.

She snorted at his casual tone. Turning her attention to the portal, she ran the knife over her palm. The process reminded Munro of the ritual cutting Eilidh had performed when she became queen of Caledonia. The old lady whispered something rhythmic, and Munro strained to hear the words but couldn't understand them. With a smooth swipe of her palm, she rubbed the blood over the curved lintel.

The energy within the portal shot out like a storm, enveloping Lisle, and the others hopped back. Arcing waves of white light crackled and danced. Beyond the light show, they saw a lush, green forest.

They all stood mesmerised for a moment, stunned. A panic swept over Munro, almost pushing him to his knees. He looked at the source of the emotion: Eilidh. She'd gone pale. "You can't," she said. "Please, dear Mother of the Earth, no." They all turned to look at her.

"Eilidh?" Munro reached for her.

She grasped his arms and stared into his eyes. "You mustn't go through that portal."

"What's wrong?" he asked. "Is it not safe?" He glanced at Lisle. Had she done something to endanger them?

"How can you be certain if it is or isn't?" she asked. "Please. Don't take the risk. Don't be the one to perform the test. I need you, Quinton. *We* need you. Not now. Please."

"Do you know of some reason the gate isn't safe? If this is dangerous, none of us can go through," he said.

"I..." she glanced around the room, as though suddenly aware of everyone's stares. "No."

"What's wrong?" Rory said quietly to Munro.

Lisle interjected, speaking to Munro. "You stay," she said. Looking around the collected druids, she pointed to Aaron and Huck. "They should go."

Munro didn't know if he could trust Lisle. She's already lied to him at least once, and he got the distinct impression she didn't want *anyone* to go to that house.

"If something they find will save my Demi, then they must go," she said as though reading his doubts. "But you have your own family to think about. Family is everything."

Munro looked into her eyes and understood that she somehow knew about Eilidh's baby. How, he had no idea. "Okay," he said. "Aaron, Huck, you up for the trip?"

Aaron's eyes shone with anticipation. "This is the coolest shit we've ever done. Hell yeah, I'm game."

"Absolutely," Huck replied.

"Rory? Is Flùranach ready?"

Rory glanced at the door. "Aye," he said with a frown. "She's in the other room." Something was clearly upsetting him, but Munro didn't have time to ask. "I'll get her," Rory said and slipped into the corridor. He returned an instant later with Flùranach, who looked red-eyed and shame-faced.

Munro groaned inwardly. They had too many distractions. "If you guys are certain, this portal buys us a lot of time," he said.

Rory nodded. "We know the flows we used."

"Okay," Munro said. He took a few minutes to outline how to search, what to look for, and how to approach the neighbours.

"We got this," Huck said. "Don't worry so much. Trust us."

Munro nodded. He didn't have a choice, did he? He glanced at Eilidh, wanting to jump through that portal with the others. He sighed. She needed him to stay behind. Even though their mission was important, she was too. "Best go then," he said. "Douglas, you're with me. We've got some investigating of our own to do." At least he could use his rune knowledge to study the Source Stone while the others were at the scene.

"Got it, boss," Douglas said happily.

With only a moment's hesitation, Aaron, Huck, Rory and Flùranach approached the portal. Eilidh spoke to Flùranach. "Mask them well, child," she said sternly. "Their lives are in your care."

Flùranach curtsied deeply. "Yes, Your Majesty. I will not fail." She stood and gestured into the air. A slight shimmer surrounded the trio, then vanished.

Without another word, they climbed into the cupboard. The electrified portal consumed them, yanking each into the darkness one at a time.

CHAPTER 16

HUCK'S INSIDES COMPRESSED and his airways closed. His eyes bulged and his ears rang. Heart hammering in his chest, he flailed in the blackness and sensed nothing. No heat, no wind, not a single sound.

Pain bloomed in his lungs. He needed air. Time stretched and thoughts grew distant. This was the end, he realised. He would die in a pastry cupboard.

Warm light surrounded him, and a firm hand slid behind his head, tilting his chin upwards. With a cough, he jolted awake. Aaron's face hovered above him, slightly altered, however, to hide his fae-like appearance. Despite Flùranach's illusion, the other druid appeared haggard and tired. Relief flooded through Huck's mind. They'd made it.

"He's alive," Aaron said, then glanced down at Huck again. "It's past daybreak. The gate's closed." He grinned.

Huck coughed a few more times as Aaron helped him sit up. Flùranach and Rory sat in the grass nearby. Huck's mind reeled. They'd travelled through not only an unstable gate, but a *closed* gate? The arches that glowed from nightfall to dawn weren't even visible in the daylight. He glanced down at his watch, a remnant of his human life as irrelevant to his existence in the Halls of Mist as electricity and the evening news. It was still set to Central European Time. "Eight o'clock?" he asked. "We were in there for two hours? How did we survive?"

Flùranach shook her head. "It felt like mere moments." She glanced at Rory.

"I dunno," he said. "I blacked out too." He stood. "I guess we'd better get a move on. We can't be sure yet we're even in the right place."

Huck struggled to stand and took Aaron's extended hand. When he had clambered to his feet, he surveyed the area. "Yeah," he said. "Damn. We made it." Elation flooded through him at the success of their journey, even if their arrival and delivery had been rough. His body objected to the harsh treatment, but urgency pressed him onward.

"You ready to run?" Aaron asked.

The concern warmed Huck. He felt a part of the group in a way he never had before, realising if he'd died in that portal, someone would have cared. "Yeah," he said.

They moved at a slower pace while their bodies adjusted to being alive, quickly finding they had landed in a forested area just outside of Mol, Belgium. Over the long run over the border and into the Netherlands, Huck noticed how quickly he was recovering. Rory definitely seemed the least affected of the humans, but Aaron struggled as much as Huck did. By the time they arrived in Amsterdam a few hours later, he felt practically normal again, albeit with a slight headache.

When they stood on Demi's street and stared her house, Huck shivered. It seemed like years had passed since he'd last been here, even though it had only been days.

Rory nodded to Aaron and Huck. "You two go inside and nosy around. I'll take Flùr and talk to the neighbours. With her knack for magical persuasion, we might get lucky and find someone who saw something helpful."

"Right," Huck said. He led Aaron up the steps to Demi's door. The doorframe had been repaired and the lock replaced. He hadn't even considered how they were going to get in. "Shit." He felt around top of the doorframe and looked under a potted plant nearby, but no key. "I guess the landlord had it fixed?"

"Maybe," Aaron said. "Or the police called a locksmith. I hope it's the latter. Less chance the place will have been cleaned up in that case. Let's duck around back. Might be another way in."

The pair tried not to look suspicious to anyone who might peer down from one of the surrounding residential buildings. Appearing innocent was harder than it sounded, considering what they were up to. They tried the back door, but found it locked. "Too bad Munro isn't here," Aaron said. "He's good with metal. Probably could have popped this lock with a touch of magic. Wait a second. There." He pointed up. In the back, on the third floor up, a window was cracked open.

"Damn," Huck muttered.

Aaron laughed. "You're thinking like a human." With a quick glance at the surrounding area, he shifted into top speed, dancing from corner to ledge to window sill. Within seconds, he'd reached the window and slipped inside. A minute later and he'd opened the back door from within.

Huck stepped in, pulling the blinds all the way down before flicking on a light. The house smelled stale, and his sensitive nose detected the tang of blood in the air, masked ineffectively by cleaning solutions. He wished he could throw open *all* the windows.

"Where do we start?" Aaron asked.

"I've not been in this part of the house," Huck said. "Never got past the living room on either visit. I guess we go by floor."

"Okay," Aaron said. "I'll start at the top and you take the bottom?"

For some reason, Huck didn't like the idea of anyone else invading the Hartmanns' privacy in their upstairs bedrooms. "Other way," he said. "I'll go up."

Aaron shrugged. "Whatever, mate."

Huck noticed a pile of shoes by the door including some rugged hiking books, rubber garden slippers, and a child-sized pair of bright blue plimsolls. The garden shoes had a layer of dust on them as though they hadn't been touched in a very long time. On a hunch, Huck squatted down and grabbed one, tipping it over. A flat, round stone the size of an American quarter clattered to the floor. Tiny carved runes covered both sides, their complexity putting them beyond his reading skills.

"What the hell?" Aaron said quietly, looking over Huck's shoulder.

"Search for these ward stones at all the doors and windows. We should take them with us," he said.

"Might be better to leave this place protected," Aaron said.

Huck pocketed the stone and shook his head. "No matter what happens, none of the Hartmanns are safe returning to this house."

"Fair enough," Aaron said. He casually poked around the small utility room. "Doesn't look like anyone's been back here lately," he said.

"You're right," Huck said. "The front entry is a floor up from here. I know Demi moved a stone like this one to let Flùranach in." Guilt surged over him. If only they'd not asked her to. "That's where Ulrich and Demi fought...and where he died."

"Okay," Aaron said. "Lead the way. Makes sense to start there."

Huck went through a small corridor and found a staircase winding upward into the kitchen. He flicked on lights as they passed through each room. Beyond that was a small dining area, which led to a landing. He pointed through an archway. "The living room is through there." He drew in his breath, preparing himself for the distasteful snooping he was about to do.

"Got it," Aaron said and made his way towards the front of the house.

Huck didn't know why he felt guilty. He was trying to save Demi's life, but he hated invading her privacy. Bracing himself, he took the stairs two at a time.

The flat only had two bedrooms, and all three shared one small bathroom. He gave the public areas a brief glance, opening the hall closet and quickly rummaging through the linens.

He went to the larger of the two bedrooms first. One of the two beds had dark blue sheets with rockets and moons printed on them. Absently, Huck closed and locked the window Aaron had used to get in. He poked around Jago's things, not expecting to find much of interest. He did discover six more protective ward stones, one affixed on each wall, another in the light fixture above, and one under the boy's bed.

Rifling through the chest of drawers, he found the top dedicated to the boy's clothing, the middle contained neatly folded women's undergarments, and the bottom held a few adult-sized sweaters. All the drawers were at least half-empty, the family having clearly packed away what they could, preparing to leave in a hurry. Guiltily, Huck ran his hands inside the drawers, through the clothes, and under the bottoms of the drawers as Munro had instructed. Nothing stood out but the discarded remnants of a life they would never return to.

Again following the ex-cop's advice, Huck up-ended the mattresses and opened boxes. Just when he was about to move on to Demi's bedroom, he came across a small box behind a stack of pillows crammed under the bed. Letters of varying ages concealed an old, leather-bound diary. Inside was page after page of fae runes. As with any runes, the magic of understanding came more from reading the intent of the creator than the characters.

Huck sat on the bed, flipping through the pages. Dread curled in his stomach. He feared the book would reveal something he didn't want to know. He forced himself to read anyway. His rune reading skill wasn't as advanced as Munro's or even Douglas', but the emotion dripping from the pages screamed at him.

He returned to the first entry. June 1957. One rune repeatedly jumped off the page in the jumble of the ones Huck couldn't interpret. Over and over, Lisle's fine, talented hand had inscribed the word *Ulrich*. Huck sat back, stunned. Lisle had known Ulrich when she was in her twenties, a young woman married to a local German man. The worst part was that she'd more than known the faerie: she'd been in love with him. Never for a moment did Huck doubt the faerie mentioned in the text was the same Ulrich who'd seduced Demi. Ulrich had been many hundreds of years old at the time of his death. How old, Huck wasn't certain, but that he'd barely had a wrinkle on his face didn't mean a thing. Not with the fae.

Huck read on. By the autumn of 1957, Lisle's infatuation with Ulrich had turned to obsession. She'd hoped he would sweep her away from her mundane life. But suddenly, towards the end of that year, he disappeared. He exited her life as swiftly as he'd entered it. Her marriage survived her infidelity, but the relationship left her with deep emotional scars.

Huck skimmed, trying to unravel the story from the clusters of runes he understood. Lisle had gotten on with her life, staying with her husband until the end, but never revealing the truth to him. Still, even with sometimes years-long gaps between entries, Ulrich's name featured prominently.

Towards the end of the journal, the entries focused more on magic, on the abilities that her contact with the fae prince had unlocked, and the insights she'd gathered through dedicated practice and study of the family documents. Even after all that time, she regarded her talents as a lasting remnant of Ulrich's presence in her life.

The regular entries stopped somewhere in the 1980s. Perhaps after thirty years, she'd given up on the idea of him returning. Then, on the very last page, Huck read one last entry, dated five years ago, around the time Demi told grandmother she was pregnant. The entry was short, one of the few of which Huck understood every rune. *My sins have returned to claim the payment due.*

That was the last entry. Huck closed the book, his hand shaking. If Ulrich hadn't been dead, Huck would have wanted to kill him all over again. Lisle had a child in 1958. Demi's father. Huck's mind reeled.

"What did you find?" Aaron asked from the doorway, his gaze fastened on the rune-covered volume in Huck's hands.

Huck stood and tucked the book into his pocket. "A potential motive for murder," he said.

"Lisle?"

The question rattled around in Huck's mind. Honestly, the situation gave both Lisle and Demi a reason to want Ulrich dead. If he had seduced his own granddaughter, and she learned who he really was, Demi had as much reason to want him dead as Lisle. If he *wasn't* Demi's grandfather, would Lisle have been jealous? Would she kill him for coming back and preferring her young granddaughter?

Judging by what Huck had learned, Ulrich had a way of provoking strong emotions.

Huck sighed. "I'm not sure," he said. "It might not mean anything."

Aaron leaned in the doorway. "Want to talk about it?"

Although he considered pouring out his story, Huck gave a shake of his head. Something in him didn't want anyone else involved. Not yet. If Demi didn't suspect Ulrich may have been her grandfather, Huck didn't want her finding out because folks were passing around Lisle's diary. If she did know... *Too many variables*, he thought. *Too many uncertainties.*

"What about you? Any luck?" Huck asked, joining Aaron in the corridor.

"Nothing useful," Aaron said. "More ward stones. Like you said, they put them by every door and window. Looks like Ulrich never got past them. I saw the bloodstain on the carpet, which someone has tried to clean up. Beyond that, nothing appeared out of place."

"Okay," Huck said, disappointed but hardly surprised. They weren't forensics experts or anything. When Munro had talked to them about how to search, the former cop seemed more hopeful they'd learn something from the neighbours than that they'd find a smoking gun.

"You done up here?" Aaron asked.

Huck glanced towards the final room, Demi's bedroom. He didn't want to rummage through her things. He'd done enough damage. "I haven't been in there," he said.

As though he understood, Aaron nodded. "I'll check," he offered. Without waiting for an answer, he stepped into the bedroom and did a quick search, running his hand under the mattress, and peering under the bed. After glancing through the remaining contents of the dressers and closet, he announced, "Not much here."

"They were already packed to move to the Druid Hall," Huck said. The realisation made him wonder why Lisle would have left the book behind.

A knock sounded downstairs at the front door, startling both men.

"That must be Flùr and Rory. Time to go," Aaron said.

"Right," Huck said. Briefly meeting Aaron's eyes, he added, "Thanks."

∞

Rory's hands shook. He banged on the door of Demi's flat, louder this time. *What had he done?*

When Aaron and Huck answered, Rory blurted out, "We have to go. Now."

The other two men stepped out and shut the door. "Shit," Aaron said. "We can't lock it from the outside without a key."

"Don't worry about that," Huck said. "We're not coming back." He turned to Rory. "The place is clean."

"We need to leave. Now," Rory repeated, glancing around. He grabbed Aaron's shoulder and gave him a light shove towards the street.

Huck and Aaron looked surprised, but nothing matched the shock on Flùranach's face. She'd worn the same startled expression for the last ten minutes, since they'd been attacked. Rory tried not to think about what had happened. They'd been desperately lucky.

The four of them left quickly, making their way through the streets of Amsterdam. Rory barely cared if they were seen. He ran as fast as his druidic magic would carry him, to the point that his legs burned with strain. As planned, they headed south and west, but not back towards the Belgian gate. They'd assumed before they'd left that the broken gate couldn't return them to the Druid Hall. After their experience coming through, Rory was convinced they'd guessed correctly.

Huck led them towards the same ferry station he and Lisle had taken to England before. This trip, they weren't slowed by an elderly human who'd never felt the touch of Otherworld air, so they didn't have to bother with trains.

By the time they'd reached the Hook of Holland, Rory's nerves had settled.

"What the hell happened back there?" Huck finally asked. "You might as well tell us. Our ferry doesn't arrive for two hours, and I'm not going to shut up until you do."

Flùranach answered for Rory. "We were attacked," she said. "Rory defended me."

Rory searched her eyes for hints of amusement, but he found none. Ever since she'd said the bonding words to him, he sensed the connection with her, but the experience was definitely different from last time. He shut the idea down. He didn't want to think about *last time*. He needed to move past those dark days.

"What?" Aaron exclaimed. "By whom?"

"I'm pretty sure it was one of Konstanze's Watchers," Rory said. "We'd only gotten through one building of flats when he came after us."

Huck looked at Flùranach. "But you stopped him?"

Of course they assumed she would have done the fighting. Rory's instinct to feel insulted melted as quickly as it appeared. He was an absolute moron. What was he thinking, punching a faerie? Punching him? A human using physical violence against a faerie was like a kitten going after a wolfhound. Oddly though, the fury of Rory's reaction startled the guy so much, Rory'd gotten in a second swing. That one sent the Watcher to the floor.

"I didn't have to," Flùranach said. "Rory had the situation well in hand." For the first time, he was certain he saw a twitch of a smile at the corner of her mouth. "Rory subdued him, then I added enough confusion to his mind to allow us to escape, should he regain consciousness before we were at a safe distance."

Huck burst out laughing and slapped Rory on the back. "Nice one," he said.

Even Aaron managed a smile. Given his distrust of Flùranach, that was no small thing.

Rory stared at Flùranach, still not believing what had happened. The Watcher had come out of nowhere. When he confronted them, he ignored Rory, clearly seeing Flùranach as the immediate threat. He started to whisper an incantation, and before Rory knew what happened, he'd decked the guy. Twice. The bones in his hand still throbbed. He wondered if he'd broken something.

The most surprising thing was not that he punched a faerie. Well, yeah, that was a shock merely by the level of the stupidity. But he'd fought to protect Flùr. Someone threatened her, and his instincts kicked in. He couldn't let anything hurt her.

When he met her eyes, he realised he loved her. Only love could make someone act like such a total knobhead. Only love might make a man grab a woman in the middle of a Dutch ferry station and kiss her like they were the only two people in the world. She was infuriating and selfish and infuriating and unruly and mostly infuriating. But he adored her.

The spell was only broken when a small round of applause broke out in the waiting room. He blushed to the roots of his ginger hair when he noticed the strangers around them. Flùranach laughed, happier and lovelier than he'd ever seen her. He took her hand and led her aside. He wanted to kiss her again, this time without an audience.

CHAPTER 17

WHEN THE GROUP TRAVELLED THROUGH the gate to the Caledonian realm, relief enveloped them all. Huck revelled in the Otherworld air. The undercurrent of magic refreshed him, like a cool drink on a blistering hot day. The transition towards accepting his role as a druid had taken awhile. In the beginning, he'd been so eager to embrace the new life, but the culture shock of leaving the human realm behind threw him off course. But now, he finally didn't feel like an outsider anymore.

"Do you remember which way?" Rory asked Huck.

"West," Huck said, pointing towards the rising moon. Aaron and Rory had used their water magic to propel the ferry much faster than it could usually travel. Their talents cut a typically eight-hour journey in half. The other passengers and the crew had seemed perplexed, but the druids had performed the art subtly. They'd decided to take the risk so they could arrive well before this gate closed at daybreak.

Huck led the group along the same trail he'd taken before, hoping he'd remember all the turns. Soon enough, the trail turned into a path, then the path became a street, which led towards a fae city. Unlike last time, however, the city was festooned with ornaments. Hundreds of faeries milled about on the smooth roadways. The night glistened with the magic of lights and subtle music like tinkling wind chimes played around the entire town.

"What's going on?" Aaron asked.

Rory's expression darkened. "The wedding," he said. His words reminded them all that the night of the wedding meant the night of Demi's execution.

Flùranach nodded as she looked around. "The queen's taking of a mate will be celebrated for several nights before and after the ceremony."

"We don't have much time," Huck said. He picked up his pace and they continued west and north towards the portal. Would Eilidh and Munro really go through with the wedding if Demi was to be killed immediately afterwards? It seemed cold, but then, Munro didn't really know Demi. If an entire population was celebrating him and Eilidh getting married, why would a little thing like an execution in a different country affect their plans? The idea that life would go on even if they failed weighed on Huck.

The group ran at a punishing pace, and Aaron and Rory's use of the water flows through the night to speed the ferry meant no one had slept in more than twenty-four hours. Huck's feet missed a step along the path at one point, and they all came to a halt as he recovered from a stumble.

"We have to rest," Flùranach said. "You're too tired to go on. It's another hour at least to the portal." She still seemed to have difficulty focusing on Huck and Aaron both, instead staying close to Rory and following his lead as they travelled.

"I can make it," Huck said.

"You're exhausted."

His emotions ran riot. They'd failed. Essentially, they'd found nothing but further motive for either Demi or Lisle, but none of her or Rory's questions had borne fruit. In fact, everything they'd learned, and what they hadn't, told him nothing new. Demi or Lisle pretty much had to be the killer. The one neighbour who'd been alerted by the noise didn't have anything helpful to add. He'd seen the Watchers go into the house that night, but had been so confused at the speed with which they moved that he'd convinced himself he'd been mistaken. Nothing he told them would help prove someone else might have killed Ulrich.

Their only hope lay in Oszlár arranging a proper trial. At least that would buy time. "I'll rest when Demi's safe at the Druid Hall," Huck said.

Her green eyes shone with compassion. "Here," she said. "At least let me give you some relief from your weariness." She tentatively reached out, but still struggled. "If you could release the ward stones, it would help. I can't seem to touch you."

He took the handful of stones out of his pocket and gave them to Aaron. She even had difficulty looking Huck in the eye until he moved several feet away.

Finally, she touched his temple. A warm, soothing energy ran into his mind. The fatigue melted. When he blinked a few times, he realised he'd almost fallen asleep standing up. Only seconds had passed, but he felt as though he'd slept for a couple of hours. "Thank you," he said. He took her hand and kissed her cheek.

Flùr blushed in response, touching her face where his lips had met her skin. "You're very welcome," she said, looking pleased. "Anyone else?" she asked with a glance towards Rory. She didn't face Aaron.

"I'm good," Aaron said gruffly, but Rory nodded.

"Please," he said. "I'm dead on my feet."

She repeated the procedure with Rory, and the colour returned to the druid's face. Rory turned to Aaron. "You're sure?" he asked.

"Aye," Aaron replied. After an awkward moment, he said, "But thanks."

Within a few minutes they were back on the road, speeding as fast as their legs would carry them to the Halls of Mist.

In just over an hour, they'd crossed the low, rolling hills in eastern Caledonia and passed through the portal. They stood in the centre of the entry courtyard to the Halls of Mist, weary from their long journey. Aaron asked, "What now?"

Huck turned his gaze towards the Druid Hall. Somewhere in there, Lisle was waiting. The diary sat in his pocket like a lead weight. He'd have to confront her with what he'd learned. He had no right, but what choice did he have? "I've got to talk to Lisle," he said. Rory gave him a puzzled frown, but Aaron nodded. It comforted Huck that someone understood. He'd explain everything to them all if necessary. For now, he needed to tackle the problem alone, for Demi's sake.

Rory said, "We didn't learn much. The others might still be at the Source Stone, but I'm not up to studying or crafting. We should get some rest."

"I think I'll head to the library," Aaron said. "I was thinking about that portal we made. I have a couple of ideas I want to bounce off the others." He turned to Huck. "Take these, would you?" Aaron asked, handing Huck the ward stones. "I don't think I should carry these into a room full of faeries. They probably wouldn't care for their effects too much."

"Sure," Huck said and took the pebbles. "I might catch up with you after I'm done with Lisle." Huck felt the pull of the Source Stone. "I've never seen it." He had been afraid of the powerful artefact changing him. Now he realised he'd already begun the process, even if the transformation didn't yet affect his physical appearance.

"You should rest first," Rory cautioned him. "The Stone will take as much from you as it gives. I was knocked flat for a full day after my first time."

"Same here," Aaron said.

Huck nodded, disappointed. He didn't have a day to lose, but he had difficulty turning away. Still, his loyalty to Demi meant he needed to do what he could for her. How he'd become her advocate, he had no idea, but he'd assumed the role willingly.

"And you," Rory said to Flùranach. "You need to get some sleep too."

"I rested on the boat," she replied. She gazed at Rory with complete adoration. She'd not been able to back off her feelings for the Scottish druid any more than Huck had backed off with Demi. In both situations, circumstances changed everything. Now, Rory looked at her the same way she did him. Whatever happened in Amsterdam made all the difference.

"Stubborn woman," Rory said quietly. "You swore you'd serve the Druid Hall. Doesn't that mean you're supposed to do what I command?"

Her voice sounded like a purr. "I am forever your servant, my lord druid. If you command me to bed, I would not refuse."

Huck suddenly felt like an interloper in a distinctly intimate conversation. Aaron backed away with a shake of his head and turned to walk towards the library.

Now nothing stood between Huck and the difficult situation in his path. He left Rory and Flùranach standing in a public courtyard, staring into each other's eyes.

∞

Aaron descended the stairs and strode past the keepers and other faeries without giving them a second thought. His mind focused on the energy of the Source Stone.

Their success with the newly created gate to Germany only excited him more. Sure, the rough passage had hurt like hell. For a horrible moment, he'd thought Huck had died in transit. Even with those setbacks, the thrill of the accomplishment helped him overcome his weariness.

A part of him wished he'd let Flùranach take the edge off his exhaustion after such a gruelling day and a half. He'd watched Rory and Flùranach, and all of a sudden, Rory was smitten with her. A rotten part of Aaron suspected she'd tricked him into falling in love. Although Rory was happier and this did mean she wouldn't be setting her eyes on anyone else, Aaron couldn't shake his distrust.

As he approached the room that housed the stone, Douglas' and Munro's voices drifted to Aaron's ears.

"I'm not joking," Munro said. "I'll clear the lot of you out if you keep interrupting our work."

"You wouldn't dare," an unfamiliar voice replied.

"That's it," Douglas, the youngest druid remarked with some frustration in his tone. "I can't work like this."

Aaron entered and saw the two druids sitting near the Stone's resting place. The artefact lay dormant. "What's up?" he asked.

Munro's face lit up. "You're back," he said, his relief visible. "The portal took you to the right area?"

"Aye," Aaron said. "Bloody well almost killed us, but the gate worked."

"Really?" Douglas asked. "Nice."

Aaron snorted a laugh. "Nice that it worked, I assume is what you meant, not nice that we nearly kicked it."

"Obviously." Douglas rolled his eyes.

Three keepers stood at the edges of the room, looking frustrated and perturbed. Oszlár, the only keeper Aaron knew much at all, wasn't there. "What's with them?" Aaron asked.

"Oh, they won't leave us alone with the Stone. We told them we'd let them stay if they would keep quiet and let us work."

"*Let us* stay," one of the younger keepers grumbled.

Another of the elder faeries was sharper and replied to what Aaron told them. "You created your own portal? To the human realm? And it functioned?"

"I'm dead on my feet," Aaron said. He couldn't say why he didn't want to share his information with the keepers. He harboured a perverse desire to thwart them. The old geezers hadn't been exactly forthcoming either. The druids' knowledge was power, and he wasn't going to give it away for nothing. "I'm heading back to the Hall for a kip, but I wanted to tell you we survived and all."

"I'm glad you did," Munro said. "We need a break anyway. We worked most of the day. This is our third session since you left, but we're not making much progress. I can read a lot of the runes, but I can't quite figure out their relationship with the stone. Honestly, it doesn't seem like any of this should work."

"I have some ideas about that," Aaron said, keeping his voice low, even though the sharp-eared faeries would hear him easily. He extended a hand to Munro and helped him up. "You know the weirdest part was when we came through the gate, it was closed. We went to the right place, but, Christ, what a rough ride."

"Cool," Douglas said, scrambling to his feet to join the other two.

The druids left the library, much to the dismay of the keepers. As much as the faeries resented the druids' intrusion with the Stone, they appeared keen to hear about the new portals.

On the walk to the Druid Hall, Aaron related what happened in Amsterdam, starting with the nasty pull through the portal. Then, he continued to what they discovered at Demi's house, which was basically nothing. He left out the strange book Huck found. Although Aaron clearly saw fae runes, the American wanted to keep it mum for now. Aaron thought Huck deserved the chance to work out whatever was on his mind before telling the others. If they expected Huck to start acting more like a member of the Hall, Aaron figured they'd need to extend a little more trust.

CHAPTER 18

LOAMY EARTH COVERED LISLE'S HANDS. Never in her life had she handled soil so dark and rich. When she'd wandered out the previous night, she'd found six young female faeries hard at work in the vegetable garden beyond this castle-like Hall of Druids. Calling her new residence a *hall* seemed silly. It was more a village. But who was she to criticise?

Since arriving in this strange place, her hands ached less than usual, and her hips didn't twinge with their typical sharp pains. She felt stronger, younger even. With little to do, she'd taken to wandering. At first, she wouldn't dare to snoop, but the Druid Hall was strangely deserted. Oh, there were servants and stewards, but they left her alone and didn't speak unless spoken to. No one told her not to go anywhere. Though they were quiet, the faeries throughout the grounds always greeted her with smiles, as though she was perfectly right to do what she pleased.

When she asked questions about the vegetables the faeries were planting, they'd answered readily, although they did insist on calling her *my lady druid* or worse—*elder*. Next thing she knew, she'd gotten on her knees beside them, listening as they taught her how to harvest the squash-like vegetables attached to the thick, creeping vines.

Lisle couldn't recall the last time she'd done any gardening. It must have been the spring before Jago was born. She laid one of the large vegetables in the faeries' basket and moved on to the next plant. The honest work satisfied her. She wasn't prone to wistfulness or regret. Life gave what it gave. Mistakes couldn't be undone, only paid for. Hard labour ordered her mind, and the sensation of earth in her hands made her feel whole and connected.

"Lisle?" Huck's voice intruded into her solace, but she had to face him.

She closed her eyes, wanting to delay, but nothing would stop what was coming. Standing with minimal discomfort, a relief in her old age, she turned towards the young man. Huck's eyes told her everything. "You found my diary," she said.

His gaze flicked to the faeries working in the gardens, then back to Lisle. He gave a sharp nod, his hand going to his pocket. *He must have the book with him.*

"We need to talk. Alone," he said.

The faeries gathered their produce and quickly dispersed, taking the baskets towards the castle's storehouse. Huck blinked, surprised, then gestured to a bench. "Would you rather sit out here or go inside?"

Lisle looked down at her grimy hands and rubbed some of the earth away. She would prefer not talk to him at all. "Here is fine," she said.

"I've never been back here before," he told her.

She didn't answer. He was stalling.

Reaching into his pocket, he pulled out the rune-covered diary. He traced a finger over a few of the runes.

Shame burned through her. "You read everything?"

He nodded, and they sat together on the curved wooden bench. "As much as I could. I'm not the most gifted reader, but I understood enough." Reluctantly, he handed the journal to her. "I'm surprised you didn't keep it with you."

"I meant to retrieve it before we left," she said. "Everything happened so fast. I didn't want my granddaughter to see it."

"Demi doesn't know about you and Ulrich?"

"Of course not," Lisle said. "My sins happened a lifetime ago. I intended to take my secrets to my grave. When she told me about Jago, how could I tell her? She needed my help. If she knew the truth, she would have run from me. Only *I* had the experience to teach her how to evade Ulrich." Her voice caught. She hated saying his name.

"Was Ulrich your son's father?" He kept his eyes down as he asked. His tone was so gentle, devoid of the scorn Lisle felt for herself.

"Does it matter?" she shot back.

"Not to me."

She sighed, setting the book on the bench between them. Part of her wanted to throw the diary away, but part of her wanted to relive the moments she'd recorded within. "He was gifted, a beautiful baby. He grew to be taller than William, but who is to say my husband would not have given me a tall, handsome child? William was a good man." Over the years, she'd watched her boy for any indication he might be different, but any signs she thought she saw, she dismissed. More than anything she ever desired in her life, she wanted him to be William's.

"And you never saw Ulrich again until the night of his death?"

She shook her head. "He disappeared. I thought he'd died or perhaps something prevented him from returning to our world. One day he was there, then he simply vanished from my life."

"Maybe he couldn't find you," Huck said.

Lisle looked up at him suddenly. "What do you mean?"

"Maybe your son hid you from him much the way Jago protected Demi."

Ulrich's absence had been a relief in one way, but devastating in another. She'd vowed never to speak of her shame. Despite the fact that she'd loved him to the point of obsession, he had always had a streak of nastiness. The anger that had ripped through her when she learned how he turned his cruelty to Demi still burned.

Lisle glanced at Huck. Something in his expression made her feel naked, as though he saw into her thoughts. She hugged herself, her dirty hands smudging her blouse with dark earth.

"Did you kill him?" Huck asked.

Lisle raised her chin defiantly. "I'm glad he's dead. He'll never hurt my family again."

Huck nodded. "When I read that," he said, nodding to the diary, "I reacted the same way. Hard to imagine anyone regrets his death." He paused. "You didn't kill him though, did you?"

Lisle sighed. "If I knew then what I know now, perhaps I'd have murdered him the day I met him." When Huck tilted his head, the unanswered question still lingering in his eyes, Lisle gave up. "No. I didn't kill him."

Huck turned and stared straight ahead, gaze fixed on some point in the distant sky. "I'm not sure what to do," he said. "Keeper Oszlár is going to negotiate for a trial. I don't even know if he's returned yet."

"What good would a trial do?" Lisle asked.

"Buy us time. Thing is, Konstanze is holding Demi as a political prisoner as much as anything else. From what I gather, it's unheard of for a faerie queen to execute a human. To kill a druid? This is a power play."

"My granddaughter confessed to killing the queen's brother," Lisle said. Even if the motivation behind Demi's arrest was political, she didn't understand how this queen could let her go.

"There are many truths Konstanze would not want revealed in a trial, such as Ulrich's fondness for human women, the nature of his azuri magic, his taste for inflicting pain. If we can make her believe pursuing her threats will lose her more than she would gain, there may be room to negotiate. Konstanze's ego has been bruised by a recent loss of territory," he explained. "If only we'd gotten to Demi first."

"What do you mean?" Lisle asked. The politics of this realm confused her.

"Taking someone from any hall would violate the Halls of Mist. No other queen would support that action. This is almost a holy city. If we'd gotten to Demi first, we'd have the upper hand. Konstanze might make demands all day long, but she could never force us to give Demi up if we kept her in the Halls of Mist."

"Then take her back," Lisle said.

Huck snapped out of his pensive state and stared at Lisle. "You want me to go to Ashkyne and break her out of prison?"

The idea sounded outrageous. Lisle knew nothing about the Otherworld kingdoms. "Yes," she said. "Go save my grandchildren."

"That's crazy. I saw where she's being held. That place is a fortress. Literally."

"What if you were invisible?" Lisle asked, growing more excited. "Then you might manage, yes?"

"Invisible?" he said, disbelief wrinkling his forehead as he frowned.

"I can make you a ward stone," she said. "Like the ones you saw at my house. Stronger, even. Bonded to your own blood."

His eyes moved back and forth as he thought, weighing, considering. "How? I don't understand that type of magic. My element is fire. How do your ward stones work?"

"The rituals are written in an illustrated storybook that's passed through many generations. There are tales, yes, but after I met Ulrich, I saw the truth in the rune drawings. It wasn't a book for children after all. I've studied and practiced the ways of my ancestors for more than fifty years. We inscribe the runes, then dedicate them with our blood."

Uncertainty became incredulity. "You are a blood druid?"

"Of course," Lisle said, puzzled at his reaction.

"Blood. Not water or air or fire or stone?"

"I don't know anything of those talents, no. Our rituals are only blood."

"And Jago's sphere?"

Lisle didn't answer. Something was wrong, but she didn't understand why he was reacting that way.

"Ulrich's talent was air, wasn't it? They were telling the truth about that?" Huck had become excited, insistent.

"Yes," Lisle said.

"This means the fae don't have to be azuri to bond with a druid. An earth faerie can bond with an azuri druid. Demi inherited your blood talent," Huck said, his gaze locked on Lisle. "And passed it on to her lethfae son."

Lisle hesitated, but then nodded once sharply.

"Demi didn't kill Ulrich, did she?"

Tears pricked at Lisle's eyes. "No," she whispered.

"That's why Demi confessed. Dear Mother of Earth," Huck said. "We must get Jago out of there. Konstanze will kill him if she finds out."

Panic rose in Lisle's chest. "You said the fae protect children. You promised he was in no danger."

"That was before I found out he's a blood faerie who killed his own father." He stood and offered his hand to Lisle. "How long will you need to make me some ward stones? I must be ready to go as soon as Konstanze arrives for the wedding. All the queens will be attending the ceremony in Caledonia. She'll likely have a huge contingent with her. Even if they do postpone Demi's execution, this diversion may offer my best chance."

Lisle stood, doing her best to steady her nerves. She wanted to put her faith in this determined young man. But she now realised that even if Demi did sacrifice herself for Jago, her death might not be enough to protect him.

"Come," she said. "The ritual book is hidden in my room."

∞

Rory lay in bed. Flùranach's mass of red locks spread over his torso, mingling with the ginger curls of his chest hair. She slept. Her eyelids fluttered as she dreamed, and Rory envied the deep, restful state. His mind raced with thoughts of the threat facing the druids, the repercussions of the portal they'd created, and the druid imprisoned in Ashkyne. Through it all, he thought about Flùranach and where they'd go from there.

A guilty conscience said he shouldn't have stopped to indulge himself with her. He ought to be at the library, working with the others. He replayed the past day in his head. Every sideways look, subtle touch, and thought led to this moment. When he brought her to his bed, she'd come willingly, even submissively. As his own desire built, whatever willpower she'd been using to restrain herself broke. She became deliciously demanding, teasing his senses, drawing out his pleasure in a way that defied any experience he'd had before.

She stirred slightly as he wriggled out from underneath her. A gentle kiss to her temple settled her back into a blissful quiet. He stood for a moment, studying her, wanting to tell her he loved her, wanting to complete the bonding process she'd begun. Now wasn't the time, though. The druids had work to do.

Was that his only reason? He considered as he dressed in the moonlight. If he was honest with himself, no. He had to acknowledge two much stronger reasons. To declare his love either during or right after sex would seem, he thought, ungentlemanly.

Another darker, more serious thought worried him. The question niggled, no matter how he wanted to ignore it. Why were the keepers so determined to for them to bond? What did they know that they wouldn't share with him? He loved Flùranach and wanted to share a bond with her. He admitted now he'd felt that way for a long time, even while he was his angriest with her. But old men plotting to *make* things happen didn't sit well. He wanted to take his time with this.

With one last glance at her naked form tangled in the blankets, he turned to go. Down the stairs he went, trying to pull his focus to the job at hand. Even in her sleep, Flùranach tugged at his concentration.

He met Aaron in the corridor. The other druid shuffled towards the landing, looking tired and haggard.

"Hey," Rory said. "I thought you were over at the library."

"I was," Aaron replied. "We all came back to the workshop, but I'm falling asleep sitting up. I'll be no good until I get a kip."

"Better toddle off to bed then," Rory said.

Despite his obvious exhaustion, Aaron stopped to flutter his eyelashes at Rory. "If my lord druid commands me to bed..." He ducked with a laugh then darted towards the stairs.

"Git," Rory called after him, chuckling. At least Aaron was joking instead of displaying the usual hostility towards Flùranach. Rory hoped the exchange signalled some form of acceptance, but he suspected any lasting change would take time.

When Rory arrived at the workshop, he was glad to find Oszlár with Munro and Douglas. "Huck's not here?" he asked.

Munro shook his head. "Aaron said he went to find Lisle. I haven't seen him since you got back."

Rory nodded to the keeper in greeting. "Any news?" he asked.

Oszlár frowned. "No good news, I'm afraid."

"Konstanze means to go ahead with the execution," Munro told him.

"No trial?"

At that moment, Huck and Lisle arrived together, both listening intently for the keeper's answer.

"No," Oszlár said, a curious expression on his face as he nodded to the new arrivals. "She kept her contempt for me under the surface, but only just. The lady will be executed tomorrow night after Konstanze returns from Queen Eilidh's mating ceremony."

Munro looked like he wanted to punch someone. Huck's dark expression matched the Scot's, and Lisle eyes carried a haunted hollowness.

"I'll send word to Eilidh," Munro said solemnly. "We'll postpone the wedding."

"No," Huck said. "Don't." With a glance to Lisle, he said, "We have a plan. It's a long shot, but our best chance is if the wedding goes ahead." He explained his intentions, holding out three ward stones, two from the Amsterdam house, one he and Lisle had just made.

"Fascinating," Oszlár said.

Munro tilted his head towards Lisle. "One of these days, I'd like to learn how you make those. I'm sure we all would."

"I'll wake Flùr," Rory said. "She can go with you and use her illusions to disguise you."

"No," Munro said, holding up a hand to stop Rory. "They'd be better off without her this time. Watchers all over the kingdoms have been training to resist astral influence, including illusion. Huck hasn't touched the Source Stone. That means faeries can't detect his flows. If those stones work as well on the Ashkyne faeries as they did on Flùr, Huck might have a shot." He turned to Oszlár. "What do you think?"

The elder faerie stepped forward and peered at the stones in Huck's hand. "Unpleasant," he said to the druid.

"Pardon me?" came Huck's astonished reply.

Oszlár turned to Munro. "It's extremely unpleasant to look at him."

Lisle smiled with satisfaction, a gleam of hope lighting her eyes.

"You think this will work?" Munro asked the keeper.

"As a Keeper of the Stone, I am sworn to be neutral to politics and national concerns. The life of one woman, no matter how I feel personally, is irrelevant in the face of my duty. I cannot, therefore, encourage you to violate the territory of any queen." He paused and held up a hand when Huck appeared ready to interrupt. "I will say this. We faeries are not adept at embracing new ideas, as you have observed. Therefore, ward stones would prove an advantage, should you find yourself in a position where you wish to move undetected."

Huck nodded. "I'll dress in black like their servants and Watchers and hope no one pays too much attention."

Oszlár tilted his head, still not precisely meeting Huck's eyes. "Remember, my lord druid. It is difficult to look at you, but not impossible. I would advise extreme caution."

Munro glanced at Huck, his mouth in a grim line. "It's a risk. Be careful. I don't want to lose you too."

"Thanks," Huck said. "You go get married. And try not to worry about us. I'm planning to bring Demi and Jago back safely."

"I'll need to tell Eilidh what's happened," Munro said. "She was prepared to postpone if things didn't work out." He flashed a tiny smile. "I confess I'm glad I don't have to cancel the wedding. She'd probably be graceful about it, but never quite forgive me." The others gave a small laugh, so he paused before saying, "Listen, I know this isn't really the right time, but people are going to hear soon. Eilidh's pregnant."

An awkward stillness filled the room as the other druids shot glances at one another.

Munro rolled his eyes. "The baby's mine," he said, and the friends all chuckled together. "Jeez," he went on. "Can't a guy have a wife with three husbands without everyone thinking it's weird?"

They laughed even louder and congratulated him with slaps on the back.

Oszlár bowed to Munro. "My deepest prayer of thanks to the Mother of the Earth for her gift to you, my lord druid. Your daughter will bless our people immeasurably."

The quick flicker of recognition indicated Munro caught the keeper's choice of words. *Daughter*. Oszlár had already known about the baby. The old faerie had a lot more up his sleeve than he was letting on.

"Keeper," Munro said, "with respect, I need a little more from you."

"Oh?" Oszlár said. "How may I be of service, my lord druid?"

"Show us the Source Stone again, and this time, tell us everything."

Oszlár hesitated, then shifted his posture slightly, standing a little bit straighter. "I'm not one to defy the draoidh. However, *everything* is quite a substantial request."

"You've been keeping more than the Stone," Rory said. "You have a lot of secrets."

"When you reach my age," Oszlár said with a wry grin, "So will you."

Hon, the Hall's steward appeared at the doorway. "Queen Eilidh of Caledonia," he announced.

Munro looked at Hon with surprise, then watched as his future wife swept into the room, her brow knitted with anxiety.

"What's wrong?" Munro asked, reaching out to take her hand.

She blinked at him. "What's wrong? My entire nation expects me to take a mate tomorrow night. The celebrations have already begun. The first royal feast commences in a few hours. Queens from every realm will begin arriving through the portal soon. I still don't even know if the ceremony will take place because one of my honoured guests has threatened to kill my new mate's comrade." Her palpable anxiety filled the room.

"Konstanze isn't backing down," Munro said. Eilidh's face fell, but Munro went on quickly. "We have a plan. At least, Huck and Lisle do."

Huck took a deep breath as though trying to steel himself. "We need you to go ahead with the wedding."

Eilidh's frown deepened as she looked at the druids one by one. She pursed her lips. "I understand. Whatever your plans, you must all return by the start of the ceremony if you intend for your absence to not be noted. All the druid lords will be expected for at least that portion of the evening."

Huck nodded, but his expression was noncommittal. "I'll do my best," he said.

Turning to Munro, she said, "We need to go, then."

"Now?" he asked. "The wedding isn't until tomorrow. We planned to do some more work at the library tonight."

Her gaze went to the ceiling as though the queen was striving not to lose her temper. "I told you weeks ago you would be expected to greet the other queens and attend the feasts."

For the first time ever, Rory thought he caught a bit of nervousness in Munro's expression. Was the unflappable former cop actually worried about the wedding?

"Go on, mate," Rory said. "We've got this."

Munro sighed. "I thought I'd have more time." He glanced at the Keeper. "I still think there's more you could tell us that would help our situation."

"Perhaps," Oszlár said. "The other keepers are buzzing about your new portal. May I see it?"

"Sure," Munro said.

Eilidh interrupted. "The others can show him. If we don't behave precisely as protocol dictates, we may arouse suspicions. Many will be watching for our response to Konstanze's manoeuvres." She paused. "And you need to change before you come to the Caledonian Hall for the first feast."

Munro looked down at his clothing, a puzzled expression on his face. He clearly thought his attire was fine. With a sigh, he said, "Rory, Douglas, will you show Keeper Oszlár our portal? Then go with him to study the Source Stone one last time?"

Douglas nodded his agreement. "I know what to do. What Aaron told us gave me a few ideas of my own."

"All right," Munro said, his inner conflict playing in his expression. Rory understood. He wouldn't want to be at a formal dinner just now either. Munro extended a hand to Huck, and they shook. "Good luck," Munro said.

"Thanks," Huck replied. "You too." Rory wasn't sure which of them looked more apprehensive.

CHAPTER 19

ONE OF EILIDH'S PERSONAL attendants arrived secretly at the Druid Hall a few hours later to inform Huck that the guests of the feast would be departing soon for Caledonia. A fleeting, crazy thought popped into his head. *Why not just kill Konstanze at the wedding? Surely that would stop the execution.* He sighed. He must really have little confidence in his plan if he believed murdering a queen in front of her honour guard would be easier than what he intended to do.

He thanked the messenger and checked his pack one last time. He'd worn black and packed only the bare minimum he thought he'd need. If everything went his way, he hoped to return in time to attend Munro's wedding. If nothing went his way, he might not come back at all. He'd seen fae combat spells. No way would he survive if one was aimed directly at him. Stealth and deception were his only hope.

When he made his way to the Druid Hall's main courtyard, he found Lisle waiting for him. The old woman stared towards the blue portal in the distance, clutching Jago's teddy bear to her chest. "Take this," she said, handing him the toy. "He will be afraid. He's just a little boy," she added.

"Sure," Huck said and took the bear. *A little boy who'd killed his father.* The thought had played over and over in Huck's mind ever since he found out Jago was a blood faerie. But what child wouldn't want to protect his mother? Huck sure as hell ld. His thoughts drifted to his own mother. She'd been one of those women who joined clubs and committees, went to parent-teacher conferences, drove him to soccer practice twice a week and games on Sunday afternoons.

Shoving the memories aside, he put the teddy bear in his pack, then slung the black bag over his shoulder. Huck strained to see the courtyard in the distance. It was too far, but he thought he saw the blue flicker of the portal. The chimes rang in the Druid Hall. Soon, the sun would rise in Caledonia. The queens and their massive entourages would make their way to their day of rest before the wedding tomorrow night. Munro and Eilidh would be paraded in front of tens of thousands of faeries.

Where will I be then? Will I even be alive?

He looked at his watch. With the sun up in the human realm, the Otherworld gates would be closed already. That blue shimmering portal would be his only way out of Ashkyne for at least the next ten hours.

"It's time," he said.

Lisle put her ropy, wrinkled hand on his arm and squeezed. She remained silent, but her expression spoke volumes. Hope, fear, dread, and a prayer for safe return all wordlessly passed between them.

Huck checked for the stones in his pocket. They were there, as they had been the first dozen times he'd checked. *One foot in front of the other*, he thought. He strode down the pathway and to the bridge over the fog that gave the Halls of Mist its name. His gaze never deviated from the portal.

He slowed when he approached the immense courtyard, surprised to find it still crowded with faeries dressed in resplendent formalwear. Moving hundreds of wedding guests would take time, he supposed. Part of him wanted to turn back to his Hall, but he had to move on. His best hope was that they would think he was going to Caledonia like the rest of them. It even occurred to him the portal might take him there. What if he truthfully didn't want to go to Ashkyne, no matter if his sense of duty told him he had to? What if he walked through that portal and ended up alongside the other party-goers?

As he moved towards the crowd, not one of the faeries acknowledged him. None bowed their heads with respect as they usually did. He looked at them incredulously, searching for a sign that Konstanze's new attitude of disdain had spread even beyond her own kingdom. But then his confidence surged. Of course. The ward stone. He'd known how they worked and even hoped they would cause him to be ignored, but wanting a thing and experiencing it were completely different.

A cluster of faeries stood between him and the shining portal globe. "Pardon me," he said quietly.

One female faerie glanced up, then her eyes darted away. She frowned as though she'd smelled something unpleasant. "We should go," she said to her companions. "I'm tired after the meal. The food, I think, was too rich. I have a headache." Her friends tutted with sympathy, but not one of them noticed Huck.

A voice suddenly rang in his head. *Your wards have a limited area of effect. Be cautious.*

He whipped around, looking for the source of the message. From the far side of the courtyard, he saw Eilidh. She met his eyes and held his gaze for a few seconds before casually and deliberately turning away.

With that sober reminder, he slipped into a group making its way towards the portal's glow.

Any fear, or secret hope, he would not end up in Ashkyne vanished. The blue glow surrounded him, and the cooler air of an Ashkyne breeze whipped at his shirt as he stepped through to the other side.

He touched the identity token beside the ward stone in his pocket, marked with the rune of the Druid

Hall. He'd decided to keep this part simple. In the best case scenario, the Watchers wouldn't even challenge him, but as Eilidh had reminded him, he wasn't truly invisible, only, as Oszlár put it, unpleasant to acknowledge.

The Watchers spotted him immediately. When he stepped closer to the one nearest him, however, Huck noticed how uncomfortably the soldiers regarded him. He picked out the one with the highest rank insignia. Lisle had explained that the more powerful the faerie, the stronger the effect of the stone, repelling their magic from a fundamental level. He only hoped this faerie had been promoted based on talent and not for something trivial like his family name.

The Watcher had dark grey skin that was almost black with a bluish tint, especially around the creases of his ears and the highlights of his facial features. He was tall and erect. Huck dropped the token into his hand.

"The Druid Hall?" the Watcher asked. He looked up at Huck and his dark skin paled a few shades, giving him a strange, gun-metal pallor. "Ashkyne's gates are closed to all but our citizens."

Huck retrieved Konstanze's letter from his pack. "Our Hall has permission from Queen Konstanze to offer final prayers for a prisoner."

Nearby Watchers subtly moved away, resuming their protection of the portal. The guard glanced at them. Huck hoped their display of disinterest made him seem less threatening.

The Watcher opened his mouth as though to speak, but then glanced away. He handed the letter and the token back to Huck. Without another word, he returned to his duty.

The abruptness of his show of disinterest startled Huck, but he shook himself into action, slipping through the ranks of Watchers. He glanced back after he'd moved away, but none came after him. Only when he'd gone some distance did the Watcher he'd spoken to relax.

The exchange weighed on Huck. He'd gotten through because of the letter. He hadn't been rendered as invisible as he'd hoped. Clearly the guards didn't want to deal with him a moment longer than they had to, but how on earth would he sneak Demi and Jago past?

He couldn't. His only option was to take them to one of the gates to the human realm. Ashkyne's borderlands covered many countries, from Germany to Romania. All he had to do was move the pair of them to England somehow. Eilidh was the only queen he could trust. He had to use Caledonia, even though some other kingdoms might be closer.

One step at a time, he told himself. He had a long way to go. Getting Demi out of prison was only the first step. Considering the way the fae guarded their young, finding Jago might prove the most dangerous part.

∞

Oszlár had agreed to dismiss all the other keepers while Rory and Douglas visited the Source Stone, but he insisted on staying as they worked. They must not, he warned them, alter the Stone in any way.

"Aaron said I should look at the runes on the walls," Douglas explained to Rory. The discovery of his unexpected talent with runes had his confidence surging. Aaron had told Douglas only he or Munro could crack the Stone, so to speak.

Rory asked the younger druid what he detected about the inscriptions surrounding them.

"They seem to be written by a lot of different people," Douglas said, careful not to touch them. Mere physical contact with a rune wouldn't alter it without deep intent accompanying the move, but the watchful eyes of the head keeper made him a little nervous.

"Druids?" Rory asked.

Douglas shook his head, his fingers hovering over the surface of the stone wall. "I don't think so, at least not these." He paused. "They're really weird."

Rory sighed. "Weird? Care to be more descriptive?"

"They seem like gibberish. Aaron said he thought so, but he wanted me to look too." Douglas felt the weight of Oszlár's gaze.

"Why didn't Munro notice that?" Rory asked.

Douglas shrugged. "None of us did. When the Stone is raised, it's hard to think about anything else. You remember."

"Aye," Rory said.

"Munro said the last time he came here, he couldn't make heads nor tails of the walls." He stopped. "I know this sounds barmy, but I sense the runes don't want to be understood."

Rory stopped dead in his tracks. "They what?"

"I'm just telling you what I feel," Douglas said, holding his hands up.

Spinning towards Oszlár, Rory's demeanour changed. "What do you know about this?" he demanded.

"I am a Keeper of the Stone," Oszlár said, as though that explained everything.

"A keeper of secrets," Rory said. His eyes reflected in the dim, misty glow in the chamber.

"Precisely," Oszlár replied with a slight bow and an amused look.

Both druids stared at him. Douglas had guarded what he said in front of the keeper, but now the old faerie dangled some truth in front of them. He wanted more.

"And the secrets of the Stone," Rory began. "Do they relate to why you want me to bond with Flùranach so badly?"

"Yes." The faerie regarded Rory eagerly, as though waiting for something important.

"What *is* this thing?" Rory asked, stepping closer to the flat top of the dormant rock. "It reads the minds of those who come near, detects where they want to go, and teleports them there. It transforms druids, chooses queens, and for some reason, it has chosen Flùranach for me?"

"No," Douglas said, realisation dawning. He looked from Rory to Oszlár and back again. "The Stone doesn't do any of those things." Thoughts whirled about in his mind, and he struggled to order them.

"What then?" Rory asked.

Excitement built in Douglas' chest. Why hadn't he seen the connection before? "The Stone doesn't do anything."

"Are you saying this rock is a fake?" Rory's mouth gaped. "That's preposterous. I can detect its power, even though it's dormant. We've all used the portal. If the stone doesn't do anything, how are people getting shifted around?"

Douglas shook his head rapidly. "No, no. You're missing my point. Okay, think of one of our talismans, like, say, the star we used to find Tràth when he was lost in the aether. Remember?"

"Aye," Rory said. "Of course."

"What did the talisman do?"

"The star amplified Griogair's call to his son, then pinpointed Tràth's location and pulled him out."

"Not really, no," Douglas said, his thoughts whirring. "Eilidh amplified Griogair's call. Eilidh found Tràth."

"You're saying she didn't need the star?"

Douglas shook his head. "Not at all. But look, let's say you want to dig a hole."

Rory exhaled his impatience. "Okay."

"You've got some dirt and a spade."

"Right," Rory said.

"Who digs the hole?"

Rory muttered, then forced himself to play along a little while longer. "I do?"

"Exactly."

"But..."

"The spade doesn't dig a hole. A spade is just a spade. Without you, the spade sits in the garden shed, leaning against a wall, giving the spiders something to spin a web on."

Rory furrowed his brow.

Douglas gestured at the centre of the room. "The Source Stone is a spade."

"This is the garden shed?" Rory asked.

"I think the better question is," Douglas said, shifting his gaze to the keeper, "who is digging the hole, and why?"

Oszlár smiled. "I confess. I thought Lord Druid Munro would work it out first," he said. "I had hoped he would not do so for some time though." He sighed and stood, lost in his thoughts, while the druids watched him. Finally, he began to explain. "In the days of the first draoidh, when our world was young and your precursors walked among us, there was one kingdom, one Otherworld. As often happens, as the centuries passed, the draoidh became divided, as did the fae who worked with and supported them. When the powerful draoidh sorcerers grew at odds, the world splintered. The Otherworld we know is a fragmented remnant of what it once was."

"And the Stone?" Douglas asked.

"The Stone is what we have always said: The Source."

"The Source of what?"

"Of all magic. Of our essence. Of the power used to create and sustain us."

"So when the fae use it to teleport from one kingdom to another?" Rory asked.

"They are channelling the Stone's memory of a place that used to be unified. We aren't teleporting. We are asking the Stone to remember."

"The Halls of Mist was a crossroads?" Douglas scratched his head.

"Exactly." Oszlár's eyes lit up. "You understand. Where the Halls of Mists is now, once stood a great city."

"So why doesn't everyone know this?" Douglas asked. "And why didn't you just tell us?"

"The Stone is the key to our survival as a race. What do you think would happen if one queen believed that by taking the Stone, she could eliminate her rivals?" He shook his head. "No. We keepers have sworn an oath. We give ourselves to the Stone. We serve our people to prevent our race from descending into chaos."

"So *you* choose the queens? You picked Eilidh to rule over Andenan lands when Vinye died?"

"No," Oszlár said. "The Stone is in some ways what it appears to be: a powerful, almost rational artefact. It does, however, draw on the keepers' knowledge and energy when making a change. So, in a small way, we do have some influence."

"Then why don't you just pick one good queen and unify the Otherworld completely?"

Oszlár chuckled. "If only life were that simple. If only we could force people to live in peace. Have you attempted such a feat in your own world?"

Douglas had to concede the point. He turned back to the Stone. "So how does this thing work?"

"I don't know," Oszlár said. When Douglas shot him a pointed look, the elder raised his hands. "I speak the truth on that," he said. "The lore of the keepers is ancient and secret, passed to us by the eldest of the draoidh, gone now for tens of thousands of years. We never thought to meet their like again. We know our duty. The Stone shows us the strength of each candidate as reflected by our own observations and experiences. But sometimes, in ages past, instead of bringing kingdoms together, the good of the race was most served by creating an entirely new kingdom with a new queen."

"If we, the new draoidh, are so flippin' important," Rory said, "How come you're willing to let one of us die?"

Oszlár's eyes flashed. "You think I didn't try to stop Konstanze? We were once the servants of the gods," he shouted. "Now we are nothing more than old scholars and you are mere fledglings. We lose one druid tomorrow night, yes, and that pains me. But we must protect your place in our world until the day when your true magic manifests. Someday you will remember what those who came before you understood. You will unlock the secrets and revive the Stone."

"Revive?" Douglas asked.

Oszlár sighed. "I have worked its magic for thirteen hundred years. The Stone grows weaker. Without your help, it will die, and the fae will die with it."

Douglas nodded. Oszlár's account explained everything, including why the keepers had been so keen to support the construction of the Druid Hall and helped to establish them as the draoidh of old. "How long do you have?" he asked.

The old faerie shrugged. "A night? A thousand years? Every time a faerie asks the Stone to remember the Otherworld as whole, it grows weaker."

"Using the portal damages it?" Rory asked. "Why not shut the thing down?"

Oszlár said. "The same reason you do not shut down the brain just because you have a headache."

Douglas pondered. "The Stone is the only thing holding the kingdoms together."

"You're saying the gates to the human realm don't work in the same way as this portal?" Rory asked.

"Correct," Oszlár said. "They are like anchors. If we tore them all down, the Source would not suffer."

"Except for the fact that faeries seem to need to visit the human realm to procreate," Rory said, muttering as though speaking to himself. He directed his next question to Oszlár. "Do you know why faeries have to visit altars to have babies?"

Douglas said, "Munro and Eilidh didn't. Ulrich and Demi probably didn't."

"I have suspicions, yes. You'll also note that the azuri fae of the Isle of Skye were blessed many more times than is usual for faerie couples. But I admit these questions do not overly concern me. My challenge and life's work are the Stone alone."

"What about the gate we created at the Druid Hall?" Rory asked.

"Like the gates from the human realm to our lands, you created an anchor. I'm impressed that you were able to affix your gate to an existing one, but that has nothing to do with the Source. Your achievement, while laudable, will not solve the problem of the faltering Stone."

Rory sighed. "We're wasting our time. There's nothing here that can help Demi."

"That's not true," Douglas said. He'd been listening, thinking, staring at the runes on the walls. He turned to Oszlár. "We can stop Konstanze from killing Demi."

Oszlár's expression darkened. "I will not risk doing damage to the Stone. We can't force it to do what we want. There are rules and structure to its magic. Konstanze is strong. She is in no danger of losing even an iota of her kingdom. She came within a breath of gaining Vinye's lands. One life, no matter how precious, cannot take priority over the lives of every faerie in every kingdom."

"I understand," Douglas said. "I won't damage the Stone." He crouched beside the artefact's resting place and ran a hand over the top. "Now...wake it up."

"No," Oszlár said. "Not until you explain what you intend to do."

"I can feel the Stone's magic calling me," Douglas said. "Can't you?" he asked Rory, hoping the other druid would play along. He couldn't feel anything unusual, but he believed that once the keepers activated the Stone, he'd know what to do. The truth teased at his mind.

Rory looked puzzled, but nodded. "It's distant, but there's something about the mist."

Douglas stood and faced the elder faerie. "I can wake the artefact, but I don't know the Stone as well as you do. We risk less if you do your part."

"What are you planning?" Oszlár demanded.

"I'm going to give Konstanze what she wants," Douglas replied. "A demonstration of why you shouldn't fuck with a Druid Lord." He turned away and returned to the centre of the room, to wait for the Stone to rise from its resting place. "Now, call the other keepers if you need to, but wake it up."

Silence hung in the room. Douglas could hear both of the other two breathe, and his own steady heartbeat. He kept as still as possible. Rare confidence coursed through his veins. He would slap that bitch Konstanze and save Demi at the same time. But only if Oszlár believed him.

The old keeper exhaled tiredly. "Very well."

CHAPTER 20

DEMI HAD GROWN ACCUSTOMED to the schedule of the various guards, but not the conditions. She was cold, despite the blanket Leocort had provided, her back ached, and her stomach growled. They fed her, but her diet was meagre, consisting mostly of fruit and bread. At least the food was wholesome. They could have given her rancid slop, she reminded herself, or worse: nothing at all.

The other Watcher who guarded her cell ignored her completely. His aloof manner didn't disturb her. She'd come to associate remoteness with the fae. Even in his scant expressions, he seemed to loathe Demi. Somehow, without saying a word, he made her understand she would find no sympathy from him.

Leocort, on the other hand, treated Demi as a guest. His polite behaviour struck her as strange, considering he didn't seem inclined to stop the queen from having her killed. After that first day, they never spoke of Ulrich or the murder again.

Instead, he would talk to her as she ate. Although she would have preferred something more directly helpful, his company prevented her from going insane with dread. When she brought up certain subjects, he would grow agitated and leave, so she avoided them. Unfortunately, the one topic she most wanted to discuss, Jago, topped that list. Leocort asked her about her life, her family's magical heritage, the Druid Lords, although the information she had of them admittedly wasn't much. Still, she told him what she could. He always thanked her as though he regarded her storytelling as a precious gift.

Although she had no view of the outside, Demi suspected night had fallen again. The hour of her execution approached, marching towards her like a dreadful spectre. Leocort must have arrived to begin the final night's watch. She could tell because a glowing haze appeared in the centre of her cell. She waited, expecting him to walk in momentarily. Perhaps, since this was her last night on earth, he'd bring her something solid to eat, even though she hadn't asked. Sighing, she pushed the thought aside. She wasn't *on* earth anymore, technically speaking. As she had every night before, she closed her eyes and prayed for Jago, that he might be healthy and happy, and that he wouldn't be afraid. Whispering in the dark, she begged her maker to forgive the boy for what he had done. The blame was hers alone.

Time ticked by, but Leocort didn't come. She worried for him, despite the concern seeming irrational. He'd been good company. She wanted to ask him to attend her execution so his would be the last face she saw. The request seemed selfish. Who would want to witness a death? But something told her he would agree. If she was going to die, she deserved one self-centred wish.

Minutes stretched into hours. Her stomach complained loudly. Sighing, she gathered the blanket and lumped one end into a pillow. She'd wasted her time thinking about her final meal. There wouldn't be one. Maybe he couldn't face speaking to her, since the conversation would be her last. Feeling alone and abandoned, imagining someone cared comforted her. How long, she wondered, before they'd come for her?

A muffled noise sounded in the corridor. Demi sat bolt upright. Had she fallen asleep? A heavy thud followed several louder crashes. The light in the centre of the room dimmed, then winked out, plunging her into complete darkness. She crawled to the back wall, drew her legs up, and hugged her knees.

A hiss came from the doorway. "Demi?"

She leapt to her feet, but stayed against the wall. For the first time in days, hope surged in her chest.

"It's me. Huck." He stepped closer. His eyes shone in the darkness, just like the fae's. "It's okay," he said. "I've come to get you out."

"Where's Leocort?" she said.

"Who?" Huck moved towards her in the darkness.

"The guard," she said.

"Don't worry. I've taken care of him."

A remote part of her brain told her she shouldn't care, but Demi couldn't help worrying. "You've killed him?" A groan escaped her lips.

Huck hesitated. "I'm not sure."

"Where is he?" she asked, stumbling towards the doorway.

"I dragged him to another cell," Huck said. "Look, we have to go. I brought ward stones for you, but they don't make us invisible. We should leave before someone sees us."

"You have a stone imbued with my blood?" Demi asked. "Give it to me." She didn't know how to make Huck understand. Leocort had been kind to her. She wouldn't let him suffer, not because of her.

Holding out her hand in the darkness, she felt the small weight of two stones drop into her palm.

"I'm not sure which is which," Huck said.

"Take me to him," she said, then added, "Please."

To his credit, the druid only gave a small grumble before following her instructions and leading her past the empty watch station. His hand was meaty and rough, but she relished his touch. Only then did she realise how long it had been since she'd touched another person.

They ducked into another cell on the opposite side. "He's in here," Huck said. "Can you see?"

"No," she told him.

"On the floor. About three feet in front of you towards the left wall."

"Guide me," she said. The last thing she wanted was to kick Leocort in the head.

Huck did as she asked and took her into the room. "Right in front of you," he said.

Demi crouched and extended her hand, reaching for the faerie's still form. She found his chest first, and she groped around until she followed his arm up to his face. His skin was still warm. He was alive.

"Leocort," she whispered. "Leocort, please." She took one of the stones, the one that resonated with her magic, and she pressed the rock against the side of his neck. The process was more difficult with someone who didn't share her blood, but she had to try. "What did you do to him?" she asked Huck.

"Goddammit, Demi," Huck said. "With the crowds and the guards, it's taken me more than a day to get here. I'm trying to save your life. Can we leave, please?"

"He knows where Jago is."

"So do I," Huck told her. "I was allowed to visit him the day I came to see you, remember?"

Demi still couldn't leave until she knew Leocort wasn't dead on her account. "What did you do to the Watcher?" she repeated.

Huck didn't answer at first, but then said, "I hit him on the head." A pause. "A couple of times. He's tougher than you'd think."

Demi had never healed more than one of Jago's occasional scraped knees. Even though Lisle had insisted the magic was safe, Demi had feared using the flows would alert the faerie who had hunted her for so many years. She understood the fear to be unreasonable, but she refused to take risks with Jago's safety.

Allowing the stone to guide the flows, she stopped the small amount of bleeding, but she had no idea what to do about the probable concussion. Anything she might try could make his injury worse. "Oh, Leocort. I'm so sorry," she said. "I never wanted you to get hurt."

His eyes fluttered open, shining green in the darkened cell. "I hear you," he croaked. "But I cannot look at you. Why do I not see you? Is this druid magic?"

"Yes," she said. "Is Jago still at the nursery where Huck and Munro first saw him?"

"No," he replied.

"Where is he?"

"I cannot betray my queen. I'm sorry."

Huck stepped forward. "I'll get him to tell us," he said, his voice terrifyingly flat and grim.

"No!" she shouted, then winced at how the sound echoed. Lowering her voice to a whisper, she hissed, "We're not going to hurt anyone."

"I know what happened in Amsterdam," Huck said. "How long before another *accident*? How long will Jago be safe? If this guy knows where your son is, don't you think we should use whatever means necessary to find out?"

Demi pressed her eyes closed and breathed. "No," she said. "Leocort was kind to me. I won't repay him by beating information out of him."

"Even if it saves your son?" Huck asked.

"Wait outside, please," Demi said.

Huck grumbled and strode towards the entry, but he didn't go through.

"You healed me," Leocort said weakly.

"I tried. My gifts are undeveloped. There are stories of great healers in my family, but I don't know their methods. I was always too afraid to explore the flows more. They reminded me too much of Ulrich. I learned what I believed would protect us and nothing more."

"It would be easier on me if you let your companion torture the information out of me. I could tell you what you want to know without betraying my queen. I want to help you," he said. "I have from the beginning."

"I know." Demi sighed. "You're a good person. You brought me flowers and told me stories. You gave me blankets and kept me company. You didn't have to do any of that. I'm sorry for your injury."

Huck interrupted. "We have to hurry, Demi. This isn't a game."

Anger surged within her. "You think I don't understand the stakes?" she hissed. Thoughts buzzed in her head. How could she convince Leocort to help her? "Leave with us," she said. "Come be a part of the Druid Hall. There must be lots of faeries there, right, Huck?"

"Yeah, there are. Stewards, scholars, teachers, scribes, cleaners, builders, gardeners, cooks...I've lost track of everyone that lives there," Huck said.

"No Watchers though," Leocort said.

Demi put her hand on his face. "You'll be the first. You can work for me if you want. Do whatever you please. Be my Watcher or become something new." She paused and bowed her head. "Even if you won't tell me where Jago is. I owe you this much. You were kind to me. I'll protect you from Konstanze."

He laughed weakly. "You amaze me, my lady druid," he said, then after a pause added, "Your boy was moved to the castle."

"Why?" Panic almost choked her. "Did something happen?"

"I don't know," he said. "It is unusual for an infant under ten years to live outside the nursery compound."

Tears stung at her eyes, but Demi blinked them back. Now wasn't the time.

"Where exactly in the castle?" Huck asked.

Leocort hesitated. "I could find out. Do you trust me?"

"Yes," Demi said.

"No," Huck said at the exact same moment.

"Can you stand?" Demi asked, extending her hand to help him up.

"Yes, my lady druid," he said. "I think so." He clasped her forearm and she lifted him to his feet. A dim light appeared in the room. Leocort stepped back a few paces. "If I may say so, your aura is most disturbing. How have you altered it?"

"Come to the Druid Hall, and I will show you anything you want about my magic. For now, I need to reach my son."

"Of course," he said. He gave a wary glance towards Huck, but quickly lowered his eyes. "At least now I don't feel so foolish that you managed to sneak up on me. I thought I heard something, but I felt a strong compulsion to resist turning around."

Huck peered into the corridor. "Is there anyone else nearby?"

"Not immediately, but as we go deeper in, we'll encounter others. Stay in the shadows and follow. I suspect your magic will shield you well, at least for now."

"Deeper in?" Huck said. Suspicion rang in his voice. "Why would you want us to go farther into the holding area? Isn't going out and around closer?"

"If we go through the cells and past the Watcher's keep, the distance upward to the royal living quarters isn't far. I suspect the boy is somewhere in there, either in the queen's wing or possibly in the guest area. I'll stop at the Watcher's keep to learn what I can."

"Are there any other Watchers we can trust?" Demi asked.

"No, my lady druid. Konstanze inspires great loyalty."

"But not in you?" Huck said, a challenge in the question.

Leocort gingerly touched the back of his head where Huck's heavy blows had landed. "My daughter is a scholar. She aspires to become a keeper someday. The keepers support the druids' claim, and she trusts her mentors' judgement."

"And you trust hers," Demi said.

"Yes. She believes your people are important to our race and accepts your claim to the title draoidh," he hesitated, trying and failing to meet Demi and Huck's eyes. "I hope they are right." Flicking his gaze to the door, he walked along. "Stay here a moment. I'll scout ahead."

He slipped into the corridor, and Huck glared at Demi. "I hope your trust in this clown doesn't get us killed. He might be going for backup. He might return with fifty faeries. If that happens, all the ward stones in the world won't help us. All he has to do is throw a shield over this door, and we're stuck."

Worry churned at Demi's stomach. Had she made a terrible mistake? She opened her mouth to respond, but Leocort reappeared. "The way is clear," he said. "Stay in the shadows. The most dangerous part will be the keep. Once we come close to the Watcher base, walk confidently and don't hesitate, even for a moment. With a bit of luck, no one will want to look at you."

"The effect of our ward stones is limited," Huck told him. "If someone sees us from a distance, they'll not have any problems recognising exactly who we are and what we're doing."

Leocort raised an eyebrow. "Interesting," he said. "Very well. We'll avoid open areas. That'll mean going around the central hall of the keep, but that's easily done."

"All right," Demi said. "Let's go get my boy."

∞

Munro let attendants help him put on the finely embellished tunic Eilidh had picked out for the ceremony. The whole process struck him as an elaborately staged farce. In all the time he'd lived with Eilidh in the Otherworld, he'd never been as acutely aware of her royal status as he was at that moment. In his younger days, he'd envisioned himself having a simple civil ceremony. But even in his bachelorhood back in Scotland, he'd understood, deep down, he'd be unlikely to get that wish. He'd compromise, he'd told himself. He'd planned to agree to a hundred or so of his and his then-unknown bride's closest friends and family. Maybe have a nice reception over at the Huntingtower Hotel.

He blew out a sigh as nimble fingers wrapped a sash around his middle. Really? A sash? A hundred of their closest friends seemed a distant dream. A hundred wouldn't even count the stewards and attendants involved in this production.

Although it was her second wedding, Eilidh didn't seem any more relaxed than he was. Oh, outwardly she was lovely and gracious. But she kept sending little messages telepathically, sometimes reminding him they had to hurry to a new location, festival, or feast, or things like, *Why have none of the druids come?* or *Try not to look as though you're in pain.* Fortunately for both of them, he couldn't reply the same way, or he'd be tempted to tell her to can it. They were both nervous. And having all those other queens around with their entourages didn't help.

The smiling and waving and acknowledging the cheering crowds when they went from place to place...his face hurt from the plastered smile. He was tired. And they hadn't even had the actual ceremony yet.

"Your boots, my lord druid," one of the attendants said with that eternally patient tone the servants often used with him.

"What?" He looked down and saw the faerie was holding out a pair of elegant leather boots. Elegant. Him. Seriously. He would never let Eilidh pick his clothes again. He'd drawn the line at flowers in his hair. No bloody way. "Right," he said. He took the boots and sat down, shoving his right foot into one and then his left into the other. The attendant looked politely appalled. Munro fought not to roll his eyes. He was *not* letting some guy put his boots on for him. "Now what?" he asked.

"This way, my lord druid," the attendant said. The whole affair was so choreographed. The upside, however, was Munro didn't need to remember anything. The attendant led Munro into a long corridor. The green of the forests shone beyond a graceful arch festooned with tiny pink roses. They walked down the hall, followed by dozens of other attendants and servants. Why, he had no idea. He walked, and they followed.

Once they arrived outside, thousands of faces greeted him. The scene reminded him of a sea of faeries. Sparkling lights wove through moonbeams on a central dais and danced in flowing swirls.

"Her Majesty will approach from the other side. You meet in the middle," the attendant explained as though Munro were a very dim-witted child.

"Right," Munro said. Of course, someone had walked him through all this before, but he hadn't been paying much attention. He scrubbed his hand through his hair and turned to the attendant. He had planned to ask something, but his mind went blank.

"May the Mother bless your union," the attendant said and bowed. Munro stared at him, then back at all the others, who mimicked the motion.

"Thanks," he said, ignoring the flicker of amusement on their faces. He knew he must look a right idiot, but this was for Eilidh. He could stand wearing this preposterous getup in front of two thousand of the most influential people in Caledonia and from across the Otherworld kingdoms if it made her happy. That didn't even include the tens of thousands of common faeries who lined the streets to catch a glimpse of them when they departed the castle. His legs carried him forward. He didn't remember taking the steps, but somehow, he managed without staggering like a drunk.

When he came closer, he recognised Elder Oron waiting for him on the dais. Oron had been Eilidh's mentor before she became queen and was now her most trusted ally on the Caledonian joint-conclave. Her father and mother, whom Munro barely knew but had met a few times, and a couple other faeries she counted as her closest friends were also with them. The one face that surprised him was Prince

Griogair's. Munro didn't mind Eilidh's other husband. In fact, they were pretty good friends. They'd saved each other's asses more than once, and were both committed to Eilidh, heart and soul. Even still, Munro hadn't expected him to stand on the dais with them.

As Munro approached, Griogair moved to meet him at the bottom of the steps. In a low voice he said, "Eilidh asked me to be ready, in the event the other druid lords were unable to attend. It would be most awkward to have no one stand for you during the ceremony."

Oron cast Griogair a glare. Munro remembered someone saying that no one except the officiator was supposed to talk on the dais. Technically, they weren't on the dais yet, so Munro ignored the look.

"Thanks. They didn't show?" Munro replied. He'd been kept so busy, being ushered from place to place the previous day and night, he had no idea none of his friends had come. Anxiety flickered through his mind.

"No." Griogair seemed worried. "And something else. There have been ripples." Munro glanced over at Eilidh, who was just stepping up from the other side. She looked resplendent in a sapphire blue gown shimmering with diamonds.

"Ripples in what?" Munro asked Griogair, both men's eyes fixed on Eilidh.

Griogair tore his gaze away and gave Munro a minute shake of his head. "In the Otherworld."

Munro tried to mask his surprise, certain this meant something was happening with the druids and their work with the Source Stone. He should be there. He glanced up at Eilidh. Despite her smile, her hidden concern heaved through their connection. "Why is no one reacting?" Munro whispered.

Griogair gave a tiny shrug. "Only the strongest will have sensed the undercurrent so far, and the disturbance has been intermittent. It started about an hour ago."

The druids had to be responsible. In their investigation with the Source Stone, they had either discovered something important or their attempts had gone wrong. Nothing else would have kept them away. "We have to go on with the ceremony," Munro said, knowing Huck counted on them to keep Konstanze and her entourage from returning to Ashkyne as long as possible.

"Precisely what my mate said," Griogair chuckled. They turned towards Eilidh and began to ascend the steps. The prince whispered, "Soon to be your mate as well, my friend. I am proud to stand with you."

Munro gave him a grateful glance. "Thanks." He looked up at Eilidh, and a smile tugged on his lips. Even with so many crazy things happening all around them, tonight was a good night. Finally, after all this time, she'd be his wife.

When the two men reached the top of the dais, Munro reached for Eilidh's hands. He took them and kissed the backs of each one. "I love you," he said softly.

Oron grumbled. "You aren't supposed to speak yet," he muttered.

Eilidh grinned. "I love you too." Her silver eyes shone in the moonlight.

Munro turned to Oron. "Okay. Let's do this, then."

The elder shook his head with dismay, but amusement shone in his eyes. He raised his voice and intoned formally, "Under the blessing of the Mother of the Earth and the watchful guard of the Father of the Sky, I bind these two in thought, spirit, and flesh." Oron lifted his hand and recited an incantation in the ancient fae tongue.

Everyone else disappeared for Munro. The worries faded to the background. His skin tingled as the joining magic danced around them. He'd understood faerie mating ceremonies weren't merely a formality, that he was entering a compelling magical contract, but he'd not anticipated the depth of the experience. As Oron spoke, Munro's will and commitment to the union were tested. He may have spoken. He wasn't certain.

Sudden silence swept around them. A reverent hush quieted the crowd as lights danced. Time seemed to stand still. Only the Elder's voice, reciting words Munro didn't understand, made him aware any time had passed at all.

"Quinton?" Eilidh said after Oron's voice faded away.

"Yes?" he replied, feeling slightly dazed.

"It's time to go," she said. "Are you ready?"

"The ceremony's over?" he asked.

With a musical laugh, she said, "Yes. Come. Now time for the fun part." She laid her hand on his forearm. "Or am I going to have to guide you to the tents where we'll disrobe? You appear slightly stunned."

"Oh, no," Munro said. "This part I'm ready for." He reached over and swept her into his arms and kissed her. A cheer went up around the crowd.

Eilidh flushed. Even still, she'd enjoyed the kiss as much as he had. She opened her mouth to speak, but then she suddenly paled and stiffened. Panic stabbed through her aura.

"What's wrong?" Munro asked. Gasps sounded around them.

"I don't know," Eilidh said. "Another ripple. This time, *much* stronger."

She looked at Oron, who snapped his fingers at one of the nearby attendants. "Gather the conclave," he said. He turned to Eilidh. "Your security is paramount, Your Majesty. We should get you to safety until we know what's happening."

The ground trembled beneath their feet, and the crowd's mood shifted. What had been a happy celebration suddenly felt like a barn full of horses had been spooked in a thunderstorm.

Munro hated to even consider leaving, but he had little choice. "I should go to the Halls of Mist," he told her. "Will you come with me?"

She glanced towards the crowd and shook her head. "My people need me. If I leave, they might panic. When you know what's going on, send word. I'll join you when I can."

Munro didn't like it, but they both had obligations. He kissed her again. "I'll see you soon. I promise. We have unfinished business," he said quietly.

Be careful, she sent to his mind as he rushed down the steps and through the frightened crowd.

CHAPTER 21

DEMI HELD HUCK'S HAND as they stood in utter darkness, pressed against a cold stone wall, waiting for Leocort to appear from the other side of the keep. She could hear Huck's breathing, even though she couldn't see him. Turning her face towards him, she whispered, "Thank you."

His eyes cast a strange glow when he looked in her direction. He blinked slowly and squeezed her hand.

They'd gotten past the keep with little trouble, doing exactly as Leocort instructed them. Once or twice, Watchers had wandered in their direction. The first time, the faerie shuddered as he walked right by them. The second time, the guard approached, but hesitated, then turned around as though he remembered he needed to be somewhere else. The two druids had been lucky. As Huck said, the wards didn't render them invisible.

After several minutes past, Demi shifted her weight. "He's taking too long," she said quietly. "He might be in trouble."

"He's adult faerie, with more magic in his little finger than you or I will master in a lifetime. He can take care of himself," he whispered. "If he doesn't return soon, we'll find our own way."

"I can't leave him behind. I don't want him to suffer for my escape."

Huck didn't answer. She suspected he thought she was being sentimental for no reason, especially considering what was at stake. But reaching out to Leocort felt right to her. He was more than her jailor. In only a few days, he'd become her friend. The situation was strange and unlikely. Before her arrest, she'd never known any faerie but Ulrich. He hadn't inspired anything but fear of his race.

The sound of voices came from farther down the corridor, slowly growing louder. "Why are you asking about the boy?"

"The human woman will die tonight. I think it's only right that she goes to the Mother knowing her boy is well." Demi recognised Leocort's voice.

"So tell her as much," came the sharp reply.

"Would the statement be true?"

"What does it matter? She killed our prince."

"Lies do not become our race, Avin."

The approaching faeries drew close. If they stepped any further, they'd walk right into Huck and Demi. She began to inch away, but Huck squeezed her hand and pulled her closer. What was he doing? Demi trembled with pent-up anxiety.

"The boy is alive," Avin said.

"Alive? Why wouldn't he be? Do you mean he is in danger of *not* surviving?"

The second faerie hesitated. "You should tell the prisoner her son is well. We do not need her causing trouble."

"Are you worried that she can? The queen said she is nothing but a human, that the druids' claims to an ancient heritage are false."

"The child has begun weeping blood," the faerie said. "Our healers have tended to him, but can find nothing wrong." He paused. "He has grown inconsolable." He lowered his voice, and Demi strained to hear. "Even the queen is afraid of him."

"What is she planning to do?" Leocort asked.

"She said she'll deal with the child after she returns from Caledonia. There are rumours that she believes the druids' story that Ulrich had ill magic. I'd not doubt the tales myself. I served as his personal guard for a time. I could tell you stories about him that would shrivel your rod for a century."

"I've heard some malicious talk," Leocort said. "No ill magic could sully the royal bloodline. It's impossible to conceive of such a thing."

"Of course," Avin said. "I'm merely relating what I've heard."

"I'll forget this conversation, my friend, but I'd caution you not to repeat baseless gossip."

Feet shuffled on the stone floor in the adjacent corridor, then one set of footfalls moved in the other direction. She prayed that the faerie who'd remained stationary was Leocort and not his companion.

After a long moment, he spoke. "I sense your presence only because I can't will myself to move around this corner."

"We're here," Demi said.

Leocort finally stepped into the intersection. "You overheard?" he asked. His expression was strained and he looked away from the pair.

"Yes," Demi said. "How long before the queen returns?"

"I don't know," he said. "The ceremony should be taking place now. I would expect Queen Konstanze to return shortly thereafter. She will not wish to be in Caledonia come sunrise." He paused. "Do you know what is wrong with your boy?"

She feared Leocort would not help her if he knew Jago had blood magic. Ulrich had told her clearly that only gifts of water, stone, earth, and air were accepted in the Otherworld. Because her druidic abilities hadn't developed until they met, she'd had no difficulty in hiding her barely emerging blood talents from him. "Jago has never cried tears of blood before," she said carefully. "Is it possible this is the result of some magic Konstanze has done?"

Leocort's forehead crinkled as he frowned. "Come," he said. "The darkest hour of the night is passing. If someone discovers our absence..." His voice trailed off. His blue skin paled.

"What's wrong?" Demi rushed towards him. She supported him as his legs faltered. "Does your head injury trouble you?"

Leocort looked past her, to Huck. "This is druid magic," he said.

She glanced over, but Huck's expression was unreadable in the dim light.

"We should hurry," Huck said flatly.

The faerie nodded. He stood upright. Whatever had caused him to falter passed. With obvious effort, he walked past the two druids. "Follow me," he said. "Quietly."

Taking a wending route through the maze of corridors beneath the castle, Huck and Demi stayed close to Leocort. When other faeries approached, they hung back, but no one challenged them. They came to a spiral stone staircase.

Again, Leocort staggered, but caught himself on the wooden rail. He glanced at Huck. "Am I not helping you?" he asked. "Why are you doing this?"

"Whatever you're experiencing isn't my work," Huck said, "but that of my comrades. They are summoning the Source Stone."

Leocort paled even further, his skin taking on a green-tinged, sickly hue. "They are draoidh," he said.

Huck tilted his head. "Of course. Isn't that why you're helping us?"

"Yes, my lord druid," Leocort said. Gathering his strength, he led them upward.

On each landing, the group paused as Leocort kept an eye out for danger. Watchers and servants went about their duties in the corridors, but Demi noticed they all had an uncertain look about them, as though they were afraid. The source of their disturbance was unclear, but anything that improved the chance that Jago's guards would be distracted or disabled suited her fine.

Leocort guided them to the top of the stairs. He nodded to the end of the corridor, where two Watchers stood on either side of an enormous arch. "Beyond are the queen's personal chambers."

"Where will Jago be?" Demi asked.

"Somewhere close, I think. She may fear him, but he is still of royal blood," Leocort said. He gestured to the opposite end of the hall. "Walk that direction. Slow and erect, like soldiers. No one should bother you. But don't turn back. I'll establish where the queen is keeping the boy."

Demi and Huck did as Leocort instructed. She fought the urge to turn and watch him as he approached the guards at the queen's door. At the far end, she and Huck came to an alcove and he pulled her within. With a swipe of his hand, Huck extinguished the torch flame behind them. "We'll wait here," he said. "I don't want to wander too far without him."

Suddenly the ground shook beneath their feet. Huck braced himself against the wall and pulled Demi close. "Earthquake?" she asked.

"I don't think so," Huck said. "Leocort is right. You can tell by the faeries' expressions around here something is up. I hope this means the other druids have found a way to stop Konstanze." He glanced at a passing faerie's stricken expression. When she'd gotten out of earshot, he said, "I also hope they can do whatever they have to without bringing the castle down on top of us."

Worry clouded her mind and grew stronger as they waited. Her desperate fear shredded any hope of patience. She needed to hold her Jago, tell him everything would be okay.

Irregular footfalls approached, and Demi's alarm rose. She stepped out of the alcove, only to see Leocort stumbling towards them. Rushing to him, she said, "What happened?"

He stared at her, puzzled. "Can you not feel the heaving of the flows?"

Demi shook her head. "Our magic is different from yours."

"It's as though the Otherworld is tearing in two."

A child's scream sounded nearby. Without a second thought, Demi broke into a run, hurtling down the corridor towards the sound of her son's voice. She heard Leocort groaning in pain behind her and the sounds of other faeries in the vicinity, all clearly in distress. "I'm coming, Jago," she called out. "Mama's coming."

∞

Aaron and Lisle ran towards the main courtyard of the Halls of Mist, following the young scholar sent to fetch them. As they stepped off the bridge, a hard tremor knocked them forward, and Lisle tumbled to the ground. Aaron's heart thumped in his chest. If that had happened even five seconds earlier, he would have finally learned how deep those foggy chasms below extended.

"Hurry, my lord druid," the faerie called, helping Lisle to her feet.

Aaron didn't like that the old lady had been summoned too. She'd never touched the Source Stone, and its magic would likely overwhelm her. If the scholar hadn't insisted all available druids of the Hall were required urgently, Aaron would have voiced his objections.

Ahead, huge arcs of electricity flared from the portal, extending beyond the main courtyard. The young scholar froze. "We can't get past that."

"Bollocks," Aaron said. He didn't like the charges the portal emitted, but neither was he prepared to turn back. "I'll go first," he said.

"My lord druid!" the faerie shouted, but Aaron had already broken into a run, heading for the runed pillars of the library entrance. He turned, one hand on a pillar, the other motioning for Lisle to come ahead. She couldn't run well. When she approached, Aaron swept forward and scooped her up, carrying her the rest of the way as a flare of light warped past. Aaron glanced back at the messenger.

The faerie inhaled deeply, then nodded, sprinting towards the druids with the natural speed of his race. Three steps in, an electrical burst struck him square on the chest.

"Shit," Aaron said. Releasing Lisle, he ran back, arriving in time to catch the young scholar as he crumpled. A treacherous light show flashed around him. Aaron tucked his shoulder down and slung the faerie over it, then carried him fireman-style to the library entrance.

Navigating the many narrow stairs to the hall below took more time than Aaron believed they had to lose. Alarm hurried him downward to the wide, open chamber of the library, with Lisle trailing silently behind.

When Aaron finally staggered in, faeries rushed forward to relieve him of his burden. "What happened?" one asked, carefully guiding the scholar's limp form to the ground.

"The portal is shooting out lightning," Aaron said. "You'll stay with him? We have to get below."

"Yes, my lord druid," she said, putting her slender fingers on the scholar's face. "We will care for him well."

"Thanks," he said, but her attention was elsewhere as she urgently snapped her fingers for two others nearby to assist her.

Aaron showed Lisle to the hidden stair that would take them below. With each step, the heavy pulse of the Source Stone throbbed waves of pressure in his chest. "You might get overwhelmed," he said to Lisle. "Don't let that worry you."

"What is happening?" she asked.

He ignored the question, instead moving as fast as possible to the Stone's chamber. He wasn't sure anyone knew what was happening.

He burst in, pushing his way past the keepers, who surrounded the Stone and chanted rhythmically. Glancing back, he saw the old woman more politely weaving through the crowd. Finally, they both arrived at the centre of the room. The Stone was raised and glowing. Douglas and Rory knelt on either side of the artefact. Sweat beaded on their skin. Their taut faces and clenched jaws showed their struggle.

Aaron went to the far side and knelt between them. "What's happened?" he shouted over the droning keepers.

Douglas strained to look at him, as though fighting the will of the Stone. "It doesn't like being told what to do," he said.

"It's breaking apart," Rory shouted. "If we let go, or they stop, the Stone will shatter."

"Jesus," Aaron said. The throbbing of the Stone's magic made his head swim.

"If the artefact breaks," Douglas said, "the Otherworld kingdoms will be splintered forever. Everyone will be cut off."

Aaron's gut tightened. Hundreds of thousands, if not millions, could die. He put his hands on the Stone, and a jolt shuddered through him. His teeth ached and his eyes bulged. With some effort, he linked with Douglas and Rory. They'd successfully joined before, but this time, the Stone fought them. He'd never experienced anything like this, never would have believed a talisman could have a will of its own, even a strong, ancient artefact like the Source Stone.

He looked up at Lisle, who stood in front of the keepers, her bright eyes fixed on the Stone. She'd proven herself a talented, capable druid, helping them when they crafted the portal. He didn't think they could have succeeded without her. Now they needed her again. "Lisle!" he shouted. She looked up at him. "Lisle! Come touch the Stone. We have to hold it together!"

The old woman knelt and, with only a moment's hesitation, put her hands on the surface. Aaron felt her energy quickly join with the men's, as though she'd been linking all her life. She shuddered with pleasure at the touch of the Stone's power. He cursed to himself. Lisle was a strong druid, yes, but inexperienced with the Stone. She'd never be able to resist its overwhelming magic the first time. Her presence in the link could make things worse.

"Imbeciles!" she shouted, her eyes gleaming. "You take without sacrifice."

Aaron's eyes clamped shut as the entire room shuddered.

Lisle looked around the room, but she didn't seem to find what she was searching for. With effort, she pulled her hand back and bit down on her palm. Breathing hard, she groaned with the effort. When she took her palm away from her mouth, blood covered both.

"What are you doing?" Aaron asked.

She put her fingers back to the Stone and then repeated the ritual with the other hand. Through their link, Aaron experienced the pain in his own palms. Nausea rose in his stomach as the Stone responded to her blood. The tremors stopped, but the throbbing of magic didn't abate. Instead, the flows turned and swirled around Lisle and, through their link, the other druids.

Sweat dripped down her nose and splashed onto the Stone's surface. Her expression grew wild with the power coursing through her. "Give to the Stone," she said. He removed his hand and began to put it to his mouth, but she stopped him. "No, offer your magic. Feed the Stone."

"How?" Rory asked, his features tight with strain.

"Every time you have come here, you have taken from the Stone. Reverse the current. This is the only way to heal the artefact."

Aaron felt a surge in the link between the four druids, and Lisle guided them expertly through the heaving flows.

When he turned his focus away from his own experience and shifted to the Stone itself, he sensed Lisle's blood, their combined sweat, the warmth of their flesh on its surface. The Stone ached.

Douglas' magic coursed first. Cool water streamed from below his hands and wormed to the centre of the Stone's surface, where the fluid met Lisle's blood. Aaron and Rory followed the younger druid's lead. But instead of the fusing liquid splashing to the floor, the Stone absorbed the solution thirstily.

A great sadness swept over Aaron, emanating from the Stone. The sensation tore at his heart and wracked his body. His soul keened and tears sprang from his eyes, splashing on the smooth rock, which took each drop within.

Injured, but sated, the Stone relented and quieted.

"Now," Lisle said in a soft whisper. "Inquire, but do not demand."

"What should we ask it?" They had to be careful. Their truce with the Stone was precarious.

Douglas leaned forward and spoke gently to the Stone. "The queen of Ashkyne has denied the draoidh," he said. "She seeks to destroy us and the Keepers of the Stone, who support us. She must be weakened, or neither we nor your keepers will survive."

The Stone turned slowly beneath their hands and a loud grating noise of rock against rock filled the chamber. Even the keepers grew silent.

The druids waited, perplexed and anxious.

"What's it doing?" Rory asked.

Douglas shook his head and glanced at Lisle. "Thinking," she said.

Aaron frowned. Powerful artefact or no, rocks don't think, not even magically imbued rocks.

Suddenly, the keepers ducked as lights shot outward from the Stone and swirled around the room. They forked like tendrils, twisting and seeking the runes on the surrounding walls. One by one, the threads of light tapped various symbols.

Douglas read them out. "The peaks of Ashkyne must not end (cease, die). The kingdom holds too much heart (life, blood). The Stone must not break."

"Jesus," Aaron whispered. Turning his attention to the Stone itself, he spoke. "We don't want you to destroy Ashkyne. Maybe just forget about it for a little bit?"

The Stone turned again, and one light streamed outward. The beam touched a symbol on the wall. Aaron turned to Douglas. "What does it say?" he asked.

Douglas looked at the symbol, then met Aaron's gaze. "Forgotten," he said.

As soon as the word slipped out of his mouth, the Stone sank into the ground, inch by inch. The druids' link melted, and the four of them sat in stunned silence.

"It didn't break," Douglas said. He closed his eyes, his relief evident.

"Well done, boy," Lisle said. She sat back on her heels, looking drained, traces of blood still smearing her face.

"We couldn't have done it without you," Aaron admitted. "Again." Her resilience when dealing with an artefact that had overwhelmed the others impressed him.

Lisle tried to stand, but faltered.

One of the keepers darted forward and caught her. "My lady druid," he said with reverence. "We can assist you back to the Druid Hall to rest, or offer you a place here."

She smiled briefly, but her expression quickly turned serious. "We don't have time," she said,

"First, we have to figure out what we've done." She made an effort to stand on her own, but her knees buckled.

Aaron said to the keeper, "Please take the lady druid somewhere safe to rest." He cut off Lisle's protest with a wave of his hand. "You proved more capable than anyone before. Every single one of us collapsed after touching the Stone for the first time. And here you are, standing and talking. We need you too much to let you drive yourself further than your body can withstand."

She sighed and nodded. "Very well. But call me if you're going to break the Otherworld again."

A smile came to his face unbidden. "I promise." He admired her grit.

CHAPTER 22

MUNRO SPED AS FAST AS POSSIBLE towards the portal to the Halls of Mist. Many of the foreign guests, including most of the royals, followed. Their voices occasionally rose in alarm behind him as further tremors rippled through the ground. Relief flooded over him when he finally glimpsed the portal's familiar blue glow ahead.

A few metres closer, however, and he realised this was not the serene globe of light he expected. The Watchers who guarded the portal had backed away from the immense round platform. Cracking bolts of lightning shot out, arcing to the earth and juttering to and fro.

By the time Munro drew near, the other queens and their entourages had caught up with him. A familiar voice came from just behind him. "My lord druid," said the young faerie.

Munro turned to see who'd spoken. "Tràth?" Griogair's son's presence surprised him. "What are you doing here? You should be with Eilidh and your father."

Tràth frowned at the angry portal. "Douglas is through there."

Munro instantly understood. The separation must have proved difficult for Tràth, considering how infrequently he and his bonded druid lived apart. Passing through the portal dampened Munro's connection to Eilidh much more than if one of them were merely in the human realm. He had to assume Tràth and Douglas experienced the same difficulty.

"Do you know what's happened?" Tràth asked.

When Munro opened his mouth to answer, he noticed several of the queens listening. He glanced at Tràth and gave a minute shake of his head as though to say *not here*.

The faerie signalled his understanding with a subtle gesture.

"Yes, what is going on?" Konstanze demanded, stepping forward from the crowd. "Your druids have something to do with this," she said.

Munro turned slowly, looking her up and down and raising an eyebrow, but saying nothing.

"Why are none of your people here?" she asked. "I find their absence at the precise moment something damages the portal to the Halls of Mist most suspicious."

Resisting the temptation to tell her to shut up required all Munro's willpower. He crossed his arms in front of his chest and stared straight at the leaping flows of the portal. Despite wanting to annoy Konstanze, the sight did worry him. What if they were cut off forever? If he'd missed the wedding, Eilidh would never have forgiven him, but he felt he should have been with the other druids. Maybe if he had stayed and helped, they could have avoided whatever had disrupted the portal.

He shoved that foolish notion aside. He wasn't the most important or the most powerful of the druids. Although he might have been the one to bring them to Caledonia, the others had proven at least as talented as he.

Konstanze's eyes flashed with anger. "Have you forgotten who I am?" she asked. When he didn't answer, she laughed shrilly. "And what about your little friend? The one who murdered my brother?" She glanced at those watching. "Did you refuse to meet my demands for her release because you understood her guilt and agreed with my sentence? Or was your pride greater than your honour?" Konstanze shook her head and tutted at him. "It's a pity that you'll take your queen down with you."

"Your brother? The sadistic bastard who got off on beating up women?"

"Lies!" she shouted. A strong wind buffeted out from her and shoved Munro back several steps. He stared at her. He hadn't expected a physical attack, but she looked poised to strike again, despite the onlookers' gasps of surprise.

Tràth stepped between them. The young prince waved a hand and a glimmering shield of air appeared around Munro. "Your Majesty, in your understandable grief for your brother, you forget yourself."

The other faeries backed away, careful to avoid the charged portal. A man in formal regalia approached Konstanze from the side and whispered in her ear. She shook her head sharply and waved him back.

Munro felt sorry for Konstanze, even though she was the source of his present problems. Had she not known what her brother was? Or had she known all too well and spent her life covering for him? Before Ulrich's death, the druids had gotten along fine with the Ashkynen queen. That one event unravelled so much.

Konstanze moved forward, so close she nearly touched Tràth. "I stayed my hand until after the ceremony out of courtesy to your mate. Queen Eilidh is not without charm…or power. But know this: the moment I return to my kingdom, the human murderess is dead." Her shimmering pale lips curled into a smirk. She lowered her voice to a scarcely audible level. A sudden shift in the air kept the sound close and prevented anyone from overhearing. "Her and her demon child."

"You would kill a faerie child?" Munro said, incredulous.

Her eyes sparkled with delight at his reaction. "A lethfae child," she corrected him. "The offspring of a murderess and a cruel, despicable faerie. My brother was a waste of royal seed. What possible reason would I have to want the abomination to live?"

Munro stared, speechless. He'd understood she was ruthless and angry, but he hadn't anticipated she might kill the boy.

"All you have to do," she said, her voice a sickening purr, "is make right the portal and allow me and my people to pass unharmed. When we arrive safely in the Halls of Mist, denounce your false draoidh claims. The woman and her child will become your problem. Keep them in Caledonia, away from my people, and I will pursue them no further."

Munro wondered what had happened to make her give up her claim on the boy. Her closed expression gave away nothing.

Long moments passed, the pair of them staring at one another with Tràth between them. Others from all the kingdoms watched from a barely discreet distance.

When he looked in her eyes, he believed she meant what she said. She would kill a four-year-old. The threat to execute Demi sickened him, but he understood Konstanze's desire for revenge. With no evidence indicating Demi hadn't committed murder, plus her confession, his hands were tied. But to kill a child? Out of pure, vicious spite? Out of anger that Eilidh had been granted the lands Konstanze assumed would go to Ashkyne?

He glanced away, repulsed. How could he not do as she demanded? How could he justify allowing her to kill a small child when he had the power to stop her by saying a few words? Surely a temporary lie was worth saving the boy. Even if it meant a setback in the druids' relationship with the fae, he had to pay that price.

He glanced up at the portal over her shoulder. The events in the Halls of Mist that confounded the portal were out of his control. All he had to do was convince her on that point. Then he'd say whatever she wanted, at least until he brought Demi and Jago safely to Caledonia.

The ground shuddered hard, then suddenly stilled. Voices around him chattered. Konstanze beamed with triumph. The portal shimmered calmly, as though the disruption had never happened.

∞

Huck stayed close behind as Demi rushed towards Jago's wailing. Other faeries raced by in the chaos. They ignored the pair, either repelled by the ward stones or too wrapped up in whatever magical force so severely disrupted their equilibrium.

Demi paused at a door which was surrounded by four Watchers. The floor had stopped trembling, but they still appeared weak and sickly. Without a thought to her safety, she ran past them. They didn't even come out of their stupor long enough to question her.

Huck followed her in. Jago lay on a bed on the far side of the room, moaning loudly. Demi let out a strangled cry as she hurried to him. Brown smears of dried blood covered the boy's pillow. Fresh red droplets balanced on his eyelashes. She scooped him up into her arms and murmured to him in German.

The child's arms wrapped around her and he clung to her. Rocking him back and forth, she kissed his face and held him tight.

"Is he all right?" Huck asked, frowning. Jago hadn't stopped crying.

Demi didn't reply. Clearly, she didn't want to say no, but couldn't say yes.

Huck understood and didn't press. "We need to get him out of here. I don't know what's going on, but Leocort seems to think it's druid magic. This could be the others working to help our escape." He slipped his rucksack off his shoulder and dug around inside, then pulled out the well-worn bear Lisle had given him. "Hey, little man," he said. "I've got someone here who's been missing you."

Jago's crying slowed when he caught sight of the bear. He snuffled and hiccoughed, but at least the gesture distracted him. He glanced up at Huck, his red-rimmed eyes wide. "Please," he said in English.

Huck grinned. "You bet." He handed Jago the bear, and while the boy cuddled his friend, Huck took a cloth from his pack and used it to wipe the stains from Jago's face.

"Mama?" Jago said. "I want to go home. I don't feel good."

Demi held him, worry playing across her face and drawing her forehead into a tight frown.

Although Huck had intended to take them to a gate to the human realm and to avoid the soldiers at the portal, considering Jago's state, time wasn't on their side. "I think we should head for the portal."

"Will it take us home?" Demi asked.

"Yes. To the Druid Hall." If she didn't want to make the Halls of Mist home, she could leave someday, when they were safe. They'd work that out later.

Demi nodded. "Thank you," she said.

"We have to hurry. Whatever is making the faeries sick appears to be getting worse, judging by the sounds outside."

"What about Leocort?" she asked. "Where is he?"

Huck held out his hand, and she took it. After all they'd been through, the contact seemed natural. "We'll look for him on the way out. But if he's sick, we may have to leave him behind. I can't carry him all the way to the portal." He looked into her eyes. "If a day comes when he wants to join us, I promise we'll make a place for him at the Druid Hall."

She pursed her lips but nodded.

Huck offered to carry Jago, but both mother and son refused, so he held Demi's hand as they left the chamber. The faeries who'd guarded the door lay unconscious on the floor. Huck frowned. Whatever the druids were doing, they weren't supposed to kill everyone.

He retraced their steps to the main stairway, suspecting the floor above the Watcher's keep was ground level and would have an exit.

They found Leocort at the stairwell, slumped in a corner. Huck released Demi's hand and knelt beside the Watcher. "Are you okay?" he asked, wary of even touching the ailing faerie.

Leocort's eyes fluttered open, but they stared out, glazed. "Our magic is gone," he said. "We've been severed from the source."

Huck's mind raced. Severed? He'd heard of that. Severing was a punishment used to separate a faerie from their magic, usually done, as far as he remembered, just before an execution. He'd heard it was a painful, terrible experience. "All of you?" he asked.

Leocort nodded. "None I've seen are untouched."

Huck worried for Jago. He had no idea what severing would do to a half-druid, half-fae child, but he was obviously in some distress. Worse, Huck had no clue if any damage caused was permanent, or if Jago and Leocort would be fine if Huck could get them to the

Halls of Mist. "Come on," Huck said. He leaned down and put his arm around Leocort's mid-section, then pulled the faerie to his feet.

"No," Leocort said. "I'll slow you down." His body was too weak to protest.

Huck didn't want to argue. Half-carrying the faerie *would* slow him down, but Demi would never forgive him if he didn't try to save the person who'd tried to save her. "Will you serve the Druid Hall?" Huck asked.

Leocort's eyes rolled back in his head. "Yes," he said.

"Then start by making an effort here. I'm not leaving you behind."

The stairs were the worst, but once they got to the main landing, Leocort at least attempted to carry his own weight. He leaned on the druid as little as possible, but was unable to let go.

They passed many faeries as they hobbled towards the portal. Most were unconscious, but some sat, glassy-eyed, as though their souls had been ripped from their bodies.

The group took twice as long to return to the portal's dais as Huck had needed to get to the castle in the first place. When they arrived, his hopes were crushed. The familiar blue glow of the shining portal had vanished. The dais stood empty. Those who guarded the kingdom lay motionless, like fallen soldiers.

Demi stared, her expression wild and desperate. "What will we do?" she said.

Huck exhaled. They would need half a day to travel to a gate to the human realm, even longer if Leocort's strength faded. They had no food and no options. "We wait," he said.

With a frown, Demi asked, "For what?" She began rocking Jago again.

"They know we're here. They'll open the portal again." *If they can*, Huck thought.

CHAPTER 23

WITHOUT WAITING FOR KONSTANZE or the other queens, Munro stepped into the blue haze of the portal to the Halls of Mist. She clearly believed the shift in the portal marked compliance with her demands. Fortunately, he hadn't said anything the others could interpret as a promise or admission.

The first face Munro saw was Keeper Oszlár's. The ancient faerie was flanked by druids. They all stood strangely still. Aaron exhaled with relief when he caught sight of Munro, who was immediately followed by Tràth. Douglas clapped Rory on the back. The new arrivals strode directly to the other druids. Keeping his voice low, Munro hurried to explain. "Konstanze has threatened to kill Demi and Jago the moment she gets back to Ashkyne unless we abandon the Halls of Mist. Tell me you have a plan. She's right behind us."

The druids all stared at the portal, waiting. Interestingly, no one materialised immediately. Either something had delayed them, Munro thought, or Konstanze was taking the opportunity to proclaim victory before passing through.

"What's happened? Why did the portal go down?" Munro asked.

"The whole thing was a battle, but if we're right, we convinced the Stone to temporarily cut Ashkyne off from the Source."

Munro blinked and looked to Oszlár. "What does that mean?"

The elder keeper appeared as serious and stoic as ever. "In truth, I don't know. Your brothers and sister have awoken an aspect of the Stone we haven't encountered before. In my thirteen hundred years of service to the Stone, I have never witnessed the artefact responding like this. We keepers are both astonished by what you have accomplished...and afraid."

The concern in his voice alarmed Munro. Aaron quickly sketched out their encounter with the Stone and its response.

Munro started to ask the keeper whether the discovery was a good thing. Before he could speak, the wedding guests emerged through the portal in small clusters.

None would meet his eyes. As he feared, Konstanze must have announced that the druids were a bunch of frauds parading as draoidh and had convinced them to admit their deception. Konstanze arrived last.

"Are you sure her kingdom is cut off?" he asked the other druids quietly.

Aaron nodded. "None of us could reach Ashkyne when we tried, not even Oszlár."

"Can you restore the connection?" Munro asked.

The other druids exchanged glances. Douglas said, "I think so."

"Jesus," Munro muttered. He didn't know what would happen to a kingdom cut off from the Source Stone. It might be simply like shutting a door. On the other hand, Oszlár had always spoken about the Stone as a more than an artefact, but almost like an anchor. In truth, Ashkyne might have been dying.

Konstanze stood in front of the portal, other queens and dignitaries fanning out from her on either side. "I believe you have an announcement?" She smiled maliciously.

"Yes," Munro said. "We do." He nodded, taking the measure of the other queens. Some wore expressions of curiosity, while others appeared disdainful or even disappointed. After a long moment, he regarded Konstanze. "We Druid Lords believe it is, for the present time, acceptable for you to retain your throne. Our decision comes despite your disrespect to us, to the Keepers of the Stone, and your threats against one of our Hall."

Konstanze barked an involuntary laugh, but stopped abruptly when she caught the expressions on all the druids' faces. The other queens glanced at one another in astonished puzzlement.

"Return the Druid Lady Demi Hartmann to us now, along with her son, the leth-draoidh child Jago. Do this, and we will restore your kingdom to you."

"Restore..." Her eyes flashed with anger. "Neither you nor the keepers have the right to deny any queen passage to her kingdom, nor even suggest taking her throne. The precepts of the Halls of Mist are inviolable. You have no authority."

"And the will of the Source Stone?" he asked, raising an eyebrow.

She gestured to the portal behind her. "I see no indication any gates are shifting. And why would they? I am one of the most powerful queens in the Otherworld. My position is secure." She sneered. "Unlike yours."

"We are draoidh," Munro said.

She threw back her head and laughed. "You are not even shadows of the great fae sorcerers of old. Now..." She glanced at the other queens. "I must take my leave. I have an execution to witness."

Munro bowed to her. "As you wish. Go. *If you can*."

Without even a trace of doubt on her face, she, her mate, and the others of her entourage turned back to the portal. Konstanze led them towards the shining globe of blue light and stepped inside. They remained on the platform, bathed in azure light.

They looked at one another, confused. The other queens who watched murmured in shock.

Konstanze spun around, fury contorting her features. "What have you done?" she demanded.

"The Stone bends to the will of the draoidh," Aaron said calmly.

The enraged queen stared at him in disbelief. "This is some kind of deception," she said. "You discovered a trick to block the portal so none can pass through."

Douglas chuckled. "Oh, anyone else can leave, *Your Majesty*," he said. "Just not you, you great cow."

Munro shot him a pointed glance, and the youngest druid shrugged but seemed abashed. Turning back to Konstanze, Munro said, "Feel free to try. The other queens are at liberty to travel to their kingdoms as always. But, until you order the release of the druid and her child, Ashkyne is cut off from the Halls of Mist…and the power of the Stone."

"Release the human who murdered my brother?" she spat.

"We both know she didn't kill him," Munro said quietly.

She strode forward, away from the portal's glow. "Someone must be held accountable."

Munro tilted his head. "Ulrich was the architect of his own demise. We can either lay out his iniquities for all to judge, or you can let his memory rest with dignity. Why not allow your people to maintain whatever esteem they still hold for him...and your family."

One of the other queens stepped closer. "My lord druid," she said to Munro. "We have your leave to depart for our kingdoms?" She bowed to him, keeping her gaze low.

"Of course," he said. "We have no wish to interfere with the kingdoms. We only seek to protect one of our own, wrongly accused, and the child Konstanze promised me she would kill alongside our sister druid."

Gasps and chatter rippled through the crowd of onlookers.

"Thank you, my lord druid," the queen said. She signalled to those near her. With some hesitation, they turned to the portal. With an intake of breath, she approached it. In mere seconds, she and her party vanished.

For the first time, Konstanze seemed concerned. She glared at Munro, then towards the other queens. "We must stand together," she said. "We cannot allow these humans to dictate to us, to murder our families."

Zdanye, Queen of Tvorskane, shook her head. "Now is the time for truth. Prince Ulrich was a vile faerie, Queen Konstanze. All who knew him have little trouble conceiving of that reality. If no evidence exists that this woman did wrong to him, and if she is a druid under the protection of their Hall, you have no claim." With a bow to Munro, she said, "My lord druid, I take my leave. I wish blessings to you and your mate."

Munro tilted his head, acknowledging her respect. "Thank you, Queen Zdanye."

After the Tvorskane contingent departed, no others left the Halls of Mist. The queens and their contingents moved decidedly away from Konstanze, taking up positions on the opposite side of the courtyard.

Konstanze simmered. "I do not believe you," she said. "You have merely performed a trick, like the illusions of an astral fae."

Munro nodded, "It could be true, I suppose," he said. "But tell me this. What if we speak the truth? How long do you think your people can survive, cut off from the Source of all magic? Days? Hours?" He paused. "Would you rather see your people die than bend, when you know you are in the wrong?"

She glowered at him. "I see nothing to indicate my people are in any jeopardy. All you have done is strand me and my royal party against our will, in direct violation of every precept of the Halls of Mist."

Aaron spoke up. "We have done nothing but commune with the Stone. The Stone chooses according to the good of the fae. Is your response to abandon your people when they are isolated from the Source?"

Konstanze hesitated, turning her attention to the portal. "You claim you can bend the Stone?"

"Why do you dismiss the evidence of your own eyes?" Munro asked.

"If this is true, then allow us to pass. How can we even consider your claims with no proof what you say is true?" Her eyes gleamed with anger.

Aaron whispered to Munro. "I don't trust her. If we let her pass, Demi's as good as dead."

"Agreed," Munro replied quietly. He glanced at Oszlár, then back to Konstanze. "Then we are at an impasse," he said. "You do not trust our word, but how could we ask the Stone to restore the portal without first receiving your guarantee of Demi and Jago's release?"

Surprisingly, her smile returned. "This proves you false," she said.

"In what way?" Munro asked.

"You claim my people are in immediate danger, severed from the Source. This cannot be the will of the Stone. The keepers have always maintained that the Stone acts for the good of the fae. Tell me, Keeper Oszlár, how would the death and suffering of hundreds of thousands of faeries benefit our race?" She looked at the other queens, then back to Munro. "Will you really condemn an entire nation to die? Do you wonder that a queen would defy you, when you hold an entire nation hostage if we do not meet your outrageous demands?"

"You cannot have it both ways, Konstanze. First you challenge us as toothless pretenders, but now you claim we are powerful tyrants. All we ask is your unbreaking guarantee of the lives of Demi Hartmann and the leth-draoidh child Jago."

"And all I ask is that first you show evidence that you are not performing your usual parlour tricks. Until I see proof, I have no reason to believe my people are in danger. If I'm right and this is some harmless deceit, then all my capitulation would do would perpetuate your dangerous mythology and elevate your false claims even further."

Munro and Queen Konstanze stared at each other intently. Munro had no desire to see her people suffer, and he was shocked she would let it go that far. What could he do to prove to her the Stone had severed her people from the Source?

The blue glow of the portal darkened, and crackling energy shimmered along its surface.

Munro turned to Oszlár. "How long can Ashkyne survive disconnected from the Source Stone?" he asked.

Oszlár shook his head. "Not long, my lord druid. I've seen many fae severed. It is a maddening state."

Munro ran his hand through his hair and paused a long time, lost in thought. He couldn't let all those people die. Finally he said, "Douglas, ask the Stone to open the portal to Ashkyne and restore her people to the Source."

"If you do that," Aaron said, "she'll kill Demi and Jago as soon as she arrives safely in her own kingdom."

"I know." Munro looked at the other queens and their worried faces. "But I can't let hundreds of thousands of faeries die to save two druids."

"If Demi doesn't return," Aaron said, "then we'll just cut off her kingdom again, this time with her trapped inside, and we won't let go."

"No," Munro said with a sigh in his voice. "Doing so might break the Stone. As she rightly said, the Stone protects her race. Besides, we have no desire to become oppressors. If Demi and Jago die at her hands, we will seek justice, but not vengeance. We must save Ashkyne, even if its queen will not."

The portal darkened further, and once more electric bolts shot out all around it. Everyone in the courtyard scurried away from it. A loud crack sounded and an arm of lightning whipped through the blue light. Several figures emerged, bathed in a blazing coil of light.

The burning glow faded, revealing Huck supporting a sickly faerie, and a frightened Demi clutching her child to her chest. The portal calmed, and a hush fell over the courtyard.

"What is this?" Konstanze demanded.

"Your proof, Your Majesty" Keeper Oszlár said.

Demi looked around wildly, until finally her gaze settled on Munro. He beckoned her towards him.

"It's okay," he said. "You're safe here." With a glance at Huck, she hurried over to Munro, clearly wanting to get as far away from the portal as possible.

"She is my prisoner!" Konstanze shouted.

"Not anymore, she isn't. You wanted proof your people are in danger? There it is." He gestured to Huck and the faerie with him.

"It's true, Your Majesty," the blue-skinned faerie said, gulping in the magical air of the Halls of Mist like a drowning man. "In our journey from the cells, through the castle, and to the portal dais, all faeries I have seen are weak and possibly dying."

"You were the agent of their escape?" she said. "One of my own Watchers betrayed Ashkyne?"

He breathed deeply and stood a little straighter. "You betrayed Ashkyne when you defied the draoidh, Your Majesty. This woman is innocent of murder. Of that I have little doubt. She killed Ulrich in self-defence, and you ordered her execution out of a reckless desire for political gain. Even now, our people are dying because of you." He tilted his head. "I have pledged my life to Lady Druid Demi Hartmann and the Druid Hall. I will not serve Ashkyne, even in its death throes, with a traitorous queen as its head."

Huck still stood beside the faerie. He looked like hell. "Munro," he said. "If there's anything you can do, you have to help them. It's bad in there."

Munro nodded. "To the library," he said. "We must open the portal to Ashkyne and save whomever we can."

He, Douglas, and Aaron started to leave, but they paused with a start when the portal grew suddenly even darker. The light disappeared completely, and the dark rune-covered disk appeared, the same disk they'd seen the day Eilidh took control of Queen Vinye's kingdom. The queens in the crowded courtyard murmured loudly.

"The gates are shifting," Oszlár said. "Keepers, we must go below."

"No!" Konstanze shouted. She glanced around quickly. "No," she repeated, more calmly. She approached Munro, then looked down, her lips pressed together so hard they whitened. With a bitter sigh, she knelt in front of him. After a long silence, she said, "I pledge loyalty to the Druid Hall, and beg forgiveness for my trespasses. As long as I am queen of Ashkyne, the crown will remain loyal to the draoidh. This I swear on my bloodline."

Munro watched the glowing disk. It didn't waver. He knew she was only doing this to preserve her crown, but she was swearing an oath he actually believed she would be forced to keep. This was more than he'd dared hope for. He met the eyes of each of the other druids before he answered. One by one, the men each gave a nod. "Demi?" Munro asked. "You are one of us now. You have a voice in this."

"Do you believe her?" she asked, holding her son and staring at the kneeling queen.

"I do," he replied. "She will be bound to her vow by the magic of the Source stone. If she breaks it, her bloodline will lose the Ashkyne crown forever."

Finally, Demi nodded. "If it saves all those people's lives, do it."

Munro turned back to Konstanze. "We of the Druid Hall accept your oath, Queen Konstanze."

She extended her hand beside her and one of her attendants helped the queen to rise. As she did, the disk vanished with a loud groan, and once again, a shimmering blue light replaced it. "Is the path to Ashkyne restored, my lord druid?" she asked.

Huck spoke up. "I'll test it." He stepped into the light and disappeared. Within seconds, he came back into view. "It's safe," he said. "The connection is restored, and it seems the Watchers around the portal are beginning to rouse."

Konstanze bowed her head once more. "With your permission, my lord druid, I wish to return to Ashkyne and see to my people."

"Of course," Munro replied. "If the Druid Hall can offer assistance, please send word." He looked around the courtyard. "I'm sure any queen would also offer the same."

"Thank you," she said, a trace of bitterness in her tone. With a gesture to her entourage, Konstanze led them through the blue portal, and one by one, they transported away.

Munro turned to the faerie who'd arrived with Huck and Demi. "And you, Watcher? I'm sure it's safe for you to return to Ashkyne. Konstanze would not dare punish you for aiding one of our hall."

"My name is Leocort, my lord druid," the faerie said with a respectful bow. "No longer a Watcher. If the Lady Druid will allow me, I will hold to my pledge and serve her at your Hall."

"Of course," Demi said with a smile. "You will always have a place with us, if you want it."

Munro nodded. "Huck, can you show them around and get them settled, then?"

"Sure, boss," he said with a grin. "You look like you're wanting to take off."

Munro chuckled. "If nobody else needs me today, I think I'll go visit my wife. Let her know everything is all right."

"Sorry we missed the wedding," Aaron said, and the others were quick to agree.

"Not as sorry as you'll be when Eilidh gets hold of you," Munro said with a small laugh. "Demi, welcome to the Halls of Mist. I'm glad you're safe and well."

"Thank you," she said.

"Thank you," Jago echoed in a small voice.

Munro tousled the boy's hair. Then waved to the other druids and gave a polite nod to the queens and keepers. "I'll be back soon."

"Not too soon though," Huck said. "Go. Have some fun. Get some rest. You deserve it."

"You too," Munro said. With that, he stepped through the portal, on his way back to Caledonia where he belonged.

∞

Three months after Demi and Jago's arrival at the Halls of Mist, Munro brought Eilidh to the Druid Hall. They travelled together more often of late. Eilidh's essence had grown stronger as their daughter grew in her womb, and Munro hated being away from them. Eilidh held his arm as they approached the Hall's main courtyard.

Demi and Huck sat together in the garden, watching Jago play with some blocks one of the druids had crafted out of a smooth, dark wood. The child seemed normal and happy. Some weeks after the wedding, when Munro returned for a brief visit to check on the new arrivals, Huck had told him what had really happened in Amsterdam and how Ulrich died. Fortunately, the boy seemed to have no memory of that night or of his father.

Jago put down his blocks and beamed up at Munro and Eilidh when they arrived. Skipping over to her, the boy took her hand.

She smiled with delight. "Hello," she said. She cupped his face in her palm. "Aren't you a beautiful child." Looking over his head, she spoke to Demi. "Are you sure you will not allow him to join the infants in the Caledonian nursery?"

Demi chuckled and shook her head. "No, but thank you, Your Majesty. Perhaps we will visit soon, though, if that's permitted. I think he'd like to be around other children."

Munro understood her reluctance to send Jago away to school. He'd explained to Eilidh many times that humans raised their own children, but she didn't understand why. She insisted any child would be better off with those whose life's work was bringing up fae offspring. At least she'd compromised some, agreeing that he should educate his daughter in human and druidic lore himself. He didn't want his kid brought up by strangers, but he planned to take each day as it came, rather than arguing over the theoretical.

Eilidh sat and chattered with Demi. While they were all distracted, Jago reached over and put his small hand on Eilidh's belly. Munro felt the jolt in Eilidh's essence as something surprised her suddenly.

"What's wrong?" he asked, his protective instinct kicking into high gear.

She stared at Jago.

The boy leaned over and whispered to her belly. "Hello," he said. With a smile at Eilidh, he said,

"When will Princess Maiya come out to play with me?"

Eilidh and Munro exchanged a glance. She frowned at Jago. "Why do you call her that?"

He furrowed his eyebrows. "Because that's her name. She told me," he said.

"I see," Eilidh said slowly.

Demi came and gently tugged Jago away. "Come sit with Mama," she said, then to Eilidh added, "I'm sorry."

"It's all right," Eilidh told her, making an effort to relax. "I was just surprised. Maiya was my grandmother's name."

Jago shrugged. "She will be a queen someday, and I'm going to be her prince. She wanted me to know her name." He went back to his blocks without another word and continued with the towering structure he was building one inch at a time.

"Oh," Eilidh said. She met Munro's eyes. "Oh," she repeated.

Demi looked embarrassed and whispered, "He doesn't know what he's saying sometimes. I'm sorry."

"That's quite all right," Eilidh replied. "Children are remarkable." Her voice sounded distant.

"Come on," Munro said. "Let's say hello to the others." He stood and held out his hand. Eilidh took it and rose to her feet, gently rubbing her swollen tummy as she watched the lethfae boy playing in the grass.

A Note from the Author

Thank you so much for reading Druid Lords, the fourth book in the Caledonia Fae series. If you enjoyed it, please take a moment to leave a review at your favourite online retailer.

I welcome contact from readers. At my website, you can contact me, sign up for my newsletter to be notified of new releases, read my blog, and find me on social networking.

—India Drummond

Author website: http://www.indiadrummond.com
Reader email: author@indiadrummond.com

The Caledonia Fae Series

Book 1: Blood Faerie

Unjustly sentenced to death, Eilidh ran—away from faerie lands, to the streets of Perth, Scotland. Just as she has grown accustomed to exile, local police discover a mutilated body outside the abandoned church where she lives. Recognising the murder as the work of one of her own kind, Eilidh must choose: flee, or learn to tap into the forbidden magic that cost her everything.

Book 2: Azuri Fae

A faerie prince disappears in the borderlands, and his father enlists the help of outcast Eilidh and her bonded druid, Quinton Munro. Tantalised with hints of a lost and ancient magic, they learn that time is working against them every step of the way. Is the prince's disappearance related to the vanishing of an entire Scottish village?

Faced with deception, assassination attempts, and a mad queen who would sacrifice her own child to keep a dreaded secret, Eilidh struggles with an impossible situation. Her people demand she commit treason and betray the man she loves. Will she do what duty requires, or throw away the chance to reunite the kingdom in exchange for the life she hadn't dared hope for?

Book 3: Enemy of the Fae

With a young, inexperienced monarch on the Caledonian throne and traitorous plots implicating those nearest Queen Eilidh, unrest is rife in the kingdom. She must sift through the intrigues and lies to survive, all while trying to discover which of her trusted companions hates her enough to commit mass murder.

Pressures threaten to overcome the young ruler, and to protect Quinton Munro, her bonded druid, she must send him away. His journey becomes a mission when he stumbles on an ancient truth that will shake the foundations of the entire faerie realm. Confronted by infinite danger and the promise of limitless power, Munro faces the most difficult choices of his life. Will he hide the truth to preserve stability in the faerie kingdoms or embrace the promise of his true druid heritage?

One friend will die because of that truth, one friend's betrayal will cause irreparable scars, and the once tightly-knit band of druids will learn that not all magic is benevolent.

Book 4: Druid Lords

The druids of Caledonia have taken their place in the Halls of Mist, only to learn that their path is fraught with many dangers. When their newest member, Huck Webster, finds a woman of magical talents in Amsterdam, their troubles multiply. Lying between them and a peaceful existence are a dead prince, a furious queen, and a druid accused of murder. Each druid must search his soul and discover where his talents, and his loyalties, lie.

Book 5: Elder Druid

As the Druid Hall celebrates the completion of the Mistgate, their leader Munro is abducted, leaving them in disarray. Queen Eilidh declares Munro dead, which threatens the fragile balance of power in the Halls of Mist. With the druids crippled by grief and uncertainty, no one notices the insidious force influencing them from a dark mirror realm.

That force has a voice, a sinister whisper in Lord Druid Douglas' ear, compelling him to feed the Source Stone and driving a wedge between him and his companions. Trath's magic could protect the druid lord, but the prince has fled heartbreak in search of a different life. But will his quest bring redemption or ruin?

Book 6: Age of Druids

Imprisoned by the demons of The Bleak, two lost druids fight to survive while Munro pushes himself to the brink to find them. In his search, he discovers a mysterious gate even the oldest and wisest of the Otherworld fear.

The Halls of Mists are in ruin, and people scheme, grasping at power as a new kingdom emerges and an ancient one reappears. Tragedy pits druid against queen, testing friendship, loyalty, and love once more.

Who will survive and who will be lost forever as desperation drives some to unthinkable ends?